HAMMERED

CATHRYN FOX

COPYRIGHT

ISBN ebook: 978-1-989374-26-9
ISBN Print: 978-1-989374-27-6

●1

TYLER

"Another night, another cold beer at Winchester's," I mumble as I glance around Blue Bay's favorite watering hole. I drain the amber liquid from my bottle and let it hit the dented, wooden table with an unnecessary thud. I give an exaggerated sigh and pick at the label, ready to call it a night until I feel a set of eyes drilling into the side of my head. I turn to my brother Jared and arch a brow. "Do you have a problem?"

"Yeah, I do. I'm tired of all your fucking moping. What the hell is the matter with you, anyway? It's nine o'clock, and you look like you're ready to crawl into bed...alone," he says, his gaze sliding to the cute brunette two tables over.

A single Owens boy spending a Saturday without a woman between the sheets is unheard of, I know. I also know my little brother will be hooking up with that well-dressed cutie tonight, or any one of the other pampered rich girls who spends their summers here in Blue Bay, Connecticut. They return every year to tan and toy with the local boys, only to up and leave for their real lives come fall. I've been home now for two years, retired from the MMA circuit to help out in the family construction business after our father died, and I can't deny that I've bedded my share of women wanting a summer fling. I also can't deny that I knew better than to get attached, and a no-strings summer hook-up was, well...a hell of a lot of fun.

Was?

Fuck, man, I don't know what's wrong with me. I used to love the attention in the cage, love the string of ladies waiting for a piece of me after a hard-earned fight. But lately, I don't know... My older brothers Sean and Jamie are proving the Owens boys do have staying power. Who would have thought? Not me. Yet they're both married with kids. Heck, Sean's wife Summer is pregnant with their second child. I sure as hell hope it's a girl. If not, Grandma Nellie will be after me to get settled and finally give her the great grand-daughter she's been wanting. I guess I used to be opposed to marriage, but lately I'm wondering how it would look on me. That thought brings on a bark of laughter.

My God, the eight Owens boys, five brothers and three cousins, have reputations a mile long. Apparently, we have authority issues, and the outsiders who have summer cottages here on the ocean have been warned to stay away by none other than Officer Walker. He and my late dad go way back, and the dispute between the two never ended with Dad's death. Nope, it extended to the eight Owens boys. He just better back the fuck off and keep his hands off my nephews as they grow up.

"Are you going to answer me?" Jared asks, holding his hand up to Stacey, gesturing for another round of beers. "The last time I saw you this down was when Rock Roberts beat your ass and stole your UFC middleweight title." I glare at my brother. Now why would he bring that up? I'd been hoping to leave the circuit with a bang, but Rock had other plans. "That girl over there is staring at you. Why aren't you going for it?"

Oh, just that maybe I'm getting played out, and while marriage is looking better and better, I'm a well-known MMA fighter—the bad boy women like to have fun with but wouldn't dare bring home to daddy.

Jared continues to glare at me, and I'm about to tell him to fuck off and mind his own damn business when the heavy wooden door swings open and hits the wall with an undignified thud. All eyes turn to the gorgeous blonde sporting big blue eyes the size of saucers as she jumps out of the way before the door swings back and slams shut against her small frame.

Dressed in skintight jeans that hug sweet curves, and a T-shirt that cups gorgeous tits, she glances around, almost frantically, and something niggles in the back of my brain as I take her in. Do I know her? Has she summered here before? I'm not sure, but there's one thing I am certain of—she's never been in my bed. That's not something I'd forget in a hurry.

She glances over her shoulder, like she's running from the devil himself and every protective instinct I possess roars to the surface. I push from my chair and it scrapes the floor loudly as I stand. I take a step toward her, my scuffing boots drawing her attention. Her gaze jerks to mine, and she takes one last glance over her shoulder, like she expects someone to rip the door from its hinges, before she comes running my way.

What the fuck?

Worried blue eyes latch on mine as she goes up on her toes and slides slender arms around my neck. "Please just go with this," she says quickly, breathlessly.

"Go with what?" I ask, my gaze roaming her worried face.

The door creaks open, and she gasps as she steals a glance over her shoulder. With her eyes back on me, she says in a loud voice for all to hear, "There you are. I've been looking everywhere for you."

What the ever-loving fuck is going on here?

Before I can ask, or even make sense of what's happening, she quickly pulls my head down, cutting off my words, as well as the flow of blood to my brain. My mouth slams against her soft lips and one strange thought hits. *It's better to ask for forgiveness than permission.* But holy hell, this woman is all over me—her softness snugly against my hardness in mind-fucking ways. My dick thickens, grows, jumps up for a front row seat. Okay, screw permission or forgiveness.

I go with it, hell, there's no way my cock won't let me, and savor the sweetness of her mouth with my tongue, a hurried exploration that I'd love to slow down. But she's frantic, and since I'm clueless, the only thing I know is she asked me to play along, I match her pace and actions.

For now.

With my arms around her waist, I anchor her to me, and don't miss the little tortured moan rising in her throat—as though momentarily forgetting she's kissing a stranger. Then again, maybe I'm not. Maybe she does know me. She links her arms around my back and holds on as I lift her clear off the floor. I turn her slightly, to glance at the door in time to see my oldest brother, Sean, enter. He's a big, bad-assed mother fucker who'd scare any woman in a dark parking lot. Wait, was she running from him? One of the lights in the lot is broken. Is it possible he'd scared her?

I break the kiss, and set her back on her feet as Sean comes our way. A strange noise, something that resembles a wounded animal caught in a trap, catches in her throat as my bro drops down into the chair next to Jared. All eyes, including Stacey's as she brings us our beers, are on the girl clinging to me like dryer lint.

I put my hands on her shoulders. "Are you okay?"

She's breathing fast and hard, her gaze going from me to Sean back to me. "Yeah, I just…"

My gaze narrows in on her. "Did my asshole brother frighten you or something?"

"He's your….your brother?"

"Yeah, Sean. Did he frighten you?"

She shakes her head fast, too fast. Okay, something strange is going on here and I damn well plan to get to the bottom of it. Women don't come running up to me, wrapping themselves around me and holding tight like two MMA fighters grappling in the ring. Not anymore, anyway.

"It's just…" She bites down on her bottom lip, no doubt trying to come up with a plausible story—unless she goes around kissing strangers for sport. I don't even bother entertaining that idea, though. This one has innocence written all over her. Yeah, something or someone has frightened her.

"Do I know you?" she asks, her eyes narrowing. I study her face, her perplexed expression, and I'm instantly aware the second recognition hits by the way her body stiffens, and those soft blue eyes go wide.

"Oh My God, you're Tyler Owens. The Hammer."

"The one and only." I dip my head, my lips once again inches from hers. "And you are?"

"Um…"

"You're Haven!" Stacey shrieks after setting the last beer on the table. "Haven Roberts."

I nod, as all the pieces fall into place. Haven Roberts. Sister of my MMA nemesis, Rock Roberts. I should have known it the second I saw her, considering how much Rock talks about her, and admires her acting abilities—and defends her when people call her a diva.

Movie trailers have been rolling down Main Street all week, a Hollywood cast and crew taking up residency in our small town to film some summer blockbuster. You'd think I would have put two and two together and figured out who she was. I guess I'm kind of stunned like that, and really, I never really paid much attention to the excitement in the air or the endless chatter about the movie.

No, these days I keep my head down; my only goal is to work hard and save harder. My plan is to save enough money to afford my own building and purchase top notch equipment for the kids who take my martial arts training classes. The one I'm in now could be taken right out from underneath us, leaving us high and dry.

Still, I should have recognized her. I guess the fear in her eyes, combined with that heated kiss, messed a little with my ability for any rational thought. I stiffen, suddenly remembering the fear in her eyes. Was it my brother who rattled this famous movie star, or something else?

Haven's smile is a bit shaky as she turns to Stacey, her shoulders not quite as tight as they were when she entered Winchester's, but still tense. "That's right. I'm here for the movie shoot. Nice to meet you all." She jerks her thumb over her shoulder. "I should get going."

She slowly inches away, but I capture her elbow. Her gaze flies to mine. "Are you okay?" I ask.

Her lashes flutter, and her body relaxes even more under my touch, and dammit if I don't like that.

"Sorry about that," she says. "It was a dare. It's ah..." she rolls her eyes. "A stupid game we play when we reach a new location shoot. You know, pick the biggest, hottest guy in town and kiss him."

Now why is it I don't believe a word coming from her mouth? Her big as fuck, mean-ass brother is nothing but a liar, too. Well, not really. We all played the name calling game before a fight. We'd hurl shit against our opponents to excite our fans and build hype. The feud between Rock and me was legendary. We both could have won an Oscar for our out-of-ring performances. When we were in the ring, there was no acting, however. Nope, we were both playing to win, but in the end the motherfucker stole my title.

Instead of calling her on her lie, I say. "You think I'm the biggest, hottest guy in Blue Bay?"

Jared snorts. "She must have lost her glasses on her way in here."

I kick my brother's boot and he's about to stand when our oldest brother Sean raises his hand. "Don't you two start."

"I...I should go," Haven says again.

I nod toward the door. "I'll walk you out."

"No need. Everything is fine. It's not like anything bad ever happens in Blue Bay, right?" She gives a nervous little laugh. "No kidnappings or stalkers." Her eyes go wide again, and she shuts her mouth like she's said too much. For a girl who acts for a living, she's not great at sticking to the script, because everything in me tells me she regrets everything that just spilled from her lips.

"Right, but I'll walk you anyway," I say, thinking back to the time Sean's wife Summer was run off the road by her ex. Blue Bay is a small coastal town, but that doesn't mean bad things don't happen.

She puts her hand on my chest, and the heat from her touch sizzles through me. She tugs it away, and from the shocked look on her face, I can't help but think it set off fireworks inside her, too. "No, it's fine, really."

I stand there, rocking on my feet for a second and she backs up, like she's afraid I'm going to follow her. She grips the door and tugs it open. I glance past her shoulder to look for something, anything that might raise alarm bells in me, but she lets the door go and bolts.

"What the hell was that all about?" Sean asks.

I shake my head and tug on my hair. "Beats the hell out of me." My boots pound the floor as I walk to the door, and pull it open. I catch a flash of her hair as she hurries down the sidewalk. Most of the trailers for the cast and crew are parked at the edge of town, not too far from the old homestead where we all live with Grandma Nellie. Except for Sean and Jamie. They have places on the water with their families.

That strange sense of longing is back in my gut as I think about settling down and marriage, but I swallow it, not wanting another inquisition from Jared...or Sean. They'd never in a million years believe I was getting played out.

"I'm taking you off the Sanderson place," Sean says to Jared when I sit back down at the table.

"Yeah, why?"

"Just returned from a meeting and I need you to erect sets for the movie."

Jared grins. "That should be fun, especially if I get to hang around Haven." He shakes his hand like it's on fire. "That girl is hot."

A fierce tug of possessiveness races through me and I try to hide it. Haven is nothing to me. We shared a joke of a kiss. If my brother wants to hit on her, no fucking problem—as long as it's through my dead body.

What the hell am I saying?

"Even prettier in person, don't you think, Ty?" Jared adds.

"Yeah, I guess." I give a nonchalant shrug, but these two assholes can read me far too well.

I drink my beer and try to ignore my annoying brother, but he continues with, "Maybe I'll build a nice cozy bed on set. You know for after the shoot." He arches his brow and I work to keep my temper in check.

"You don't have a problem with that do you, Tyler?" Jared asks.

I shrug. "Why would I?"

"You have something you want to say, Tyler?" Sean asks, and tips his bottle to his lips.

I go back to peeling the label on my bottle. "Nope."

"Good, I'm reassigning you, too."

I'm about to protest—I don't want to work on some dumb-ass movie set that will get torn down when it's no longer needed—but can't bring myself to do it. Oh, and why is that? Because there is more going on with Haven than she's admitting, and I have this strange, innate need to watch over her, and keep my brother far away.

And no, it has nothing at all to do with my cock wanting her. I mean, come on, just five minutes ago I said I was played out, and this is a woman with a reputation for falling for her leading men. But that fucking kiss. My stupid dick twitches, and if the bastard could speak, he'd call me out so fast my head would spin—the one on my shoulders. Okay so yeah, maybe I do want her, but I *am* also worried about her safety. I'm kind of a nice guy like that.

"Fine," I grumble.

"Have you heard?" Sean asks.

I eye my brother. "Heard what?"

"Grandma Nellie is housing a couple of the cast."

My head snaps up. "Why the hell did she do that?"

He shrugs. "Hotels and cottages are all booked, and you know Gram, that's what she does. She's never met a stranger."

"Do you think Haven is staying at the house?" Jared asks, and jumps to his feet.

"I'm not sure," Sean says.

He arches his brow again, the brunette he'd been eyeing earlier no longer his focus. "Maybe I'd better go check."

I put my hand on his shoulder and push him back into his seat. "Sit down, little brother."

Jared laughs. "Yeah, that's what I thought."

2

HAVEN

Stars twinkle in the velvety sky overhead, and crickets chirp in the nearby fields as I hurry down the long, dark road and try to put that awkward encounter at the Winchester behind me—not an easy task when my lips are still tingling from the atomic kiss. Who the hell kisses a stranger with a passion so off the charts it's a wonder we didn't blow the place up? Cripes, I can't even imagine what his kisses would be like if he meant them, and don't even get me started on the way my body is still responding, right around the juncture of my legs.

With trees hugging either side of the winding road, I round the corner to find a big old homestead rising up in the distance. The swing on the wide expanse of porch, along with the welcome sign above the door instantly puts this out-of-tower at ease. Everything about the place exudes warmth and contentment—a happy family—and I smile as I let it wrap around me like a comforting hug.

I grew up in California, and both my parents are managers in the movie industry. My older brother Rock—his stage name, of course—and I definitely didn't have what I'd call a normal upbringing. Heck, I'd been starring in commercials since I was four months old and schooled every afternoon on the set. Rock acted right along with me, until my parents discovered his fighting skills, and redirected his talents. Fame and glory, that's all they ever cared about. Raising well-adjusted kids—not so much.

In a small town like Blue Bay, and in a homestead like this one, I just bet they had sit-down dinners where they all talked —about real things, important things. They probably all swam and fished in the lake just beyond the house, and Christmas mornings were undoubtedly filled with love and laughter around a gigantic fir tree picked out by the kids and cut down by the father. I bet it was just laden with home-made decorations.

I chuckle slightly. I'm going all Hallmark here, but I can't help it. I want to picture a home with a menagerie of happy kids, because it's something I've always wanted. I love my brother dearly, and would be lost without him. Heck, with absent parents, Rock and I were there for each other through thick and thin, relying only on one another, because how could we possibly trust anyone in the cut-throat world we were thrust into? I shiver as I think about the kinds of people we've dealt with over the years.

This big homestead, however, probably housed a dozen siblings, boys and girls who fought like cats and dogs, and loved and trusted just as hard. I always wanted a sister—or even a friend who wasn't nice just to my face. Will I find that here in this big house, in this small town, or am I simply channeling that old Norman Rockwell calendar I had in my teens? Lord knows I try to romanticize everything—my way of escaping reality, I guess. But lessons learned have taught me happily-ever-after only exists in the movies.

With no available accommodations in this former whaling village, a few cast and crew members are now making this gorgeous home our headquarters until our trailers arrive. Apparently Blue Bay Construction is run out of this place and the guys, I think someone said they were all brothers and cousins, will be working on building sets for us. Seriously though, opening your house to strangers is such a hospitable, small town thing to do, isn't it? I don't mind hunkering down here for a bit, as long as I have a soft bed tonight.

A yawn pulls at me as I take the last step up the porch and catch the voices spilling from the open window. The laughter and comradery coming from inside eases the tension inside me, although the voices don't sound familiar. But the happiness does remind me of home and hearth—safety—everything I'd imagined as a child.

As I consider my safety—my stalker—I recall the apprehension creeping through my bones earlier. I jumped to conclusions, assuming that big hulk of a man following me from the parking lot at the Winchester was the same one leaving threatening notes. He was simply Tyler's brother, and no doubt harmless.

Tyler Owens.

What were the odds that I'd run straight into his arms?

My cheeks warm, ribbons of embarrassment careening through my blood as I recall my kiss with him—my God, did I really do that? Yeah, I did and damned if I don't want to do it again.

Get yourself together, Haven!

I didn't recognize him at first sight, probably because I was so scared. Some part of me thought a solid guy like him would scare off whoever was following me. Or rather, not following me. It was a ridiculous thing to do, but I wasn't thinking with clarity, and fear was guiding my actions.

To add insult to injury, I lied about it, telling him I had to kiss the biggest guy in the place. Hello, dim-witted moth to light. Nevertheless, he turned out to be the biggest guy in the place, and the hottest—at least to me, and to the girls two tables over. Yeah, I saw the way they were drooling over him, as well as the other Owens brothers. Not that I can blame them. The man is drool worthy, sexier than any leading man I've ever collaborated with.

Maybe you should collaborate with Tyler—in the bedroom.

No, no, no, I am not going to do that—he's my brother's enemy—and it would be in my best interest never to set eyes on him again. In a small town like this, I fear that might be impossible, though. I'm just glad I'm staying on the outskirts of town. I'm guessing he doesn't venture too far from the action at Winchester's.

I take another glance over my shoulder, and as I peer into the dark night, the hairs on the back of my neck stand on edge again.

You will be mine.

My God, I guess that last threatening letter frightened me more than I want to admit. By rights, I should go to the police, or even the director and tell him I'm getting letters from some crazy stalker, but after the trouble on set during my last movie, I can't rock the boat. Honestly, in this business, you're only as good as your last movie, and not only was mine a flop, the off-set feuding between me and the male lead —who just happened to be my ex—was tabloid fodder. I'm lucky any director wanted to work with me after that.

Now my motto is head down, work hard, no relationships of any kind during a shoot, and especially no relationships with anyone involved in the industry—ever. With that last thought in mind, I plaster on a smile and work to shake off my discomfort as I reach for the door to let myself in.

My hand stills when gravel crunches behind me. I turn, search the dark driveway, and see one headlight slowly coming down the lane. My thoughts instantly go back to Tyler Owens. I honestly had no idea he lived in Blue Bay, but

I'd bet my warm bed tonight that the town's bad boy drives a motorcycle. But he's probably already between the sheets with one of those girls who'd been admiring him from across the bar.

Why the hell does that bother you, Haven?

It doesn't!

Or at least it shouldn't.

I'm not about to get involved with a man who was my brother's mortal enemy in the cage. I can't even imagine what Rock would say if he knew I'd kissed his nemesis. Not that he needs to know. What happened between Tyler and me was a one-time thing. He's the kind of guy with a revolving door, and I have no desire to find myself on either side of it. Seriously I could make myself a scarf with the number of red flags he gives off.

If he's such a bad boy, why did you feel safe with him?

Why indeed?

Ignoring that inner voice, I open the door, expecting to see my co-star and director sitting around chatting, but when my gaze lands on a group of strangers, I stiffen. Oh my God, it's late and dark. Did I wonder down the wrong driveway, enter the wrong house and crash a family party?

"Um...I'm sorry. I thought this was where..."

An elderly lady stands and comes toward me. Her slippers scuff on the polished wooden floor as she shuffles close. "You must be Haven." Her smile is as warm as her demeanor. My jumping nerves settle slightly, but that still doesn't mean I'm in the right spot. Perhaps she recognizes me from my films.

"I am," I say. "I thought this was where..." Backing up, I reach into my pocket and pull out a slip of paper with the house address. The door creaks behind me, and before I realize what's happened, I back right into a brick wall.

"Whoa," a man says, his mouth by my ear, the heat of his breath doing ridiculous things to my body. I don't need to turn to know I've backed straight into Tyler Owens. So it *was* him on the motorcycle. Honestly, what are the odds I'd run into him—literally—two times in one night, and that he and his family are the ones who will be working on the sets? Is *he* the one stalking me? I gasp at that thought and spin around. His face softens, his eyes narrowing in on me.

"Haven, are you okay?" he asks in the softest, sweetest voice, and despite his big presence, the way his strong, protective hands are touching me, all the stress of the last week, and all the threatening letters comes racing back in a whoosh.

You'll be mine.

As tears threaten, I blink my eyes to dull the vision of those words found on the sheet of the paper shoved under the bathroom stall at the airport, right after I landed in Connecticut. Someone knew exactly where I was going to be. Were they on the plane with me, or were they waiting in the terminal? A hard shiver races down my body and I shake, almost violently.

"Haven," he says again, and that's when I realize I'm causing a scene. Calling on all my acting skills, I push my hair back and fake a smile.

"Sorry, you frightened me."

He doesn't smile. Instead, he angles his head, those gorgeous green eyes of his moving over my face in a careful assessment. I stiffen, willing myself not to squirm, to show any sign of nervousness. He doesn't need to know about my problems. "You seem to be frightened a lot lately."

Shoot, I didn't think he'd be able to read me so easily.

"No, it's…I didn't expect anyone to be behind me."

"And at the bar?"

I give a dismissive wave of my hand. "Oh, like I said, that was a silly dare," I blink to hide my discomfort, but I'm wasting my time. This man can see right through me. I don't know how, and I don't know why. I only know that I'd have more luck convincing a room full of movie critics that I was acting on a dare, before this guy.

He lifts his head, ending the staring contest, and he exchanges a look with the elderly lady beside me. Whatever they just silently telegraphed sets her into motion.

"Haven," the woman says. "Come in, come in. You're in the right place. Don't let my grandsons scare you off. They might look like ogres, but they're all sweet boys."

"Hey who's calling me an ogre?" one of the guys sitting around the table asks, and I note he has the same eye color as Tyler. In fact, all the guys do. I'm not a writer, I'm an actress, but if I had to describe it, I'd say it was the color of dark moss with speckles of molasses, everything about them reminding me of the green of spring after a harsh winter. The kind of eyes that can see all the bare patches of the soul.

Tread carefully, Haven.

"Hush, Jacob," the woman says. She smiles at me again. "I'm Grandma Nellie. You can call me Gram."

"Nice to meet you, Gram?"

She points. "My grandsons, Carter, Jace, and Jacob. There are more—"

"Really?" I ask, my heart jumping. Maybe I was right about this place. Maybe it is hearth and home and maybe there are some women I could bond with—Lord knows it's nothing but competition between women in my world. "You have granddaughters too?"

A series of groans roll around the room. "What did I say?"

"Don't ask," Tyler says, and I laugh at his exaggerated groan, instantly feeling a comradery with these guys.

"I have grand-daughters-in-law, but one of these days, these boys will give me a great-granddaughter." Another series of groans roll across the room.

"How many grandsons?" I ask

"Eight grandsons, and two great grandsons." A warm smile takes over her face and it's easy to see how much she loves her family, and how much they all love her. "They'll all be around sooner or later to say hello, or you'll run into them on the set, but I take it you already met Tyler."

"Tyler and Sean," I say.

"And Jared," Tyler rumbles. "We ran into her at the bar. Actually, she ran into us. Me specifically and literally." He exchanges another look with Gram.

"Are you hungry, child?" She points to Jace, at least I think it's Jace. It's hard to think straight or remember everyone's names with Tyler standing close. Cripes, it's like my skin is on fire, a deep scorching burn that caresses all my erogenous zones. "Back in New York, Jace was an award-winning chef," Gram says as she beams at Jace with pride. "He'll whip you up something delicious."

"Oh wow, really?" I ask, curiosity racing through me. If he was a prize chef, what brought him back to Blue Bay? I guess I can understand why Tyler is here. After losing the championship title—to my brother, no less—he returned to his roots. I'm not about to ask questions, though, or delve into their personal lives. I'm only here for a short time and really, their reasons are their own. Just like my reasons for keeping my stalker a secret are mine alone.

As Jace makes a move to stand, I hold my hand out to stop him. "No," I say quickly, noting the way Tyler continues to stay close, all solid strength and power and damned if I don't like it. A lot. "I think I'm going to call it an early night and you're all doing enough for us as it is." I stretch my arms out. "It was a long flight and I have an early start tomorrow."

Carter jumps to his feet. "How about I show you to your room?"

A noise, a growl of sorts rumbles up from behind me, and I turn to see Tyler glaring at the man standing.

"Sit down, Carter."

Carter smirks and my gaze goes back and forth between the two men. Am I missing some secret joke here? Does Carter know something I don't?

"Sure thing, cuz."

Gram fills a kettle. "Don't mind them. Too much testosterone in the room. Tyler, why don't you get Haven settled in your room? You can bunk with Carter tonight."

"Have you heard him snore?" Tyler blurts out. He rakes his hand through his hair, mussing it up and damned if that doesn't just make him look sexier. "Jesus, I need to get my own place."

"Language," Gram says, and I can't help but laugh.

"You're one to talk," Carter says. "You snore loud enough to wake the dead over in Hope Falls."

"You want to take this outside?" Tyler asks.

"You don't want me to embarrass you in front of Haven, now do you?" he asks, and places both hands on the table. That's when I notice the tattoos on his forearms. I resist the urge to scan Tyler's body for ink.

Tyler cracks his knuckles. "You could try."

Unable to help myself, I laugh. "You're right, Gram. Too much testosterone." I glance at Tyler. "Do you think you could show me to your room before you two take this outside?"

"You don't want to see the show, watch me knock your boyfriend down a peg or two?" Carter asks with a smirk.

"He's not my boyfriend," I say quickly. "I just met him at Winchester's tonight."

Grinning like he really does know something I don't, Carter opens his mouth to say something, and Tyler points to him. Through clenched teeth he says, "Leave it, Carter." Tyler turns to me, and his voice is softer when he says, "Come on,

I'll take you to your room." He searches the floor. "Where are your bags?"

"Jonah dropped them off earlier," Gram says.

Tyler glances at me. "Jonah?" he asks.

"He's the male lead in our movie." Tyler's eyes narrow, then he nods, like he just put two and two together. What, does he think I have a thing for Jonah? I have no idea how that rumor ever started, but for some reason, everyone thinks I fall for the leading man. I only did it once and that was the worst mistake of my life. "He's staying here too, but not in my room," I add quickly. What the hell am I doing? Tyler doesn't care if I'm with Jonah or not. Why I'm trying to clarify it is beyond me. "We'll only be here until our trailers arrive. I don't want to put you out any longer than I have to."

The guys at the table chuckle, and one whispers, "No worries, Ty likes to put out."

Gram glares at them, and runs her fingers over her knuckles. "Do I need to gristle you?"

All the guys stiffen and sit up a little straighter, and a series of 'hell no' goes around the table.

"What's a gristle?" I ask, amused at the way Gram handles all her grandsons.

"You don't want to know," Tyler says, his body bumping mine as we continue to linger in the doorway, the warm night air breezing through the place, carrying the scent of jasmine and fresh cut grass.

"I put Jonah in Sean's old room, and Mason is in Jamie's," Gram supplies. "Your bags are already in Tyler's room, Haven."

Tyler gives me a little nudge, and the warmth of his flesh races through me. I bite down on my tongue to stifle a moan, or some other telltale sign that his touch, innocent or not, is messing with my traitorous body. "Come on, I'll show you to my room," he says.

We head up the long staircase. "Who's Mason?" he asks.

"He's the director," I supply as I run my hand along the wooden rail. "So, Carter is your cousin?"

"Yes."

"You guys all work construction?"

"Do now."

I nod, understanding that Tyler was a fighter before coming home. "What did Carter do before?"

"Firefighter."

"Oh, yeah, here in Blue Bay?"

"Jacksonville."

"Oh, wow, nice. Did you all grow up in this place?"

"Yes," he says again, his feet stomping on the steps behind me.

"It's gorgeous." I take in the gorgeous curve of the rail. "How long has it been in the family?"

"Forever."

"Did a family member build it?"

"Grandfather."

"Is he still alive?"

"No."

"What about your parents? Do they live—"

"Gone."

I glance over my shoulder and take in the tightness in his jaw, the way his muscles ripple as he clenches down.

"I'm so sorry."

"Thanks."

His green eyes lift, and I bite back a gasp as he zeroes in on me. Holy hell, being the sole focus of this man's attention is...a bit intimidating, and a whole lot stimulating.

"What?" he asks.

"Do you always give one-word answers?"

"No."

I laugh at that. "You're the strong silent type, huh?" I say, hoping he can't hear the arousal in my voice. Then again, a guy like him is probably used to it. Coming from the MMA circuit, he's used to women throwing their panties at him. I am *not* going to be one of those women. Ever.

His hardened demeanor changes, and he offers me a grin that is so playful, so downright sexy and mesmerizing, it's all I can do to stop myself from ripping my panties clear from my hips and tossing them at him.

No, no, no, Haven.

I am here to work, not to get involved with a local, no matter how good looking, and...sweet, he is. Really, beneath that rough and tough surface, I think maybe Gram was right, and he is a softie.

"You think I'm strong?" he teases.

All the tension from the day spills out of me and I laugh. "I think you're something," I say.

"You're something too," he responds when we reach the top step.

"What's that supposed to mean?"

"Nothing." He scrubs his face. "I'm just tired. I don't know what I'm saying."

I stretch out my arms and stifle a yawn, and his glance drops to take in my chest as I expand it. Holy shit, I'm not sure any man has ever looked at me with such desire in his eyes. Truthfully, most men don't look at me—Haven. They see the movie star actress, the character I played. Then again, am I ever really myself anymore? Do I even know who Haven is, or what she wants, after all these years of pretending to be someone else?

I follow him to a room, and he stands back, gesturing for me to enter. I walk past him, my body brushing his, and I'm certain he just cursed under his breath. Is he feeling this 'thing' between us too? Could that be what Carter was picking up on?

He looks like he's about to leave, and even though I should let him, I find myself saying, "Gram said there were eight of you. Cousins and brothers?"

"Carter, Ryan and Jace are cousins. They grew up with us after their parents died."

I touch his arm. "I'm sorry, Tyler." His gaze drops to my hand and I pull it back.

"Sean, Jamie, and the twins, Jared and Jacob are my brothers. I'm the middle child."

I groan. "Ugh, the dreaded middle child," I tease. "Did you feel left out?" His face drops, and my pulse jumps. Holy God, did I hit on a sore spot. I quickly try to backtrack. "Tyler, I was just—"

"Night, Haven."

He turns and I say, "I...um...do you think I could have a shower first? I feel icky after my long flight."

He scrubs his chin and angles his body. I study his strong profile when he says, "Yeah, sure."

He points to the door to the bathroom. "Shower is in there, and you'll find towels in the closet."

I put my hand on his arm before he leaves and his gaze jerks back to mine. "Thanks Tyler, for this...and earlier."

"No problem," he says, his voice a bit gruffer. "Get some sleep."

I watch him walk away, my gaze latched on his backside, pulled by the easy way he walks. The stairs creak as he descends and I back up, step into his room. A grin plays on my lips as I take in his space, and before I touch his bedding and run my hand over the sheets, I glance over my shoulder. I have no idea why I feel like I'm invading his privacy.

After a thorough inspection of his room, and the view of the lake out back, I grab my bag, toss it onto his bed, and pull out my pajamas. I hurry to the bathroom, shower quickly, and then climb between Tyler's sheets, which smell freshly laundered. I close my eyes, secure in this room with all the big Owens boys milling about. It doesn't take long for me to fall asleep, but then suddenly a crashing sound outside my window pulls me awake.

I sit up, and rub my eyes, not sure if I was dreaming or not. I listen for a sound, and something creaks outside my door.

"Hello?" I say, and glance at the clock. It's well after midnight, surely everyone has gone to bed by now. Moving as quietly as possible, I reach for my phone, pad across the wooden floor, and press my ear to the door. Silence meets my ears, so I quietly open the door and glance down the long length of the hall. Swallowing against a dry throat, I turn on my flashlight app, tiptoe to the stairs and head to the kitchen for a drink.

The light over the stove provides a path to the cupboards. I turn off my flashlight app, and after searching for a glass, I fill it with cold water. The house creaks, and I nearly jump a foot off the floor when something bangs outside again. Breathing deeply, I drop into a chair at the big oaken table and take a fast drink to calm myself. The floor creaks behind me, and I spin so fast, water spills all over me, drenching my pajama shirt.

"Tyler," I gasp, as his big presence eats up the doorway.

"Sorry, I didn't mean to scare you. I heard you get up."

"I didn't mean to wake you," I say quickly and work to regulate my breathing.

"You didn't. I was awake."

"Carter's snoring?" I tease, hoping to lighten the mood.

He takes a step closer, hovers over me. My pulse skyrockets as my gaze drops to take in the gorgeous man before me, dressed only in a pair of jeans, which he wears entirely too well. From the dim light over the stove, I count eight abdominal muscles.

My gaze lifts back to his, and he's not smiling. Nope, not smiling at all. There's a new kind of ferociousness about him. In fact, he's looking at me with murder in his eyes and a shudder goes through me.

"Are you okay, Haven?"

"Oh yeah, sure. I...I heard noises."

A moment passes and he finally says, "This is an old house. Things creak, pipes bang."

"Right," I say with a shaky nod, as I work to pull myself together. "That bang was probably just a water pipe. Sounded like a damn gunshot."

He sits down in the chair next to me, his solid presence offering comfort, and my shoulders relax. "You want to tell me what's going on?"

3

TYLER

I have never in my life seen anyone this spooked. I'm not sure what's going on with her, and from the way she's wrapping her arms around herself in a defensive move, I'm not so sure I'm going to find out. All I know is something is wrong, and if she wants to open up to me, maybe I could help her. Or maybe I should reach out to Rock, let him know his sister might need him.

"What do you mean?" she asks, and I take in the dark circles under her eyes. When was the last time this woman had a good night's sleep?

I hand her a napkin from the holder Gram keeps on the table. She presses it to her wet pajama top and I do my best not to stare. I just wish my *best* was better than it is. Goddammit, what kind of man am I? This woman is frightened and I'm staring at her damn breasts.

Looking for a distraction as she dries herself, I run my thumb over the old table, touching the dents that have been made over the years by one brother or another. Warmth touches my soul as I recall the fights and fun we had around this table over the years.

My gaze cuts back to her once she finishes drying herself. "I think you know what I mean," I say.

She blinks rapidly as she sets the napkin on her lap, and reaches for her glass, swallowing what's left so hard that the sound reverberates around the big empty room. "It's just..." she begins and stops, her brow furrowed. For a second I think she's going to tell me, but then she says, "Just a big old house and I'm not the best sleeper, anyway."

I watch her for a second, note the way her dark lashes are fluttering rapidly. In the cage it's my job to read my opponent's body language, and right now hers speaks volumes. "It's not my business, but if you're in some kind of trouble, maybe I could help."

"Why would you want to help?" she blurts out, her gaze jerking upward. "What is it you want?"

My head rears back. Whoa, what the hell did I say to put her on the defense? I hold my hands up, palms out. "Okay, not my business. Just wanted to make sure you were okay." I make a move to stand and her trembling hand on my arm stops me.

"I'm sorry. I didn't mean to yell like that." She briefly closes her eyes and shakes her head, obviously sorry for that outburst. "It's just...I guess it's the world I grew up in. It's tit for tat you know. No one does anything altruistic. So, I guess I just assumed..."

"Assumed I wanted something," I say, finishing her sentence. "I don't, Haven. Despite what you think of me, or what you've heard about me," I say, knowing her brother talked trash about me for years, even though that was for show. It certainly doesn't mean the world didn't believe it though, or that Haven doesn't think I'm a world class prick who preys on the dreams of innocent children. "I was raised to do the right thing."

She nods, and tucks a strand of hair behind her ear. She looks down for a second and when her head lifts, the worry on her face hits harder than one of Rock's haymaker punches. My brain is still rattling around in my skull from the last one.

The freckles around her nose bunch when she says, "I...I can't really say anything."

"Okay, you can have your secrets, but you're in my house. I can't have you bringing trouble here, Haven. I have brothers and cousins to think about. I have Gram to watch over. Here in Blue Bay we protect what's ours."

She nods, and goes quiet again. "I'm sorry, Tyler. I'd never want to do anything to jeopardize you or your family, especially after everyone has been so kind, opening your home to strangers."

My heart pinches at the worry in her voice. I have a feeling Rock was right when he told me his sister was one of a kind, a girl who cares more about others than she does herself. "There are no strangers in Gram's life," I say, and it brings a smile to her face.

"She's really sweet. She's like the grandmother I never had."

I nod, sad that Haven never had anyone like Gram in her life. Honestly, she's the glue that holds the family together. After Mom died, she stepped right in to keep us boys in line. "Yeah...," I murmur.

She glances at her hands as she twists them in her lap. "It's just if my director ever found out."

Tabloid pictures fill my brain. Ah, now I get it. Haven is worried about bringing more trouble to the set, and losing her career. Shit. She's definitely caught between a rock and a hard place. I touch her chin, lift it until those pretty eyes of hers are on me again.

"Your secret is safe with me. You have my word on that."

She nods, picks the wet napkin back up and nervously plucks at it. "I've been receiving letters...threatening letters."

Fuck. I exhale and sit back in my seat. "Did you go to the police?"

She shakes her head fast. "No, I can't. I can't do anything to lose this job. My career..."

"That's why you kissed me at Winchester's? You thought Sean was some sort of stalker, and thought if he saw you with me, he'd back off."

"After I landed, someone shoved a letter under the bathroom stall. It said, *You'll be mine*."

"If it was the woman's bathroom, do you think it was a woman?"

"I don't know. I guess."

"Well, a guy could have paid someone to do it, I suppose. A beautiful woman like you, I can see it being a guy, especially saying you'll be mine."

"Yeah," she says with a nod. "I just don't know."

As a jolt of anger rushes through me, I shake my head, my fingers curling into fists. She notices my reaction and gives a megawatt smile, like she's said too much and wants to backtrack. Her switch in demeanor happens so fast it catches me off guard.

"I'm sure it's nothing," she says quickly.

I narrow my gaze. "If it was nothing, you wouldn't be so frightened."

She continues to smile, but when I arch a brow, refusing to let her off the hook, she gives in and her face falls. "Yeah, you're right."

I lean toward her, and brace my elbows on my thighs. "How long has this been going on?"

"A couple of weeks now."

"Do you have enemies?"

"I...I don't think so. Rock does, but—"

I consider our MMA fans. Would one go so far as to threaten a fighter's sister? "You think someone who has it out for Rock would come after you?"

"I really don't know." Blue eyes full of vulnerability search mine, and my gut twists. "Do you think it could be?"

"I don't know either, Haven. Do you think you should call your brother?"

She shakes her head. "He has a big fight coming up in Vegas and I don't want to worry him."

"He'd want to know. You're everything to him."

A small smile touches her mouth. "I know. He's everything to me too. He's the only guy..."

Her words fall off, but she doesn't need to finish for me to understand, her brother is the only guy she's ever been able to count on. Well, that changes right now.

"Okay, then it's settled. From this second until the movie finishes up and you leave Blue Bay, you're with me. I'll be that boyfriend you were seeking at Winchester's. Whoever gave you that letter will have to go through me to get to you, I won't let anything happen to you," I say.

I'm not doing this just because Rock is my friend—yeah, we put on a good show, but he's the guy who stayed with me all night when I found out my dad died. I'm doing it because she has no one else to turn to and I don't want anything to happen to her.

"What do you want in return?" she asks.

"Your safety. If I had a sister in trouble, I'd hope someone would do this for her."

Her entire body tightens, and her eyes narrow in on me. That obviously wasn't the answer she was expecting. Confused, she stares for a good solid minute, or at least it feels like that, and then she shakes her head, like she can't seem to wrap her brain around anyone not wanting something from her. That totally pisses me off. What kind of world did she grow up in where she can't count on people? Christ, I could call any one of my brothers right now, for anything, even a paper cut, and they'd be here in a second.

"What's the problem, Haven?" I ask, since I'm a no bullshit kind of guy.

"I can't ask you to do that and not do anything in return," she says. I'm about to tell her it's fine when a loud bang reverberates through the house. She just about jumps three feet in the air.

I put my hand on her shoulder, to calm her. "It's probably just an animal in the trash. You stay here, I'll go look."

"Are you sure?"

"I'm sure." I push from my chair, and open the door, which isn't even locked. Hell, no one locks the doors in Blue Bay, but maybe we'll have to change that for the time being. Outside, I find the garbage tipped over, and I pick it back up and secure the metal lid. Back inside, Haven is still sitting in her chair, her eyes wide.

"Breathe, Haven," I say when I reach her, and she sucks in a breath. "It was likely just a racoon." I stifle a yawn and she stands.

"Thank you, Tyler. I've definitely kept you up long enough."

"Wasn't sleeping anyway."

She puts her glass in the sink, and gives me a weird little finger wave as she starts toward the stairs. I follow behind her, and try not to look at her sweet ass in those short pajama bottoms. A groan I have absolutely zero control over rises in my throat and I fake a cough to cover it. Haven momentarily stills on the steps, and I nearly crash into her.

"You okay?" she asks.

"Fine."

She starts up again and I follow her to my bedroom. She enters and I step inside with her, shutting the door behind us. She turns to me, her eyes wide. "What are you doing?"

"I'm staying in here tonight." I gesture to the chair in the corner. "I'll sleep there."

"Tyler—"

"I don't want anything from you, Haven," I say, although that's a big fucking lie. I want her in my bed, beneath me, but that's not going to happen. "First nights in strange beds aren't easy." I almost snort at that. How many women have I gone home with and jumped straight into bed with, no problems at all? Although I never stay the night and sleep wasn't what we were after. The women who get involved with me know straight up I don't stay. I leave before they have to explain I'm not 'meet the parents' material.

She looks at the chair. "No, they're not, but I can't ask—"

"You're not. I'm offering."

"What will your family think?"

"I'm a big boy, Haven. I don't have to answer to anyone but myself."

She nods in understanding. "How about you take the bed and I'll take the chair?"

Okay, so she's not opposed to me staying with her, she's just opposed to me being uncomfortable, and I like that about her. She's definitely not a pampered princess like the media makess her out to be. My heart softens as she moves toward the chair.

"Not happening, Haven," I say and capture her hand. I spin her to face me and that's when I see it—lust in her eyes as our fingers connect. She doesn't pull away. Nope, instead she weaves her fingers through mine, and damned if that doesn't stroke my cock.

With my traitorous dick thickening, I stand over her, hover close, watch a streak of pink crawl into her cheeks.

"I just don't understand why you would do this," she says so quietly I have to strain to hear.

"Because it's the right thing to do," I say.

Her tongue caresses her bottom lip, like she's moistening it, for me, and so help me God, if I wasn't in that chair tonight, I'd be rubbing one out.

"Do you...always do the right thing?"

"No," I say flat out.

I let her hand go, and move around her before I show her just how often I do the wrong things. "Get some sleep, Haven." I plunk down in the chair.

She hesitates, her gaze going from me to the big bed, back to me. "I mean..." she begins. "This is your room and your bed. Maybe we could share it. Put a pillow in between us or something.

I laugh again. "You think a pillow is going to do anything?"

"What do you mean?"

"Haven," I say. "If you haven't figured it out by now, I'd really like to fuck you. I'd like to fuck you into next week until you can't remember your own name, but never forget mine. But that's not part of the deal here. I'm going to take care of you because I want to. Wanting to fuck you is something different."

"Oh," she says and takes a fast gulping breath.

"Oh, is right and you need to understand this. If you invite me into that bed, a pillow isn't going to keep me from you. Fuck, a goddamn brick wall wouldn't be able to hold me back." My gaze drops, takes in her damp pajama shirt and the way her nipples are puckering so beautifully. I fist my hands and release them again, eager to touch her, taste her, put my cock deep inside her until her walls clench around me in orgasm. My gaze travels back to her face, and while I know this is my buddy's sister—bro code and all—and would rightfully hand me my ass if I touch her, I can't help but want her. My dick has been hard since that kiss at the Winchester. But she's vulnerable right now, afraid of her own shadow and I'm not a guy to take advantage of the situation. "Do what you want with that information," I say.

HAVEN

Do what you want with that information.

As Tyler's words ping around inside my lust-rattled brain, I move to my suitcase and pull out a dry T-shirt. I hug it to my chest and note the way he's scrubbing his face like he's in total agony as he watches my every movement carefully.

I inhale, sucking in a breath of courage. Honestly, I cannot believe what I'm about to do. Seducing a stranger is not my style, but why can't I have a night with this guy? The second I pressed my lips to his, felt his strength—his protectiveness—it filled me with a kind of want I'd never experienced before. He's big and tough, and like all MMA fighters, he's scary and threatening, buzzing with power and control, but there is another side of him, one that draws me in and wraps me in safety. I'm not asking for forever here, just one night. One night to feel wanted, comforted—sheltered—in his arms.

"I...um...I need to change my shirt."

"Yeah," he says and turns his head and a small smile touches my mouth at his gentlemanly manners. He's a fighter.

A guy like him takes what he wants. He doesn't ask for it, doesn't let anyone or anything stand in his way. I've seen him in the cage, seen him knock teeth out with a single punch, his every hit deliberate and thorough. Would he be like that in bed? A fire burns low in my belly, eager to find out.

"The thing is though, Tyler," I say, and his head slowly swivels back until his eyes are locked on mine. "If you *were* my boyfriend, you probably wouldn't turn your head while I changed, right? I mean, if we were to really convince people, especially my stalker, that we're a couple, we should probably be familiar with each other. Or at least display some type of intimacy in public." I open my mouth to continue, but stop when the green in his eyes deepens.

"Do you know what you're doing, Haven?"

I gulp. "Yes," I say and as my gaze drops to take in the rippling muscles on his chest, I've never been more sure of anything. This man is a work of art, absolutely gorgeous and I want to touch him more than I want my next breath.

He tilts his head. "I'm a prick. You know that, right?"

I give a nervous laugh. "I've heard, but you've been nothing but nice to me."

"I don't always do the right thing," he says, his voice rough and edgy.

"Maybe that's okay with me. Maybe I'm not looking for Mr. Right tonight, Tyler."

His green eyes go dark, feral almost, and he waves a finger back and forth between the two of us. Even though he's warning me against getting involved, he wants this every bit as much as I do. It's written all over him, and of course, he'd told me so with his own words.

"You've had a rough night. Trauma and emotional exhaustion can make you do strange things," he says. "I need you to be sure."

He's right. I am emotionally exhausted, and that can make

a person do strange things, but the way he's checking in with me makes me want him even more. "My night hasn't really been that rough," I say, and slide my teeth over my bottom lip. His resulting growls sends shivers through me. "It could be rougher."

Good Lord, what am I saying? Do I want it rough with this guy? I take in his mouth, his big hands. Do I want him to take me with that sexy mouth, demand with those rough hands? My God, I do, and honestly that surprises me. I've never wanted it like this before...then again, do I even know who Haven is, or what she wants? I don't but tonight is a different story. Will I regret this come morning? I guess I'm going to find out.

"Tell me what you want," he says.

"I want you."

"If we start this, the second I get my mouth on you, there'll be no stopping."

"I have no intention of tapping out, Tyler," I say. He angles his head, his gaze roaming my face, and I think back to what I know about this man. "Just one night," I say quickly. "I'm not looking for a future, Tyler."

His brow furrows and something dark and dangerous flashes in his eyes before he quickly blinks it away. "No future, got it."

I remember the women on his arm, a different one every week. "We're on the same page here." Feeling brazen under his heated stare, I toss the dry shirt to the bed, and toy with the hem of my wet shirt, ready to peel it over my head.

"So you think you know me then?" He stands, stretches out his long length, and my sex quivers.

"I know enough."

"You don't know anything about me," he says. "But know this. The only man who's going to put his hands on you while you're in Blue Bay is me." Before I can respond, his hungry lips are on mine, his hands sliding around my back to grip my ass roughly. I yelp with excitement. He's right. I don't know anything, and this man is going to use me, abuse me, give everything he's got and take everything he wants.

I can't wait.

He pushes my hands away and grips the hem of my shirt. His rough knuckles scrape over my sensitive flesh and I whimper with need and he tugs the shirt up. "We need to get you out of this," he says with a growl. "And not because it's wet."

Don't even get me started on wet, or the tremendous heat pooling between my legs. He lifts my shirt, and I put my arms up in the air, letting him undress me. His eyes blaze with need as he pulls the material over my head and tosses it onto the chair he'd recently occupied.

"Fuck," he says under his breath as his gaze drops to my breasts. They're not overly big, and despite the industry, I will not enlarge them. From the look on Tyler's face, the way he's gazing at me with raw hunger, it's clear I made the right decision. "Perfect," he says and lightly brushes his hands over the sides of my breasts.

I suck in a fast breath, my nipples puckering before his eyes and the pleasure radiating from his body lets me know how much he likes that. I arch my back a bit, offering myself up to him and he growls deeply before bending forward and sucking one nipple into his hot mouth. My hands go to his shoulders as he swirls his tongue over my bud, teasing and tormenting, and sucking so hard I feel the pull between my quivering legs.

"Tyler," I whisper, and race my hands over his broad shoulders, scraping his skin with my nails, clawing at him for more. He slides a hand into my sleep shorts, and a little breathy whisper catches in my throat.

Wasting no time, he parts my wet lips with his scalding

fingers and caresses my clit. Molten heat blisters through my body. I moan as he mutters curses under his breath. "So good," I whimper, and move against his finger shamelessly. With his mouth still on my nipple, his rough finger swipes my clit, then circles it until I'm damn near delirious. My God, it's been so long since I've been touched—and never like this— I'm about to climax.

One glorious thick finger slides inside me, and he presses the palm of his hand to my clit. I practically shake against him, a hard tremble from deep inside vibrates through me as he reduces me to a needy, quivering mess.

"Ty," I say, and his head lifts, his eyes meeting mine, the curve of his mouth tightens—so does my sex.

"You like this, Haven? You like me fucking you with my finger?"

I put my hands on his chest, race them over his hot flesh and revel in the way his muscles flex beneath my touch. "Yes," I say and buck against his finger as he fucks me with it. "I'm so close..." I murmur and nearly cry out in distress when he pulls his finger from my shorts, leaving me empty and aching.

The next thing I know I'm on the bed, flat on my back, and he's peeling my shorts from my hips. He hastily removes them and tosses them aside, leaving me completely naked. "I want my mouth on you," he growls. "When you come, it's going to be all over my tongue."

"Oh my God, yes," I blurt out and it brings a small smile to his face. He stands over me, takes a moment to look at my body, and the lust reflecting in his eyes washes over me like a hot caress. Arousal pulses through me, a hot burst of need that scalds from the inside out.

"Open your legs. Show me that pretty pussy." I widen my legs, giving him what he wants—what I want. I lay there, wide open and vulnerable—things I normally go out of my way to avoid. Honestly, I've never put myself on display, probably wouldn't with any other man either. There's just something about Tyler that brings this out in me. I barely know this ferocious fighter, yet I like who I am with him. No pretense, no acting, just the two of us being totally honest with one another, giving and taking what we need—abiding by the rules.

He scrubs his chin and curses under his breath. "Something wrong?" I ask as he takes deep breaths, like he's trying to get his raging need under control.

"Yeah," he says his gaze slowly moves down my quivering body. "I need my mouth on you, I need to taste every goddamn inch of you, but my fucking cock, greedy bastard that he is, wants inside."

"Show me," I say, shocking myself. "Show me your cock, Tyler."

His gaze is dark, intense, ravenous as he tracks back up my body, until we're staring at one another. I have never seen a more beautiful man. Everything about him is hard, lethal, intense. A caged animal seconds from becoming untethered. "You want to see it?"

"Yes, please."

He rips into his jeans, and tugs them down, releasing his gorgeous cock. He takes his thickness into his hand and pumps a couple of times. I sit up, wet my mouth, and reach for him.

"Do you think I could have a little taste before you fuck me?" I grin as dark lashes fall over hard eyes blistering with heat. I like that I can do this to him.

"Jesus, Haven," he groans, and steps closer.

I angle my head and open my mouth to catch the cum pooling on his crown. He pumps again, squeezing his shaft until the droplet lands on my tongue.

"Mmm," I say as I swallow his tangy saltiness.

"That is the hottest thing I've ever seen," he says, his voice thicker, rough with want.

I glance up at him as his cock pulses, eager for more. I widen my lips to accommodate his girth and slide him to the back of my throat. His fingers coil in my hair and tug my curls to the side, giving him a clear view of his cock sliding in and out of my mouth. I relax my throat and take him a bit deeper, and his body shakes as I slide one hand around him.

"Christ," he murmurs through grit teeth. "That is so good." I fuck him with my mouth, and he thickens, his veins filling with heated blood and I love how fast I'm able to take him to the edge.

He tugs on my hair, pulling me off him, and heat blazes in his eyes when he says, "On your back," he growls. "Legs wide open."

A hard quiver goes through me at the ferociousness in his tone. I can't believe how much I love it when he talks to me like that. No finesse, no poetry, no practiced words or hidden agenda. Just blunt, straight up what he wants. I'm definitely not used to that. What you see is what you get with Tyler. It's a goddamn refreshing break.

He kicks his pants off and rubs his cock as his big body stretches my legs out even more, to accommodate his width. With the tip of his cock, he taunts me, rubbing that hard, swollen crown of his over my clit, before tapping me with it. He groans as he slides it along my wet folds, and I shake beneath him.

"More," I say, and go up on my elbows to watch the way my wetness glistens on the tip of his cock.

"You're soaked, Haven. So fucking wet for me."

"Yeah," I say.

"Have you been hot since you kissed me?" He angles his head, when I bite down on my lips. "Don't bother coming at me with any bullshit. I only want the truth."

"I have. I couldn't stop thinking about that kiss," I say. "What about you, Tyler?"

"If you're asking if I wanted to fuck you the second you came through that door, the answer is yes. So did every other guy in the place," he says, ownership in his voice and his gaze.

"The only one I want is you, Ty," I say, and his mouth tightens again.

"This pussy," he says and pets me lightly, toying and tormenting every nerve in my body. "It's all mine."

My God, the way he's looking at my sex, like he's going to wreck me, sends shivers of excitement down my spine. He drops down, slides his hands under my ass and lifts my sex to his mouth, like I'm a buffet and he's about to eat his fill.

That first sweet touch of his tongue pulls a moan from deep inside me, and my clit swells beneath his scalding hot, open-mouthed kisses. My entire body jolts and I grip the bedding and tug as I toss my head from side to side.

"So good," I murmur as he sucks on me, twirls his tongue around my plump clit, before grazing it with his teeth. He gifts me with one thick finger, sliding it all the way inside me, and stroking the bundle of nerves that most men can't find. I tighten beneath him and let out a breathy little moan.

"I fucking love the taste of you," he says and lifts his head and when I see my moisture on his face, my sex clenches around his finger.

He groans as my muscles squeeze his slippery finger as he works it in and out of me, until I'm panting and jerking against him, begging for release. He inches another finger in for a snug fit, and the world around me disappears. I put my hands on his body, splay my fingers, and take pleasure in the play of his rock-solid muscles beneath my touch. I push and pull, need making me lose my damn mind.

Drenched, and delirious, I buck, and squirm. "Please," I cry out.

"Is this what you need?" he asks and applies the perfect amount of pressure to my clit, so beautiful and glorious it sends me toppling over the edge until I'm freefalling without a parachute.

"God, yes," I cry out as the ripple pleasure of release grips me hard.

"That's it, Haven. Take what you need," he says, and I heave in a breath as I ride out each sweet pulse. He stays between my legs, prolonging the pleasure with his finger and tongue. As I sail back to earth, basking in my post-orgasm bliss, he climbs up my body, stopping to swipe his tongue over my nipple.

"Jesus, I did not spend enough time here," he says. "Damned if I don't want to rectify that." He sucks my nipple into his mouth, and the sensations rocket straight through me, settle deep between my legs and arouse me all over again. My sex quivers, and I gasp. I have never come twice in one night before. Then again, I've never been with a man like Tyler, either.

"Is there a problem?" Tyler asks and lifts his head.

"No problem," I say, and his chuckle vibrates through me as I guide his head back to my breast. I wrap my legs around his body, my wet sex drenching his stomach. I roll my hips and he groans as I rub against him like I'm a cat and he's a damn scratching post.

"Hot for it again, Haven? Need my cock in that tight pussy?"

"I need you to fuck me," I say, breaking this right down to the core of what I need—what we're doing here. This is no damn romantic movie. This is basic fucking. Dirty. Raw.

Primitive.

He reaches over me, pulls a condom from the nightstand and bites into the wrapper. He tears the foil with his teeth and sheathes his big, beautiful cock. As he prepares himself, I touch his face, take in the sheer strength of his powerful body. My God, I have never wanted anyone more.

He takes my hand from his face, threads his fingers through mine and puts them over my head as he presses his crown to my opening. I wiggle, trying to force him inside, and cry out in bliss when he powers into me, stretching me in unimaginable ways that amp up my arousal, and bring on a hard quiver.

"Fuck, you are tight," he growls into my mouth as he stares at me. He pulls out, only to slam back in again. With our hands still linked, he fucks me like a man on a mission—a wild animal acting on baser needs.

I whimper as he pounds my cervix, hitting so hard and deep my entire body trembles with the approach of another climax. My muscles ripple as his big cock sears every nerve ending until flames spark anew inside me. He shifts his body, removes one hand from mine, and trails it down my neck to my breasts, going lower and lower, stopping only when he reaches my puckered clit.

"God," I cry out as he touches me instinctively—determined and thorough—like he's known my body for years, like I'd been his partner, his lover a million times before. How is he so good at this? Actually, I don't really want to think about that.

He slams into me, and I lift my hips to meet his every punishing thrust. Hot, wild and ravenous, he pistons high inside, and I ride along, panting for each and every breath as I follow his rhythm, my need matching his.

Pleasure takes hold, races through my entire body, steals the air from my lungs as I orgasm around his bruising cock. A sound I've never made before, something between a keening cry and a garbled moan, rips from my lungs, as I shudder. Hot cum drips over my flesh, and Tyler clenches down on his back teeth. I put my hand on his shoulder, dig my nails in and hold on as my world narrows to nothing but pleasure.

"Haven. Fuck," he says his raging eyes still on mine, as he stills inside me, and pulses with his own climax. My mouth falls open, wave after wave of pleasure washing over me as he presses his forehead to mine. "So fucking beautiful," he says and I'm not sure if he's talking about me, or his release. Maybe he's talking about my climax, the way my muscles squeezed around him. I swear I've never come so hard or so long in my life.

He stops coming, buries his face in my neck and grazes his teeth over my shoulder, like he's branding me as his. I put my hands on his back, lightly run my fingers over his damp skin and smile when he quivers.

"That tickles," he mutters.

I change tactics, and scratch his back and he nips at me. I bask in the weight of his body pressing me down, and instantly miss his warmth when he shifts and pulls out of me.

"Fuck," he says, obviously still sensitive as he frees his cock. Sitting up, he disposes of the condom and tugs on his pants. The bedroom door creaks as he leaves without a word and for a second I'm not sure he's coming back, but a heart-beat later he's back in the room, a wet cloth in his hand.

He sits on the edge of the mattress and puts his hand between my legs to wash me. His touch is gentle, soft on my sex, a complete contrast to the way he fucks, and I get a little pang, right around the vicinity of my heart. I blink, wondering if I'm dreaming, because I swear to God this guy is too good to be true.

"Do you have a problem, Haven?"

I shake my head, and he tosses the cloth into his laundry basket. "Good," he says and pulls the blankets up to tuck me in. He stands again, and I watch him wide-eyed as he makes his way to the door. Lord, I really shouldn't be feeling such a deep sense of loss.

"Good night," I say.

He flicks the light off, and in the dark I listen to the rustle of his pants as he removes them. "You're staying?" I ask, wishing I was better at hiding the joy in my voice.

"Yeah." The bed dips beside me, and I lay there staring at the ceiling in the dark. Even though I'm tired, my mind races, wants to relive every minute of tonight. I just had sex—the best sex of my life—with a man I barely know. A man who is going to pretend to be my boyfriend to protect me from whoever is sending threatening letters.

He shifts and his voice falls over me. "Go to sleep, Haven."

"You're awfully bossy."

He effortlessly moves me around with powerful arms, until I'm the little spoon and he's the big one. "You don't know me," he says as I melt into his warmth. "But know this. We'll be doing this again."

"This?" I ask, as we snuggle, and try not to get my hopes up. "Do you mean snuggling or sleeping together?" Yeah, I need to clarify.

"I'm talking about fucking. We'll be doing that again," he says, a statement not a question. "I'm not nearly done with you, Haven."

I bite down on my lip and resist the urge to scream, YAY!!

5

TYLER

The early morning sun shining in through the crack in my curtains slants on the wall and pulls me awake. I'm about to stretch when I realize there's a hot body next to me. I peel one eye open and my heart beats a little faster as memories of last night come racing back, pushing the early morning fog from my brain, allowing lust to take its place.

I want her again.

"Jesus," I murmur silently. You'd think I'd be sated this morning, but nope, my cock is up cock-a-doodling, ready to go another round. Footsteps sound in the hall, and by now, my brothers and cousins will have figured out where I slept last night. Good. At least now they all know Haven is hands off. The first one to say a word about me sleeping in here—or rather my bed—for the night, I'll take out back for a goddamn beat-down. Yeah, it's true I don't spend the night, but the circumstances are different here. Haven is in some kind of trouble.

Yeah sure, Tyler. Go ahead, just try to convince yourself that's why you stayed all night.

I shift to take in the way her blonde hair is falling over her face, one wispy strand moving back and forth as she breathes. A ridiculous, village-idiot grin spreads across my face. With the slightest touch, I pull her hair away so she doesn't snort it into her brain.

She stirs under my touch, and I lightly graze my fingers over her delicate shoulder, take pleasure in her soft skin. That's when I notice the teeth marks on her flesh. I chuckle slightly, but I hope the damn bites don't interfere with her filming today. She's probably supposed to be blemish-free for this sweet romantic comedy she's starring in.

She rolls toward me and I take a breath as her eyes open and meet mine. A part of me expects to see regret lingering in those baby blues, but instead I'm met with pure satisfaction. She gives a lazy, cat-like stretch.

"Morning," she says softly, and my chest squeezes, a strange little tug around my heart as I take in her pretty eyes.

"I didn't mean to wake you."

"I don't mind you waking me." She shifts to see the clock on my side of the bed. "What time is it?" she asks.

I brush her hair back and she leans into my hand, her cheek warm and flushed from sleep—maybe still from sex. "Still early. Why don't you try to get a little more sleep."

She nods and stretches. "Why are you up?"

"I'm headed to the gym." In the summers I start my weekend classes early, before the heat of the day, and before I'm required to check in for work. Yeah, in the summer, the Blue Bay Crew Construction company works around the clock, seven days a week, and I'm okay with that, considering I put all my money into the company to get it back in the black. We all did. It's healthy and thriving now, and we're all going home with a damn fine paycheck, which I only touch for basic necessities.

The truth of the matter is, I'm good with my hands and I

don't mind helping out in the family business. Big brother Sean has really done a great job filling Dad's shoes. But as I think of my Dad, and how we all up and left as soon as we were old enough, my throat tightens.

He was such a hard-ass man. None of us could ever do right in his eyes, but he was still our father, and not one of us was here when he died. All he ever wanted was for us to be together, working in the family business. He got what he wanted. Unfortunately, it came after his death. As the oldest, Sean was the first to leave and first to come back. I think he took Dad's death the hardest. He blames himself for setting an example for the rest of us.

"Of course you're going to the gym," she says sleepily. "You don't get a body like yours from sleeping all day. I should probably go too." She reaches out and a hard quiver cuts through me as she races her fingers down my chest, to my abdominals.

"Want to join me?" I grin as I think about putting her through one of my workouts.

"Yes," she says, and a smile touches her face as she puts the pillow over her head and gives a muffled, "No." She laughs, and I laugh with her.

I tug the pillow away and drop a soft kiss onto her lips. "You don't have to come."

"Maybe another time." She goes quiet for a second, her gaze dropping to take in my bare chest. "So this," she says, her questioning eyes lifting to me. "We're doing it again?"

I chuckle at that, and I don't even have to ask if she's game. Nope, the second my lips touched hers, I tasted the hunger, the need lingering below the surface. I'm not being an asshole here. I'm not even being a narcissist—I'm the furthest thing from it. In fact, I'm a realist and I understand women want me for my body. Back in the day, everyone wanted to sleep with the Hammer. The Hammer is a great guy to have fun with and nothing more. I used to be okay with that.

Wait, what?

I'm still okay with it, I guess. I don't know, like I said already, I'm getting a little played out. Haven though, she needed me last night, and I jumped on it. I'm not going to lie and say it was only to give her what she wanted. I damn well wanted it too, and I'm not going to forget for one second that she wants me for my body, and for protection. It's ridiculous for me to think she might want more. Hell, I don't even want more. I just met the woman. Yeah, sure it's like I know her after listening to her brother, but still, she's basically a stranger.

"That's the plan." I touch her face, run the pad of my thumb down her soft cheek until I get to that hollow spot on her neck she liked me kissing. She frowns and my fingers still as I study her tightening face. "Do you have a problem with that, Haven?"

"A big one, actually."

Shit, no way did I read her wrong. I'm an expert at body language. A guy doesn't win a title fight if he can't read his opponent—although she's anything but the enemy. I go up on my elbow, wanting to know what's going on inside that head of hers. Everything in her body says she wants this with me. Why the hesitation all of a sudden? "Talk."

She bites her lips to hide a chuckle and I follow her gaze down...to my cock. I shake my head and laugh. "Okay. Never mind. I get it."

My cock thickens impossibly more beneath her inspection, and a groan of pleasure rises in my throat when she takes my length into her small palm.

"The problem is, I can't let you out of the room like this. What kind of a girlfriend would do such a thing?"

"A really shitty one," I say, playing along.

She frowns. "Too bad you have to hurry to the gym."

"Fuck," I murmur at the reminder. I have ten kids waiting for me but... "If we hurry..."

Before I can even finish the sentence, she's between my legs, pushing me until I'm flat on the bed. Her long hair tickles my thighs as she poises her mouth over my crown. "I never got to finish what I started last night," she murmurs, staring at my dick with obvious appreciation. She parts her lips, and I grip the sheets as my cock sinks to the back of her warm, wet mouth.

"Jesus, Haven, that is good."

She takes me deep, her tongue doing the most insane things to me, and I grip her hair, pull it from her face to watch her take me in. Women have given me oral sex before, but Jesus, I don't think any of them have ever really enjoyed it. Haven, with her half-lidded eyes, her soft sexy moans, is between my legs worshipping my damn cock like it's a prized possession. I shouldn't like that so much.

Ravenous, she sucks and licks and makes carnal noises like she's eating an ice cream cone during Blue Bay's worst heat wave. Speaking of heat... My body burns, blistering flames racing through my veins and coaxing my climax. I try to hold on, I'm usually pretty good at that, but this woman, with those gorgeous plump lips, natural breasts the right size for my mouth, and a body made for sin...well, how the fuck is a guy supposed to hang on when he's battling this kind of perfection?

I touch her hair and my balls tighten as she takes me so deep she nearly chokes. A hard quiver goes through me and my hips jerk forward as I tremble.

"I'm there, babe. I'm fucking there." I try to tug her away, wanting to pleasure her first. Christ, I'm not a guy to take without giving and never a guy to take first. That's not how I roll. She refuses to budge, in fact, she wraps her hand around my shaft and moves it up and down, following the motions of that sweet mouth of hers. I'm a goner. I give it one more attempt, but she sucks harder. Okay, she has other plans, she wants me to come in her mouth, and I'm too damn weak to put up a fight.

I grip her hair and clench down, totally giving myself over to the things she's doing to me. Mumbling curses under my breath as she cups my balls and massages lightly, I let go. I grunt, and my body jolts under her sweet ministrations, my release so powerful and pleasurable it's all I can do to find my next breath. I pant and gasp as she stays between my legs and licks me clean, and I sit there, a little dizzy, a little out of touch with reality as her sexy moans dance like musical notes before my eyes.

"Wow," I finally manage to say as I exhale a fast breath, only to drag in another. She glances up at me, a satisfied gleam in her eyes. "What a way to wake up," I say, and she crinkles her nose, those blue eyes once again going glossy as she thinks about something. "What?" I ask and reach for her.

"You've never woken up like that before?"

"No, have you?" I ask, my voice a bit thick and accusatory. Jesus, am I jealous? Jealous that this woman might have woken up with a man between her legs?

"Actually, no," she says, either ignoring or misinterpreting the hardening of my tone. "I just thought you—"

"Past relationships stay in the past, but if you're asking if I do sleepovers, the answer is no."

Her head rears back a little. "Oh. That surprises me." She looks at the mussed bed. "Then why..."

"This is kind of my bed, and you don't snore quite as loudly as Carter," I say, and she nods, the tiniest of frowns plucking at the corner of her mouth.

Fuck, that didn't come out right. I need to explain this better, and be careful not to tell her I *wanted* to stay in her bed, mainly because I wanted to wake up with her, and that's never happened to me before. This is just a damn fling. I'm her bodyguard, so to speak. But I don't want her to think she was just a body, a goddamn sperm bank. I know what it's like to feel like a slab of meat and nothing else, and it's just shitty.

"Haven," I say and touch her chin. "I also stayed because you were scared, and I'm your boyfriend, remember?"

She gives a small nod, and even though she doesn't look convinced—I have no reason to lie about that—she says, "Now you can go to the gym and not worry about having a big boner."

I eye her for a minute, and get she wants to move on to a new topic, so I chuckle with her. "Every time I think of this, I'm going to get hard. Now get over here, so I can get my mouth on you."

She glances at the clock. "Can't actually. I have to be on the set bright and early."

I shake my head and try to wrap my brain around what just happen. "Seriously, you just woke up, decided to give me a blow job, and expect nothing in return?"

She plucks at the linen, and puckers those lush lips. "Maybe I wouldn't say that."

"Good, because I want my mouth on you. Now get over here and don't make me ask again."

"You are so bossy." She chuckles and shimmies off the bed. "I honestly have to go, but I'm going to take a raincheck."

"You can't be serious, Haven. Fuck."

"What?"

"I can't just let you give me a blowjob and leave. I'm not that guy."

She glances down, her brows knitted together. Jesus Christ, I hate every guy whose come before me, every guy who was okay with taking and not giving. That stops now.

"Get your ass over here."

"I really can't, Ty. If I'm late..." She tugs on a robe and gathers up some clothes. "I showered before bed, but I...I definitely have to shower again. Do you think it's okay? Will a shower be interfering with anyone's schedule?"

"Yeah, mine, because I want my mouth between your legs."

Her body quakes. Yeah, she wants it too, and she needs to learn that sex with me is give and take. "I really have to go."

"No, you really have to come." I climb from the bed and tug on my jeans. I open the bedroom door and wave my hand.

"What are you doing?"

"The lock on the bathroom door is a bit tricky. At this time of the morning, they'll barge in without thinking."

"I noticed last night it was wobbly." She chuckles and shakes her head. "A house full of guys, construction workers at that, and not one of you can fix the lock."

"Not much need to. Like you said, a house full of guys, but I'll fix it for you tonight. Right now, I'll give you a lesson on how to make sure the lock stays in place."

"Thanks, I appreciate it."

She steps from the room, the sweet scent of her hair tickling my nose, and arousing all my senses. I follow her down the hall and step inside the bathroom with her. I shut the door, and put my hand on the lock.

"Tug the door like this, and then slide the bolt across. It will keep it from unhinging. Try it," I say and back up. As she plays with the lock, I reach into the shower and turn it on.

She turns back to me. "I think I got..." She blinks as I tear my jeans off and check the water temperature. She points a finger at my body. "Uh, what are you doing?"

"You asked for a rain check, but it's not supposed to rain for a few days," I say. I put my hand under the warm spray. "This is a good substitute, don't you think?"

She shakes her head. "We can't—"

"Yes, we can, and we're going to."

She jerks her thumb over her shoulder. "What about your family?"

"I'm a grown man. You're a grown woman. But yeah, I really need to get my own place." Honestly, I never had a reason to before. If she's going to be here for a while, and obviously she's a bit uncomfortable showering in the family homestead with me, then I better make that move sooner rather than later. I crook my finger, gesture for her to come close as an idea forms. "No girl of mine is going to give me a blow job and go without because she's short on time. You shower, I'll take you where you need to go. Two birds and all."

"Tyler..." she murmurs breathlessly and grabs the sink to hold on.

"You better get used to that because that's the way it is." I wait for her to answer and when none comes, I ask, "Do you have a problem with that?"

"Two birds...one rock." She takes a breath. "One very big rock."

I grin. "Right, now get that sweet ass of yours over here."

She drops her robe, saunters up to me, and steps into the shower. I follow her in and adjust the spray to fall over her body. "Mmm," she moans and puts her head under the spray. I stand there for a moment, taking pleasure in her naked body and the way the warm water pools on her puckered nipples before spilling to the floor.

Her eyes open. "You coming?"

I laugh at that. "Already did, now it's your turn."

"You're a bad boy, Tyler."

"You don't know the half of it," I growl into her ear, and nibble the lobe.

I move behind her and slide my hands around her body to cup her gorgeous breasts.

"I know some things."

"You don't know anything," I tell her. Truthfully, she only knows what the media prints about me, what's said about me on the MMA circuit.

"I know that you're the poster boy for authority issues." I laugh and her body vibrates as it trickles through her.

"That could be true," I say and move her hair to kiss her neck.

"You don't know anything about me either," she moans, and I slide a hand down her stomach until I reach her puckered clit. I consider what I know about her, and it's a hell of a lot more than she thinks. Her brother adored her, protected her. Fuck, he's going to kill me for having my hands and mouth all over her right now—never mind last night. Then again, Haven is a grown woman and can sleep with any guy she wants, as long as it's me.

"I know you like this," I say and slide a thick finger inside. Her whimpering little moan pleases me and I hold my finger still. "Unless I'm wrong?" I tease.

"Not wrong," she says.

"Show me how much you like me in here, Haven," I say, my voice rough and thick against her ear.

She moves her hips, her sweet ass rubbing up against my thickening cock with each movement, but this is for her. I might have to jack off later, but that's fine. Better yet, maybe I'll find a quiet spot on the set today and put my dick inside her.

My finger sinks in and out of her tight channel, and I brush my thumb over one nipple and press the pad of my thumb to her clit.

"Tyler," she moans.

"You need to get showered, Haven. Two birds, remember." I pull my finger from her tight pussy. "Grab the body wash and get to work. You can just pretend I'm not even here."

Yeah, I'm playing with her, and when she angles her head, catching the teasing on my face, she nods. "You're right. I don't want to be late."

She squirts a generous amount of body wash into her hand and begins to hum. I circle her body, until we're face to face and my heart hammers at the lust in her eyes. I like having her like this. Getting ready for work, getting her mind on something, while I take full ownership of her pleasure.

She washes her arms, and her breasts, as I widen her pussy lips and run the rough pad of my thumb over her swollen clit. She moans, and I hush her.

"Shh, I'm not here remember."

"Right," she says so low I have to strain to hear her. I toy with her clit, and push a finger inside her. She quivers around me and closes her eyes as she continues to lather her sweet body. She leans back and lets the spray wash the suds from her breasts and that's my cue to take one into my mouth. I suck hard, nip and then lick lightly to ease the sting. The pleasure pain combination does something to her. With her eyes still closed, her throat makes a sound as she gives a hard swallow.

"I'm still not here," I say and push another finger into her tight pussy. She bites down on her lips and reaches for the shampoo. She pours it into her palm and lathers up her long locks, piling them on her head and arching her back as I fuck her with my finger. A little faster now, a little more purpose to my movements. She whimpers, and the sound strokes my swollen cock.

She goes back to humming, and the sound is choppy, breathy, a little off kilter, and I love that I can do this to her. With my finger still inside her, her body so damn close to shattering, I drop to my knees and suck her clit into my mouth.

I roll the nub between my teeth and lean back, to enjoy the way my fingers move in and out of her. Christ, I wish it was my cock, but there is no time for that right now and besides, I didn't bring a condom. Her hands fall to my shoulders and she holds on as her entire body shudders around me.

"Fuck yeah," I murmur, and glance up to see her staring at me, those blue eyes of hers hazy and half-lidded.

"Ty," she says, and I love the way she shortens my name. She wobbles a bit, and I stand and slide one arm around her.

"I'm here now. I've got you. I won't let you fall and nothing bad is ever going to happen to you as long as I'm around."

She presses her face to my chest, as she rides out the waves, and I cradle her to me, and hold her until she comes back from heaven. A moment later, she takes a deep breath and pushes away from me.

"That was..." She shakes her head, like she's unable to put it into words.

"Get used to it, Haven. Don't even think you're going to get away with giving me a blow job without letting me have my fill of you. That's not how this works."

She blinks up at me, like she really doesn't know me at all, and she doesn't. "Yeah, I'm never making that mistake again."

6

HAVEN

My God, it's hard to think straight, and I can forget about remembering my lines. How a girl is expected to recall anything with Tyler so close, looking damn hot while working on a gazebo structure for the movie, is beyond me. I steal a fast glance at him as the warm summer sun shines down on me and almost warms the chill in my bones. I suppose nothing will do that until the letters stop, and I really hope it's nothing more than some asshole trying to scare me for kicks. I can't consider the alternative. I'd never sleep. Then again, with Tyler in bed with me...

"Are you okay?" Olivia, the girl who plays my best friend in the movie asks. I turn to her and nod.

"Yeah, just didn't get much sleep last night."

She gives me an all-knowing grin. "If I were in Tyler's bed, I wouldn't have gotten any sleep either."

I stiffen, my mind going back to the loud noise I heard outside the house. Was she out there watching? No, of course not. This is a small town and obviously news travels fast. "How do you know I was in Tyler's bed?"

"Oh, you are so busted, Haven." She laughs and takes a big bite out of her cranberry muffin. Around a mouthful she says, "I had no idea who's bed you were in, but from the way you keep staring at Tyler, I just guessed it was his..." She snaps her fingers. "And damn girl, nice going. That man is fine."

"Technically I was in his bed," I hedge. "He gave it up for me."

"Oh, I just bet he did," she says with a hard eye roll that almost gives me a headache, and I just laugh. Everything that comes out of my mouth sounds sexual, probably because I can't stop thinking about last night, and really, there's no point in denying it. We're playing boyfriend and girlfriend for my safety. Everyone might as well know.

It just seems weird to talk about sex with Olivia, and everyone is very well aware that I just met Tyler—and probably that my brother hates him. I don't usually jump into bed so fast. Not that there is anything wrong with that, it's just not me. I'm glad I changed my stance on that. Although I doubt I would have done it with any other man. Just then, Shannon walks by and I give her a smile. I don't want to talk about my sex life in front of her. She's in her early fifties, with a daughter my age, and I'm sure she's not interested in hearing about my sex life. She always played younger, so twenty or so years ago, I have no doubt she would have had the lead in this romantic comedy. She was huge in her day— Hollywood elite—and I've admired her for years. She's one of the people who's always been truly nice to me. Her daughter hasn't quite achieved Shannon's success. I like her though. We were in a movie together a few years ago, when I mistakenly fell for the leading man, which created chaos on the set, and our ugly breakup landed on all the front-page spreads. Ugh. I wish I could forget that mess. I'm sure the cast I worked with at the time could too. They were all hounded by the paparazzi, which proved unfavorable for them all.

Olivia gestures with a nod after Shannon disappears. "What's the story on his brother, Jared?"

I shrug. "I don't really know him. Only met him for a few minutes," I say, as Mason, our director, comes over to us, mumbling curses under his breath. He came in after I'd gone to bed last night and both he and Jonah were gone before I made my way downstairs this morning. According to Gram, she fed them both before they started their day.

"Is there a problem?" I ask, and a shiver wracks my body. Tyler's asked me that question a lot in the last twenty-four hours.

"Yeah, our damn choreographer for the fight scene broke his arm motocross racing." He pours a cup of coffee and frowns. "I suppose I could get Feldman."

"I actually think he's on his honeymoon," I say. "Didn't he just get married?"

Mason looks at me. "Right, shit." His gaze lifts, locks on mine. "Any ideas?"

"Actually, yeah," I say. I shift until I'm once again looking at Tyler, and as if feeling my eyes on him, admiring his big arms as he reaches for a piece of lumber, his head lifts. I quickly turn back to Mason. "What about Tyler Owens? You know, The Hammer."

He nods like the pieces are falling in to place. "I thought I recognized him. What the hell is he doing in Blue Bay? Wait, didn't your brother steal his title?"

"He didn't steal it, he rightfully won it, and this is his hometown."

He gives a half laugh, half snort. "Yeah, I'm sure he sees it that way too. Watch out for him, Haven. There's a lot of hatred between the two."

I stiffen at the warning, although there's nothing for me to be worried about. Tyler is a nice guy, doing me a huge favor. What's between my brother and him doesn't extend to me, right? I shove that thought away and say, "As a former MMA fighter, I'm sure he can help us put together a fight sequence."

He scrubs his chin, and his brown eyes narrow, the way they always do when he's running something through his mind. "Not a bad idea. Do you know him?"

Intimately.

"I met him at the house last night."

He plucks a croissant from the tray of breakfast sweets. "Good, make it happen."

"I'm not sure—"

"Make it happen, Haven," he says, the finality in his voice shutting me down. Always the pleaser, always the girl to do what she's told, I nod and watch him walk away. I sigh, forgetting Olivia is there until she speaks.

"That guy is an asshole."

"Yeah, well. He's taking a chance on me. It's not like I've been in demand lately and I really need this movie to be a blockbuster."

"Yeah, I know, but if he talked to me like that, I'd tell him to fuck off." She pops another bite of muffin into her mouth and I wonder what Haven would do, the real Haven, the one I don't know. This Haven, the actress, goes along to get along. Acting is all I know. Without it, I'm nothing. Sometimes I even wonder if I enjoy it anymore.

"I guess you'd better go charm lover-boy. While you're at it, get the deets on his brother, for me." I'm about to tell her no until she turns those pleading eyes at me. I like Olivia, I do, but she has a habit of picking a local from our shoot location and sleeping with him during filming, and then dumping his sorry ass before riding off into the sunset, alone. The Owens boys are nice, and I don't want to see her hurt any of them. Although I suspect Jared isn't the type looking to settle down, so maybe the two can have a little hook-up fun.

"I'll see what I can do." I fill two paper cups with coffee, remembering from our breakfast around the old oaken table this morning that the boys all drink their coffee black. I carry them over. Honestly, it was fun sitting around the table with them, although I only had a few minutes, but listening to them all carry on like brothers filled my heart with warmth. It's hard to believe they don't have any sisters. "You guys looked like you could use a cup," I say.

They both graciously accept and thank me. "Hey, Jared," I say and don't miss the way Tyler's eyes are drilling into me, like he has something on his mind. "My friend over there, Olivia. She wanted me to say hello."

A big, goofy adorable grin spreads across his face, and I'm sure he has no trouble finding women on his own. "Thanks for letting me know." He goes back to sorting lumber, and I turn to Tyler, and try not to react to his close proximity, or how his scent of pine and testosterone turn me into some sort of nymphomaniac. But yeah, I want him again.

"What's going on with him?" Tyler asks and gestures over my head. I turn to see Mason talking to the lighting guy. "Seemed like he was giving you a hard time."

"No, it's not that," I begin, a little surprised by his protective side, even though I shouldn't be. "It's just, well..." I really hope I'm not overstepping here. Tyler is doing enough for me as it is, and I feel like a jerk putting his name forward without asking first. "He wanted to know if you would be open to helping our leading men with the fight scene."

"That's not really what I do," he says. "Besides, I'm busy building some structures for the set. Sean put me on these projects."

"No worries, bro." Jared wipes his brow with his forearm. "Carter is about to finish up on the Mackenzie cottage. I'm sure he could help if you're needed elsewhere." Tyler glares at his brother. "What? You've got a problem with Carter help-ing?" he asks with a smirk.

"Fuck you," Tyler says and Jared laughs. The two are clearly sharing some inside joke. "I'd ask Jace, but he's been hired as cook for the crew. He's set up at Gram's. Cast and crew will be headed there for all their meals."

He runs thick fingers through his damp hair and my body tingles, awakening in awareness. "All the more reason for me to get out."

"What's that?" Jared asks.

"Nothing." He turns back to me, and stares so long and hard, I begin to fidget under his questioning green eyes. "Is this important to you, Haven?"

"In a sense, yes. I suggested you, because..." When he arches a brow, I hold my hands up and say, "Because he was in a bind. I'm sorry. I shouldn't have put your name out there without asking."

He takes a drink from his paper cup, and glances around. "Coming to Mason's rescue gives you points, huh?"

I make a mental note never to try and pull one over on him. Not that I would ever want to deceive him. But the man is intuitive, that's for sure. "Yeah, again, sorry to use you like that. I can't lose this job—"

"Why?" he asks, his question cutting off my train of thought and totally catching me off guard.

I blink several times as he waits for me to explain. "It's my life, Tyler. I've been acting since I was four months old. I'd be lost if I wasn't on set. You of all people must understand that, coming from the cage. Fighting is your life. I mean it was, and I guess now you've found a new purpose. But I don't have..." I let my words fall off and he arches his brow as I go on the defense. Why the hell am I getting all worked up? He was just asking a simple question. "If you don't want to—"

"I never said that." His voice drops an octave as he scrubs his chin.

"So you will?" I ask. The muscles along his jaw ripple, and I add, "I'll make it up to you. Somehow."

"Yeah, you will, and I have one condition," he finally says.

I eye him, having no idea where he's going with this, "Okay, what?"

"You come to the gym with me."

My heart sinks into my stomach, and my blood drains to my feet. I mean I know I put a bit of weight on, stress eating when I started seeing those letters, but come on. He angles his head and grips my elbow to pull me back. My body collides with his and a little gasp catches in my throat.

"I train kids. Teach the basics of MMA a couple times a week," he quickly explains, like he was privy to my self-conscious inner thoughts. I might present confidence to the world, and maybe always pretending to be someone else is easier than figuring out who I really am. What if people don't like that girl?

"Oh, I didn't realize that." A smile touches my mouth as I visualize this big hulk of a man teaching children.

"Something funny?"

"No, it's just I think that's really nice. I bet the kids love having a former MMA fighter teaching them."

"I want to teach you some moves, you know, just in case," he says lowering his voice as his brother starts hammering a nail into the wood beside us.

"All these years, I managed to stay out of a cage and not even twenty-four hours after meeting you, I'm doing something completely out of character." I give a humorless laugh. "My brother would be shocked."

"Your brother never has to know if you don't want him to."

"You're right. If he knew you were the guy who talked me

into climbing into a cage after always saying no to him, it might piss him off. Especially considering your history."

He laughs lightly at that. "I just want to teach you some moves." Heat crawls into my face as I consider this man's moves. My God, the things he did to me between the sheets, in the shower. Once again, as if reading my mind, that sexy, all-knowing smirk is back on his handsome face when he says, "I'm talking about in the cage."

"I know," I say breathlessly.

"Although I'm not opposed to showing you a few more moves in the bedroom," he teases, but then a frown tugs at the corners of his mouth. "Your brother never has to know about that, either."

His heat goes through me, warm sensations awakening the needy spot between my legs. "Last night, that was out of character for me too," I say. Why on earth am I telling him this? He doesn't need to know any personal details about me. We're having an affair while he's pretending to be my boyfriend, and whether he believes the rumors that I fall for every leading man isn't important. We're together for the duration of this movie—for my protection—we've made that clear.

"Um, yeah," I mumble. "I'll let Mason know you agreed."

He glances over my shoulder, and his eyes telegraph a message that I can now understand. "No letters today," I say. "Maybe you already scared him off."

He nods, "It's not that I think you'll need to fight, Haven. I don't plan to let you out of my sight, but it's always a good thing for a woman to have a few self-defense lessons. I made Summer and Kylee take them."

"Summer and Kylee?" I ask, working hard to ignore that ridiculous jolt of jealousy nipping at my gut.

"My sisters-in-law, Sean and Jamie's wives. You'll meet them." My shoulders relax, a strange sense of relief moves through me. I'm sure women throw themselves at Tyler, and the thoughts of him being with another woman while we're pretending and sleeping together doesn't sit all that well with me.

He cocks his head. "What?"

"Nothing," I say quickly.

He steps closer, crowding me, and a few eyes turn our way. I guess maybe this will put the rumors to end that I always sleep with the leading man—Tyler is anything but. Wait, maybe that didn't come out right. He's definitely leading man material, he's just not into acting. Then again, we are acting here. What's going on here isn't real.

"Just you and me, Haven. For the duration of this movie. Agreed?"

I swallow at the intensity in his eyes as they move over my face. "Agreed," I say.

"Good, because I'm not good at sharing. When you're in my bed at night, you're mine and mine alone. Got it."

"Got it," I croak out and as my entire body damn near liquifies beneath his hungry gaze, one thought races around inside my lust-addled brain.

What the hell have I gotten myself into?

7

TYLER

There's nothing I'd like more than to take a fast break, head to one of my brother's places on the ocean, and dive in, but I promised Haven I'd watch out for her and that's what I damn well plan to do.

I reach over my head and stretch, having momentarily lost sight of her as she heads inside one of the trailers. Her leading man Jonah follows her in, and my nerves ramp up. I don't like her alone with him, and not because she's known to fall for her co-stars, but because he could be the asshole sending the letters. I wish I could convince her to go to the cops, but I have to respect her wishes. I don't want to go behind her back, but...

"Hey," Carter says, coming up behind me. I spin around. "Jared says I'm needed here."

"You finish the Mackenzie place?" I ask.

He links his fingers together, stretches them and cracks his knuckles. "All done."

"Good, you can take over for me here. Once this gazebo is finished, they want to construct the outside of a bakery, and a strip mall."

"Fuck man, I hate this shit. When I build something, I want it to last. I hate all these temporary structures."

I put my hand on his back totally understanding where he's coming from. "Me too, cuz. All this effort to build and tear down again. What a waste of manpower and lumber." I shake my head. "Dad would have hated this." My stomach cramps and Carter goes quiet at the mention of dear old dad. He was pretty much a father figure to my cousins too, considering they all moved into the homestead when their folks died. They were on the receiving end of his tirades as much as his own biological children were. Fuck, man, we could never do anything right.

Jared steps up to us, and I glance past him to see a reporter trying to snag an interview. They must have come in from the city, looking for a big news event. I hate the paparazzi, hate how they twist a story just to sensationalize it. Christ, a few cameras were set up outside the house this morning. There was a time I played to the cameras, but now, I just want to be left alone. I can't even imagine what it would be like for Haven. Never a moment's peace.

"You two losers just going to sit around knitting all day or are you going to help?" Jared asks.

I catch Haven coming from the trailer, and drop my hammer. "I'm taking a break," I say.

"So you and Haven, huh?" Carter says with a knowing grin.

I turn to him and consider what I'm about to say before saying it. Trust and honesty is a big factor in my life, and while I promised Haven her secrets were safe with me, I need my brothers with me.

"Listen, can you keep your eyes open for anything strange, anyone who doesn't seem like they belong here."

They both stare at me for two seconds, and then, without question, nod their heads. My heart squeezes tight. We might all fuck with each other, tease and torment the shit out of one another, and even though we've all been away, doing our own things, any one of my brothers would drop what they're doing if I was in trouble, no questions asked.

Jared nods, his face a measure harder. "Yes."

"You got it," Carter says, his grin long gone.

"Just, ah, watch the crowds, okay?" I say as I look around at the locals and news crews watching the action from behind a cordoned off area.

I spot Officer Walker watching us. The damn man is always watching us. He eased off a bit after my big brother Sean dropped a criminal in his lap, and all the papers deemed him a hero for the bust. I take a step, and Carter's hand on my arm stops me.

"We're here for you. Whatever you need."

I nod, glad that they're not pressing for answers. "Thanks." I'm about to leave again, and turn back. "Have either of you been to the fishing cabin?" Two sets of eyes stare at me like I just sprouted a second head. "What?" I ask.

"Nothing," Jared says. "Why are you asking about it?"

I shrug. "I was just thinking about camping out there until the shoot is over. There's no privacy at Gram's now that she opened the house to all these people."

"Been locked up for ages, Tyler." I don't miss the worry in Jared's voice. "You sure you want to open it up again?"

When he says open it up, I get the sense he's talking about past hurts, not the cabin. "Yeah," I say, and turn from them as old wounds that have been taped up and closed off, slowly begin to seep. I walk away, not wanting them to see the pain in my eyes. Christ, the last time I stepped foot in the cottage, I was only ten. Sean and Jamie were fourteen and thirteen respectively, out chasing girls and the twins were only seven and with Mom.

A smile touches my mouth as I recall my mom. Jesus, I

miss her. Absentmindedly, I cross the road, and head toward Haven as memories bombard me. My mind flashes back to our old man. He was a hard son of a bitch and I don't know where everyone else is mentally. I only know that Sean and Jamie have mellowed since coming home, but I still harbor a lot of pain, unable to move past the hurts Dad inflicted on me, especially that morning at the cabin after I tried to impress him. I don't know why I bothered; I was never good enough, could never do anything right by him. So yeah, it's been a long-ass time since I stepped foot in the cabin, and to be honest, I'm not sure if it has something to do with needing my privacy, or if it's something I think it's time I faced.

As I think about that, a small hand lands on my arm and pulls me from my stupor. I blink, and focus in on Haven. Fuck, how am I supposed to protect her when I drift off like that?

I shake my head to clear it, glad she interrupted my trip down memory lane. I don't want to remember—which makes me question my sanity. I fled the fishing cabin at ten, and never stepped foot in it again. As my head pounds, working hard to push down the memories, I turn my attention to Haven.

"What's up?"

She eyes me. "Are you okay? You looked like you were a million miles away for a second there."

I shove my hands in my pocket. "Just a lot on my mind."

She goes quiet for a second, and nods, and I'm grateful she's not prying. "You look hot."

I know what she means, but I grin at her and tease, "You think I'm hot."

It pulls a laugh from her and lightens my insides. I laugh with her, so at ease around her. I like that. A lot. "How's it going anyway?"

She tugs her phone from her back pocket. "I'm not needed for about an hour. Want to grab something to eat?"

"Yeah, and how about a swim? It's a thousand fucking degrees today."

Her eyes widen, gloriously. "I would love to swim." She inhales deeply. "Funny, the Atlantic smells different than the Pacific." I give her a look that suggests she might have been dropped on her head as a child. She laughs and says, "What?"

"You're kind of a weirdo."

She whacks me and I capture her hand. "I'm serious. The Pacific is saltier."

"You're saltier."

"How does that even make sense?"

I laugh, and it's so strange. I grew up in this town, spent my days biking and skateboarding down Main Street, greeting those who summered in Blue Bay. Officer Walker didn't quite think of it as a greeting though. No, he preferred to call what we were doing, 'terrorizing the vacationers', but nah, we were just having fun. I haven't felt like that kid in a long time.

"It doesn't make sense," I say, embracing the childish side of myself.

She shakes her head, amusement dancing in her eyes. "Are you twelve?"

I pull her to me until our bodies are aligned, meshed. "Want me to prove to you I'm not?"

Heat moves into her face, and it's not from the sun. "You kind of already did that, and to be honest I'm not opposed to learning that lesson again."

I laugh out loud at her playful response, and tug on her hand. "Come on. Let's go jump in the less salty Atlantic."

She laughs as we take off, and a strange sense of freedom washes over me as we head down the road, walking quickly as we pass through main street, passing by Sugar, the ice cream shop, and Benny's, the main grocery store.

"Should we grab something to eat?" she asks and points to Brewed Awakening, our local coffee and sandwich shop.

"Nope."

My stomach takes that moment to growl. "You must be hungry."

"I am."

"Then why can't we—"

"Why would we pay for food, when we can get it for free?" Hey, I'm not a penny pincher—well okay, maybe I am. I have been socking away all my cash, wanting to build a better facility for my club. The one I'm in now is temporary, pretty much loaned to me by the town, but as soon as someone wants to purchase it, I'm out on the sidewalk. I can't let that happen. I love giving back to the town and giving the kids purpose, something to do other than terrorizing the vacationers. Okay, maybe we flexed our local muscle a time or two. Sometimes those rich motherfuckers who flashed their money and thought they were better than us needed a lesson or two.

I practically drag Haven through town, and she stops when we see the ocean in the distance, all the cottages lined up. I tug her to me, and point. "That house there is Sean and Summer's, and that one there is Jamie and Kylee's. Pick one. We'll raid the fridge."

She laughs. "We are not doing that."

"Yeah, we are."

"No—" she begins, but I give her little choice. Fuck knows why I want to bring her to meet Summer or Kylee, or both. It's not in my nature. I chalk it up to the fact that she's staying at Gram's and my sisters-in-law would like to meet a famous movie star. I mean, what other reason could there be for it?

"We can't just invade unannounced," she says when we

reach Sean and Summer's home, the chiropractor sign hanging from the door. "She could be working."

"Yeah, right," I say with a laugh. Haven however, sees no humor in the situation. A dog barks before I can knock, announcing our arrival. "That would be Scout," I say. "She's a golden retriever, and you will love her. Wait, do you like dogs? 'Cause if you don't like dogs," I wave my hand back and forth between us, "I can't be with any girl who doesn't like dogs."

"Of course, I like dogs," she says and whacks me.

"He probably deserves that," Summer says as she swings her door open and backs up to let us in. Before we can take a foot in, Scout comes running over. She gives me a quick look then turns her attention to Haven, sniffing out the new girl.

"Hello there, cutie," Haven says and bends to pet Scout as she wags her tail so hard, she nearly knocks me over.

"Don't bend over too much," I tell her.

"Why?" Haven asks and tucks her hair behind her ear, just in time to get a big tongue across the face.

"Ohmigod," she says.

"That's what we call an SSL," I tell her as I pull Scout away.

"What's an SSL?"

"Severe Scout licking."

She laughs. "Oh my God, you *are* still twelve."

I laugh with her and give Scout a rub, right around her ears as she likes.

"You could have warned me five minutes ago," Haven says, and I glance at Summer, who is standing there taking in our exchange with a smile on her face.

"Yeah, but where's the fun in that?"

She gives me a whack, and I let loose a loud oomph. Scout barks, like she's laughing right along with the two women, and I start to feel outnumbered.

"Hey, where's your loyalty, girl," I say and she runs off to grab one of her toys.

"Get inside already," Summer says.

I put my hand on Haven's back and usher her in as Summer rubs her protruding stomach.

Summer's eyes go wide and her hand freezes mid-rub. "Omigod, you're Haven Roberts."

"That's me," she says, her sudden bout of shyness taking me by surprise. I think there might be a lot more to this girl than she lets people see.

"What are you doing here?" Summer asks, blinking rapidly as she tries to piece it together. "I mean, I know why you're in Blue Bay. But what are you doing here?"

Haven backs up. "I'm sorry, I didn't…"

"No, no. I didn't mean it like that. I mean, welcome. I'm just surprised to see you here, at my house, and with this clown, nonetheless."

I grab hold of Summer, fake a choke hold. She just shakes her head and taps my arm three times. "He's such a goofball, Haven. You should run while you still can." Haven laughs at that as Summer puts her cheek out for a kiss and I lay one on her. "Have you two eaten?"

"See, I told you she'd feed us."

Summer rolls her eyes at me. "All he does is eat. If he doesn't eat every two hours, he gets hangry. But I guess as his girlfriend, you've already figured that out."

"Oh wait, Tyler and I—"

"Oh, I'm sorry. I heard him say he couldn't be with any girl who didn't like dogs, and with the way you two bicker, I just assumed." She gives me the evil eye. "Did I assume wrong?"

"No," I state quickly.

"Then why didn't you tell me you were dating this gorgeous, talented woman?"

"It just sort of happened." Haven meets my eyes, and she slowly blinks, as the realization kicks in. If we're pretending, we have to pretend with everyone. I snap my fingers. "Haven met me last night and she knew a good thing when she saw it."

"My God, that ego of yours," Summer says and whacks me. "It's more like Tyler knew a good thing when he saw it," she says and glances at Haven. Summer holds her hand up for a high five, and Haven slaps palms with her as a wide smile lights up her face, the two instantly hitting it off like I knew they would. I'm not sure why that's important, I only know that it is. Strange, I know.

"What's with all the stomach hits?"

Completely ignoring me, Summer says, "Follow me, girl-friend, I was just about to make a sandwich." Haven follows Summer to the kitchen, leaving me behind like I'm the ugly cousin, but I can't stop smiling as I watch them go. Scout comes back with her toys.

"At least someone loves me," I shout after them as I try to tug the ball from Scout's mouth.

"Oh, stop fishing for compliments," Summer says.

"How far along are you?" Haven asks.

"Eight months, but it feels like twelve, especially in this summer heat." She laughs. "Why am I always pregnant when one of the guys introduces his girlfriend?"

"How many kids do you have?" Haven asks.

"Oh, just two, and of all eight Owens boys, only two of them are married. I just happened to be pregnant with Devon when Jamie finally found love with Kylee. Wait until you meet her. She's a sweetheart."

Speaking of hearts, mine, for no reason at all, beats double time as I watch the two women bond. Maybe they'll stay friends after Haven leaves. She might be surrounded by people, but I get the sense that she's alone in a crowd, missing that one true person she can be honest with, one she can be herself with.

Damned if I don't want to be that guy.

"Can I help?" Haven asks as Summer pulls a bowl out of the fridge, along with a pitcher of lemonade.

"Sure, why don't you get the glasses down and pour us all some lemonade."

"What's for lunch?" I ask, stepping into the kitchen.

"Well, I'm making chicken salad. Does that meet with your approval?" Summer asks.

"It'll do," I tell her and open the cupboard and pull out three glasses, saving Haven from blindly searching.

"Thanks," Haven says, and a shiver moves through her as I lightly brush my hand over her sweet ass.

Summer clears her throat. "Don't think I can't see you, Tyler."

I laugh and pull my hand back. "This one has eyes in the back of her head," I say to Haven when Summer points to the cupboard.

"If you want something to do with your hands, grab the plates."

"Is Devon sleeping?" I ask as I lay out the plates. Just then, Devon cries out from his bedroom.

"Well he was, and he still would be if you knew how to use your indoor voice."

"I'll go get him."

I take off to the bedroom as Summer and Haven talk, probably about me, and prepare lunch. I head down the hall. I honestly love this cottage on the ocean. Hanging with Summer is one of my favorite things to do. She's a huge part of our family, and she's the sister I always wanted. Sean is one hell of a lucky guy.

"Hey little man," I say quietly, as I slowly open the door, not wanting to startle him.

"Ty. Ty. Ty," he says and jumps up and down and holds his arms out to me.

"Who's your favorite uncle?" I ask.

"Ty. Ty. Ty."

"That's right," I say. "Uncle Ty is your favorite." I pick him up, and drop a kiss onto his forehead. "Want to go meet my girlfriend?" I ask, trying that out on my tongue and liking the sound of it.

"Mom. Mom. Mom," he says, and I carry him down the hall. The second he sees Summer, he reaches for her and she takes him in her arms, struggling to carry him around her protruding stomach.

"Hello there, handsome," Summer says, and my gaze goes to Haven, who's watching the exchange with a tender smile on her face.

"Can I hold him?" she asks.

"Yes, please," Summer says and hands him over.

Haven takes him, and sets him on her knee. He grabs her hair and tugs. "Easy there, little one," she says and tugs her hair free. "Wow, he has the same eyes as you, Tyler. He actually looks like you."

"It wasn't me," I say and hold my hands up.

Summer rolls her eyes. "He looks like his father. All the Owens boys have those green eyes. I'm jealous."

"Me too," Haven says. "Do you know if you're having a boy or girl?"

"I sure as hell hope it's a girl," I say. Haven glances at me, and I add, "If it's not, I'm the third oldest, so Gram is hell bent on seeing me married and giving her a great-granddaughter."

Summer sets our sandwiches in front of us and gathers up Devon. She sets him in his high-chair, and pours him a bowl of cereal. He digs right in, and Summer just smiles at him for a moment, the love and bond between mother and child filling my heart with happiness.

"He has an appetite like his uncle," she tells Haven.

"He's adorable."

"I just need to keep him away from Tyler's influence. I don't want him acting like a twelve year old when he's a grown man."

Haven laughs, and Summer goes serious. "Honestly though, Tyler would be a great dad, even though he says he'd only screw the kids up. It's not true. Devon loves him."

I probably would screw a kid up, and while I know that, over the last couple of months there's been a shift in me, one I can't explain. Do guys have maternal, or rather paternal, ticking time clocks?

"I—" I begin, but Summer cuts me off.

"I know, I know. I don't need to hear you say you don't want kids. I've heard it enough already." She gives a hard eye roll.

What I was going to say was that I might want kids someday, but it's best to keep my mouth closed. I don't want my pregnant sister-in-law going into shock and giving birth in her kitchen. Summer turns her attention to Haven.

"Do you want children someday?" she asks, and a pained look comes over Haven's face. "I'm sorry." Summer gives a fast shake of her head and holds one hand up, palm out. "You don't have to answer that. It's a very personal question to some people, and honestly it's none of my business."

"No, it's okay. It's just with my career, a family isn't in the cards." Warmth and longing dances in her eyes as she gazes at baby Devon. "I don't want to bring a child in the world if I can't give him or her the attention they deserve."

I take a big bite of my sandwich and take in the way Haven is tearing at the napkin. Summer obviously hit a nerve with her question. Yeah, there's definitely more to this woman than meets the eye. But I'm not going to dig too deep. Her business is hers, and mine is mine. I've never been deeply involved with a woman before, and I'm not going to start with one who has a career on the road. I might be a lot of things, and been called a lot of things, but stupid isn't one of them.

Summer puts her hand on Haven's and gives a little squeeze. "Totally understandable." She smiles and changes the subject. "Okay, now I need to feed this little one," she says and takes a bite of her sandwich as she rubs her stomach.

We spend the next fifteen minutes chatting and eating and once we're done, I help clear the table. "Do you want to come for a swim with us?" I ask Summer.

"No, you two go. I need to give little man here a bath, and then we're headed out with Gram to pick up some things."

"Haven is staying at the house for a bit," I explain.

"I heard that." She laughs. "Leave it to Gram to invite the cast and crew to her place."

"I'm moving out for a bit," I say, and Haven's head snaps my way. "No way am I staying there with everyone coming and going all the time. I had no privacy before this, and I am not bunking with Carter."

"Really?" Summer asks. "Where are you going to go? I'd offer you a room here, but still, no privacy."

"I thought I'd go to the fishing cabin, stay a while." Summer goes quiet for a second and I can tell her mind is racing.

"You sure that's a good idea?" she asks quietly, and I don't miss the way Haven is watching the exchange, and likely picking up on the worry in Summer's voice.

"Tyler, if you want your bed back," Haven interjects.

"I want peace and quiet," I explain. "That won't happen whether I'm in my bed or not. Did you see the paparazzi outside the house this morning? I'm so over that shit."

Haven nods, understanding firsthand what it's like to be hounded, to have stories made up about you. "Hard to get away from them."

"Yeah, well, I know a way."

She gives a half-hearted laugh like she doesn't believe that's possible. "I'd give just about anything to have a bit of privacy."

"Oh, yeah?" She nods, and I grin at her, and say, "I'm going to hold you to that."

HAVEN

"Okay, Haven, take five," Mason says with a grumble, and I let loose a breath as he walks away. My God, what is wrong with me? If I don't stop jumbling my lines, I'm going to be cut. I catch the way Shannon is watching me, concern all over her pretty face as Jonah, my romantic interest in the movie, steps closer.

"You okay?" he asks.

I glance around the set, and my gaze lands on Tyler, who's been watching the scene while helping his brothers with the exterior strip mall. They've yet to use him for the fight scene, so until they do, he continues to work, helping his brothers with set design, and it's insane how much of a distraction he is. Although I have to say I do like having him close, and he's not my only distraction.

"Yeah, just didn't get much sleep last night," I tell him. "Strange place, strange bed, and a busy racoon outside my bedroom window." While all that is true, it's not what really kept me up at night

"I slept great," he says and stretches his arms over his

head. "I don't care if my trailer ever arrives. Gram's home cooking is the best I've ever had."

"Yeah, it sure beats donuts and croissants for breakfast. Everyone I've met here has been so open and welcoming."

"I hear Tyler is going to be helping me with the fight scene." He lightly nudges my chin. "You know for when Zander and I have that fight outside the bar, both vying for your love." He snorts. "What a weird coincidence that the guy your brother stole the title from is going to be working with us. I bet your brother would have something to say about that."

"What he doesn't know can't hurt him," I tell him and present him with a smile that doesn't quite reach my eyes. Rock would lose his shit big time, but honestly, I'm a big girl and I can sleep with whoever I want. The truth of the matter is, I adore Rock. My whole life he's been my, well...rock. I'd never want to disappoint him or create any kind of conflict.

Tyler picks up a piece of lumber and casts me a fast glance. Our gazes meet and linger a moment too long, letting anyone in close proximity know exactly what's going on between us.

"The Owens' are a very talented bunch," I say. "We're lucky to have come across them." I take a breath and let it out slowly. "It's such a nice small town, don't you think?" I turn back to Jonah, and his head dips, a half-smile playing on his mouth.

"Since when did you like small towns?"

Always, but why would he know that? He has no idea who I really am, and when it comes right down to it, neither do I. "I like this one," I say and leave it at that.

"Other than Gram's cooking, this place is bust. Boring as fuck. What's with Winchester's anyway? There's hardly any action there. I'll be glad to be back in the city."

"Blue Bay is what you make of it, Jonah," I say, and

smooth my hand over my short dress when a breeze washes over us.

His gaze slides to Tyler's, and for a brief second the men lock eyes. "I know what you're making of it," he says teasingly, but there's a measure of warning in his eyes. "Just tell me you know what you're getting yourself into. I might have a reputation for being an asshole, but I don't want to see my leading lady get hurt." Lines crinkle around his eyes as he narrows his gaze in on me, a cautionary look around those baby blues. "Plus, you know, you can't really afford any more drama, and I want this movie to be a success, Haven."

Don't screw it up, I get it.

"It's not exactly as it looks," I tell him, realizing his concern for me is more about his paycheck. Not a surprise, really. If I've learned anything it's that people care only about their own best interests. Tyler, however, seems different. Then again, what do I really know about him?

He waits a minute to see if I'm going to explain, and when I remain quiet, he adds, "Yeah, well, whatever it is, be careful. That guy has a reputation. Not a good one. He fights dirty, will do whatever it takes to get what he wants."

I nod. "I know, I heard the rumors."

"Maybe they're not rumors." He runs his hand through his hair. "Look, all I'm saying is it's day one of the shoot, and you can't even get your lines right. Maybe you don't need that kind of distraction."

"You're right," I say. While Tyler is a distraction on the set, I'll be able to get a good night's sleep when he's beside me and won't feel the need to continually look over my shoulder.

He puts his hand on my shoulder, and with his Hollywood handsome face, stares at me. "If there's anything I can do, just let me know, okay? I need this film to be a success as much as you do."

I nod, hating how I fumbled the lines so much today. I

need to do better. No, I need my very best. "I think I just need another cup of coffee." No sooner do the words leave my mouth, but I spot Gram coming our way, a tray filled with coffee in each hand.

I glance past her shoulder into the trees, where I spotted someone watching Jonah and I in the middle of our scene. No doubt it was a local, just fascinated by the process, and I need to stop worrying and get my head into the game. It's not too late to recast and I can't forget Tyler, my knight in shining armor, or rather my knight in low slung jeans and T-shirt that showcases his hard body, is right by my side. My ovaries vibrate as I watch him hammer a nail into the wood.

"Thanks, Gram," I say when she holds the tray out and I take a cup. Jonah grabs two and saunters off. Gram's gaze moves over my face, like she's assessing me.

"Bad news," she says and shakes her head, her eyes solemn.

My entire body stiffens. "What's going on?" I ask and look around the set, expecting to find my stalker coming my way.

"I'm going to need Tyler's room back, I'm afraid."

Disappointment sits heavy, but I push it down. He said he was headed to the fishing cabin anyway, so it's not like he'd be sliding between the sheets with me every night. His conversation earlier today with Summer comes racing back. She seemed awfully concerned about him going there. I honestly have no idea what that was all about, and I'm not sure I ever will. I admit, I'm curious, but really, it's none of my business and it's probably best I don't get too close to a guy whose stage name was Hammer. I used to wonder if the girls called him that for another reason—a sexual one. Last night I found the answer out in the most delightful way.

"Something funny?" Gram asks.

I wipe the smile from my face. "No, nothing, and it's okay." I shade the sun from my eyes and search for Olivia. I catch her walking toward Jared as he sits shirtless on the steps of the gazebo and opens his water bottle. My God, the Owens men are gorgeous, but Tyler is the one who I want to be with. Temporarily, that is. Until the shoot is finished. "I can probably just bunk with someone else."

Gram nods in approval. "Heard you met Summer."

I smile. "Word gets around fast in this place."

She grins. "No need for secrets. We're all family here."

My heart lurches at that. I love how she takes everyone in and makes them a part of her already large clan. But really, I'm not a part of her family, even though I like the idea of it. I'm just passing through, a life on the road.

"You're right and yes, I met Summer. Tyler and I had lunch there today, and I also met Devon. He is so incredibly sweet. He has the Owens eyes."

"That means he'll grow up to be a handful like the rest of them." She purses her lips and shakes her head, but it's clear she wouldn't change a thing about any of her grandkids. "When Summer delivers her baby, she'll be coming to stay with me, so I need to have that room ready for her. Sometimes babies come early, you know, and I wouldn't want to have to put you out at the last minute." Gram, the matriarch of this big family, beams, obviously loving her caregiver role and it's easy to tell how much they all adore her. "I'm hoping for a great granddaughter this time. But no matter. If it's a boy I'll love him just as much." She glances down, pinches her lips and goes quiet, like she's deep in thought. Her head lifts, and there's a hint of mischief there. "Do boys or girls run in your family?" she asks.

I laugh, and I'm about to answer, tell her I'm not really sure, when Tyler comes up, a smirk on his face as he takes the last coffee in the tray and shakes his head. "Gram, don't you have another tray of coffee to distribute?" he asks as he gestures to the full tray in her other hand.

"Mind your manners, Tyler. Just having a conversation with my new friend Haven."

"What you're doing is sizing her up to see if she'll give you that great granddaughter. She's only here for a short time, and you are not setting her up with one of your grandsons."

"Don't tell me what I can and cannot do." She holds out an arthritic hand. "Or I'll gristle you."

Tyler laughs at that, but backs up just in case. "Haven already said she didn't want kids, so stop wasting your time."

I frown. Did I say I didn't want kids? No, I think it was more the case I said I wouldn't bring one into the world if I couldn't be there for it. I think it was Tyler who said he didn't want kids and was just reminding me of that.

Gram frowns at me. "You're young yet. One of these days you'll see things differently." She looks at Tyler. "I'll see you both for Sunday dinner tonight," she says.

"Not tonight, Gram. I'm going to get Haven settled into the fishing cabin. She'll have her privacy there."

"Wait, what?" I ask. I didn't realize he wanted me there with him.

Before Tyler can answer, Gram says, "I think that's a good idea, Tyler." She points a gnarled finger at him. "I'll let you both out of Sunday dinner this time."

Tyler grins and takes a sip of his coffee. "Listen, I think Olivia has a thing for Jared. Why don't you go see about her giving you a great granddaughter?"

Her eyes light up. "Oh, and where might I find Olivia?"

Haven points the way and lets loose a loud laugh when Gram scurries off. "Jared is going to kill you, you know."

His grin is full of mischief and promise when he looks at me. "I'm not afraid of him," he says. "Sorry about that, though. She's trying to marry us off one by one."

"It's fine," I wave a dismissive hand. "She's a sweetie, Ty." As soon as I say his name, he steps closer, and the air practically vibrates between us. "So about these new sleeping arrangements," I say.

He laughs. "When I told Gram I was moving to the cabin, she then proceeded to tell me she needed my room, or rather your room, for Summer. I wanted you at the cabin with me anyway, but she didn't know that, which means, she was trying to get us together, in the same room, and the same bed. She's clearly matchmaking, again."

"I could bunk with Olivia," I tell him as my body tingles all over, simply from being in his presence. "I don't want her to get the wrong idea here. I'm not about to stay in Blue Bay, and give her the great granddaughter she's after."

"No, you're not. But that doesn't mean we can't have some fun while you're here."

"I'm not opposed."

He goes serious for a moment. "I want you with me at the fishing cabin. It's private, away from the reporters. No one will ever be able to find the place, especially if they're from out of town. It's on a back road off the beaten path that's not marked and grown over. I can guarantee we'll have the place to ourselves, and I can't be your bodyguard if I'm not by your side twenty-four-seven, right?"

"Ty," I say and go up on my toes. If we're pretending to be a couple, then who cares if I kiss him with an audience. "You don't have to convince me. I'm all in."

"No baby, as soon as this shuts down for the night, it's going to be me who's all in."

I can't help but laugh at that, even though his eyes are full of need and hunger, and laughter is so far removed from his expression, I should probably be afraid—that he's going to eat me alive, and leave me a shell of my former self.

He puts his hand around my head and he's about to kiss me, but pulls back abruptly. "Shit, we're being photographed. I'm done with the spotlight, Haven." He inches back.

"Remember where we were. I want to pick up right here once I get you alone tonight."

"Okay," I say, breathlessly.

Mason calls out for me. "Back to work," Ty says, and turns to give me a whack on the backside. "Just remember, the sooner you're done, the sooner my mouth is on you."

I smile as a rush of want careens through me. "That's incentive for me to get the lines right."

He grins and walks away, taking my focus with him. As Tyler goes back to working, I take my script, read through the next scene and step up to Jonah. Soon enough, my lines are flowing, much better than they were earlier, and it could be from Tyler's reassuring pep talk. A warm sense of security wraps around me, and I try not to think about what things will be like in a couple months when we wrap up the movie. Hopefully the letters will stop once whoever is sending them sees me with Tyler.

Minutes turn to hours and the sun drops lower in the horizon when the director calls it a day. The cast and crew are all headed to Winchester's for a drink and a bite to eat, and I go along, even though I'd love nothing better than to hang out with Tyler in private. But he and Jared and Carter follow along, and plunk down at a table not too far from where I'm sitting with the crew.

Looking completely star-struck, Stacey brings us our drinks, and we put in our orders. I nurse a beer as everyone talks about the day's shoot, and while I try to involve myself in the conversation, my gaze keeps straying to the Owens boys.

In no time at all, a group of girls are sitting themselves at their table and a ridiculous jolt of jealousy sparks inside me.

"You must be happy about that?" Mason says and nudges me.

"Sorry what?" I ask.

He looks at me as he takes a mouthful of beer and swallows. "Our trailers will be here tomorrow. You can move out of the Owens house." He laughs. "But don't worry, Gram will still be cooking for us."

"That's great," I say as some cute blonde puts her hand on Tyler's shoulder and offers him a big smile. His head lifts, like he can feel my gaze on him, and I quickly look away. "If you'll excuse me, I have to run to the ladies' room." I stand and dash down the hall. I hurry into the washroom and check myself in the mirror. Heavy boots pound down the hall behind me and I stiffen. I probably shouldn't have run off like that. If someone was out there watching me, they know I'm alone.

Knuckles rap on the door and I freeze. "Haven, are you okay?"

I relax at the sound of Tyler's voice. "I'm okay," I call out.

A moment of silence and then the door inches open. I gasp as Tyler's big, steady presence takes up space in the small bathroom. "You can't be in here," I say, catching his eyes in the mirror.

"Clearly you don't know me at all," he says, another reminder. What I do know is with Tyler, what you see is what you get. I just wish I knew myself as well as he knows himself, and honestly, while I'd like to know more—everything—about him, it's probably not in my best interests. Sharing our physical bodies is one thing. Sharing our hopes, dreams, and future is another.

That thought almost makes me laugh because while I'm sure he has his all figured out, mine is a blank slate, chalked in when the next movie opportunity arises. My agent controls my every movement. I follow along like a little lamb. I remember there was a time when I used to like that. Or maybe I never did. Maybe it was just what I grew up doing. My normal.

He stalks closer and my body reacts to his closeness. "I know a little," I say when I catch the worry in his eyes.

Other than my brother, when was the last time someone actually worried about me? It's sad that I can't answer that.

"Then you know a woman's bathroom isn't going to keep me away when it's clear something is wrong." He puts his hands on my arms, and spins me until I'm facing him. Those green eyes of his move over my face, a careful assessment. "Did you get another letter?"

"No, thank God. I'm just praying they stopped."

"If that's not what's upsetting you, what is?"

"I'm not upset," I say quickly, and lift my chin to display a confidence and composure I really don't feel. But I'm an actress and if I can't pull this off, maybe I should quit.

He exhales sharply, and I sense his frustration. My God, the man is disappointed in me. That's worse than anger, and why the hell can't I get anything by him? "Why are you lying to me, Haven?" he asks, his voice a measure softer.

I glance at my feet, like a kid caught with her hand in the cookie jar. "I...I..."

"If you didn't like that woman putting her hands on me, just say so."

My head snaps up, and he's not grinning, not teasing, not making fun of my ridiculous jealousy. No, there's no ego at play here. He's sincere, totally accepting of my feelings. Most guys would laugh, tell a girl to get over it, invalidate her feelings, but not Tyler. He values my emotions and as much as I don't want it to, it plucks at my heart.

He lightly rubs my arms. "I never asked for her to touch me. I never encouraged it. If we're doing this, Haven, if we're going to be involved while you're here, and I'm going to be your bodyguard, we need to be honest."

I nod in agreement. He's absolutely right. "I don't know

why I was jealous. We're having sex. Nothing more." I crinkle my nose. "But I guess I'm not really into sharing either."

"I told you I was the only man who was going to put his hands on you while you were in Blue Bay, but what you need to know is you're the only woman I *want* to put my hands on. Got it?"

My pulse leaps, and deep between my legs I grow wet. "Got it," I say, feeling a little silly for the way I acted, but at the same time excited to know it's me, and me alone he wants —for the next few months, anyway.

"How about we get out of here." He steps close and I gasp as his hardening cock presses against me. "If we don't get somewhere private, like ASAP, I'm going to bend you over this counter, lift this little dress up and sink into you."

9

TYLER

I stand back as she says goodnight to her cast and crew, and they carry on with their drinking and conversations as I lay my hand on the small of her back and lead her out into the night. I catch Jonah's eyes as we go, and I pull her in a little closer. Am I showing possession? Damn straight. I want everyone to know she's with me, and oddly enough, I'm not one-hundred percent sure it's because someone is after her.

Outside, streaks of pink and purple bruise the night sky and Haven's shoes tap quietly on the cement, breaking the quiet around us. She glances around the parking lot and arches a brow as she turns to me.

"No motorcycle tonight."

"Nope. Why, did you want a ride?"

"Honestly, I've never been on one before."

"No?" I keep my hand on her body and she leans into me. "Rock's never taken you out for a cruise?"

She almost cringes when I bring up her brother, and really it's not her who should be worried. He's liable to hand me my ass on a platter for sleeping with her, but again, I'm sure he'd want me to be watching over her like any good friend would do, but sleeping with her, not so much. Nevertheless, she's a grown woman who can make her own choices.

"I wouldn't go anywhere near his motorcycle. I'm pretty sure he has a death wish," she says with a laugh.

Rock is reckless, that's for sure. "Do you trust me enough to ride with me?"

"I don't know you, remember?"

"True, how about we give it some time. I can tell you I'm trustworthy, but you should decide for yourself."

"I trust you, Tyler," she says quickly, blinking up at me with eyes so full of vulnerability—so lost—I could fucking sob.

"Okay, good," I say, for lack of anything else. "Where we're going, we can't take the motorcycle."

She arches a brow. "Oh, are you taking me to some dark back road, or something?"

"No, we're going straight to the fishing cabin," I tell her. "I promised you a place where you could find peace and quiet, didn't I?"

"I'm not quite sure you promised me that, exactly. I said I'd give anything for privacy, and you said something about holding me to it."

I grin. "Yeah, I did say that." A wave of need careens through me as I think about the ways of holding her to that, as I hold her against me.

"Do you really think we should go to the cabin, though?"

Beneath the streetlamp, I catch the worry in her blue eyes. A few more steps takes us to my truck and I open the door. "Sure, why not?" I ask, but there is a part of me that freezes up at the thought of stepping over the threshold. But I'm a damn grown man now, and I haven't been there since I was a kid. Surely, I can walk into the place without old hurts bombarding me, and I'm not sure why, but the thought of facing the place with Haven by my side seems just a little bit easier.

She gives an easy shrug, but her shoulders are tight. "I just...Summer seemed worried about it." She slides into the cab of the truck. "It's not like that movie, Cabin in the Woods or anything, is it?" she asks, half laughing, half frowning.

I laugh at that. "You watch too many movies."

"It just seemed like Summer was worried about you going back there. Did something bad happen?" she asks in a soft voice.

I circle the truck, a goddamn lump climbing into my throat as I slide in. "I'd never put you in a dangerous situation, and you don't have to worry about me."

She frowns at that. "I'm allowed to worry about you, Tyler."

Warmth moves through me at the conviction in her voice. I put my hand on her thigh and give a little squeeze. "I'm fine," I say, even though that might not be entirely true. My whole life I was taught to be tough, taught to hide my emotions because real men never cry, never show fear. I might have taken that advice to heart in the cage, but it's a whole different game when you're a kid in the woods.

Beside me, Haven stifles a yawn, and I shift the conversation, no longer wanting to talk about me. "You guys have long days on the set, huh?"

"Early starts and late endings." She gives a heavy sigh, a weariness about her, like exhaustion is seeping into her bones, or maybe it's more than that.

I cast her a quick glance as I maneuver down the winding road, passing a few of Blue Bay's summer vacationers. They wave as I pass, and I wave back in return. "Do you enjoy it?"

She goes quiet, too quiet, and when I glance at her again, she smiles but it's strained.

"Most days," she says.

I nod, and sense she doesn't want to talk about it. We both sit in comfortable silence, lost in our own thoughts until I come across the long dirt road leading to our secluded oasis. Grandad bought up this land years ago. Dad once talked about parceling it off and selling lots around the lake. Maybe that's something my brother Jacob might want to do in the future. He dabbled in the real estate market when he was in Florida, although I wouldn't like to see the land go to anyone other than the Owens family. I drive deeper into the woods, until the road narrows and the trees close in on us.

"If we're going overnight, I probably should have stopped to get clothes." She gives me a playful look. "Then again, I have a feeling I don't need them, but I could use a toothbrush."

"Already done, toothbrush included," I say and gesture to the back of the truck.

She shakes her head like me thinking to pack a bag is ludicrous, but I don't miss her grin. "Looks like you thought of everything." The smile on her face fills me with pleasure. Honest to fuck, how can such a little thing make her so happy? I guess she's been fending for herself for a long time now, unable to rely on anyone else. Dammit if that doesn't piss me off, make me want to be the guy she can count on, at least while she's here in my neck of the woods.

I follow the path, and soon enough my headlights illuminate the cabin. Haven sits up a little straighter, her eyes wide.

"I...I thought this would be like a run-down fishing cabin."

I take in the well-made cottage, the wide expanse of deck on the front which overlooks the dock leading to a gorgeous lake. Our old boat bobs in the water, and creaks against the wharf. A mixed bag of emotions, everything from happiness to grief, rips through me. Nothing has changed since I'd been here last, yet everything is different.

"I have no idea why I had that image in my mind, but it's gorgeous, Ty," Haven says, pulling my thoughts back. I swallow down the unease punching into my throat, turn the engine off and sit there for a second. I glance at the place again and try to see it from Haven's eyes.

From the pristine state, it's obvious someone has been taking care of the place. There's a fresh coat of Cape Cod grey on the cedar shakes, and blossoming white and purple flowers decorating the window boxes. Maybe one of the guys has been here, or maybe Gram tends to the upkeep. Either way, I'm surprised to see it so pristine.

"Did one of you guys build this?"

"Actually, this is where Gram and Granddad used to live when they first married. Granddad worked and saved and eventually built the homestead after my Dad was born."

"It's lovely, Tyler." I catch her smile as she takes it all in. "Ohmigod, look there's still a rope in the tree over there."

I laugh. "We had fun on that thing. Well, except Jamie. He got all tangled up, couldn't jump off, and nearly broke his neck when he came back and smacked into the tree."

She covers her face and laughs. "I can't even imagine eight boys. I have one mischievous brother, and all his antics were enough." She shakes her head. "It's a wonder you didn't kill each other."

I laugh with her. "I know."

She exhales a contented sigh. "I'd give anything to have those kinds of memories, Ty." The smile falls from my face and I swallow, hard. I let her indulge in that dream even though not all the memories were idyllic.

My gaze goes to the old bird feeder that I made in school. I laugh. "I can't believe that's still there," I say and gesture to the feeder shining in my headlights. "I made that."

"Really?"

"Yeah, I made it for Mom in school. I think it was for Mother's Day or something like that."

"It's sweet. I bet she loved it."

"Yeah, she did."

"You two were close."

I nod as my chest tightens, right around the vicinity of my heart. "You would have liked her. She was really sweet. My asshole brothers called me a mama's boy. Age difference and middle child thing. I think my mother took pity on me, but don't worry, I put them all in their place when I got older."

A small smile touches her mouth. "I bet you did and your mother sounds like an amazing woman, Ty. I'm so sorry you lost her when you were young."

"How about you, Haven? Are your parents around, still in your life?"

She opens her mouth like she wants to say something, closes it for a second and simply nods. I'm not sure what it is she was going to say, and right now, with my insides a little raw, I'm going to let it go. She pinches her lips tight and glances around again, like she's looking for a distraction, a change in subject.

"It's a bit crowded at the old homestead. I can't understand why one of you guys haven't claimed it as your own by now."

My smile fades from my face. "I can," I say, and clench down on my jaw as those two words come out a bit shaky.

She frowns and her hand tightens over mine. "We don't have to go in if you don't want to. We can go back—"

"Come on. I'm fine. Let's go check it out."

I hop from the truck, grab our bags from the back and meet her on the wooden walkway leading to the front porch. The aged boards groan beneath my weight as we both go quiet and make our way up the path. Someone has been keeping the place up, but more needs to be done. We walk along the boards, and in the distance, water laps on the sandy shore and crickets chirp in the tall grass nearby.

"A porch swing. I love this," she says and drops down into it. "Can I sit here for a minute?"

"You can sit there all night if you like, but the mosquitos might eat you."

"Come sit with me," she says and pats the seat beside her. I plunk down and give us a slight push. The old chains groan as a comfortable silence envelopes us. She breathes in deep, like she's sorting and examining the different scents surrounding us, and I can almost feel the tension leaving her bones as she exhales. I like that she's comfortable here, with me.

"You want to hear something funny?" Haven asks, breaking the quiet of the night.

"Sure, tell me a joke."

"Well," she begins as I kick my legs out. "I always wanted to have an apiary."

"Really, you want a bee farm?" She nods and I try to figure out the punch line. "Why is that funny?"

She thinks about that for a second. "I don't know, it just seems silly, I guess."

"Nothing silly about that, Haven. If you want an apiary, you should get an apiary. What made you think of that tonight, anyway?"

"I was on this set once. I was only around five, I think, and we were in a house on a lake, with lots of flowers. I used to watch the bumblebees in between scenes. They just went from one flower to another, like they didn't have a care in the world. I think I used to envy all that freedom, to be honest."

I nod as I let that sink in. Life couldn't have been easy for her. Always in demand, always faking a smile, even when she didn't feel like it. "I can understand that."

She blinks and looks at me with hopeful eyes, like I might be the only person in her entire life who sees her for her, and not an actress. It pisses me off so much, I swear I could punch something. "You can?"

"Five years old is pretty young to be on the set."

"Tyler, I've been acting since I was four months old. Do you remember that old tissue commercial? The one where the baby is pulling them all from the box?"

"That was you?"

"That was me. I was practically raised on the set. Rock was with me up until we were pre-teens, until he took up martial arts."

"Was that lonely for you? I mean did you have any close friends?"

"I had my tutor. She was really nice." When I frown, she hurries out with, "Seriously though, I was used to it. I didn't know any other way of life."

Jesus, she was raised on the set. My life was far from perfect, but hers sounds like a goddamn nightmare you can't wake up from. I don't say that. Who am I to judge her life? Instead, I smile at her and say, "You were cute in that commercial."

"Hey, what do you mean *were*?" she says and whacks me again.

I laugh. "If you want to go fishing, you need a rod and a worm," I tell her. "But you'll only catch trout, not compliments."

"Hey, I wasn't fishing," she says with a laugh.

I grab her and pull her onto my lap. Her knees press onto the swing on either side of me, and she drops down, her hot core centered on my thickening cock. "For the record, you're not cute anymore." She opens her mouth, and I kiss away whatever it was she was going to say. She softens in my arms and I slide my tongue in to taste her, deepening the kiss until we're both breathless. I inch back, press my forehead to hers and say, "You were cute when you were little, but now you're beautiful, Haven. You light up a room when you walk into it. I almost had to hammer two brothers and at least one cousin."

"Oh please," she says with a laugh.

"I'm sure you're told that all the time, though."

She frowns. "People say nice things when they want something from you."

"Fuck." I curse under my breath. I hate her fucking industry and she deserves better than that. "When I tell you you're beautiful, it's because I mean it. Lip service comes later, when you're beneath me in bed, got it?"

A fine quiver moves through her and she grins at me. "Got it, and for the record," she gives me a teasing wink. "You're not so bad yourself."

I arch a brow and run the rough pad of my thumb over her wrist. "Not so bad? What happened to the biggest, hottest guy in the room?"

"Right, wasn't that what I said," she teases.

I cup her cheek, and she leans into my hand. "So you really want an apiary."

"It's a pipe dream, Tyler." I hate the defeat in her voice, the fact that she's given up before even trying. "How can I possibly have an apiary in my line of work?"

"I don't know. All I do know is life is short, and you should go after what you want. Even if you don't get it, you should still go after it. It's no fun spending your life wondering what if..."

She slides off my lap, and stares out into the lake. "You're not wrong."

"Do you still like acting?"

She frowns. "I don't know who I am without it, you know." She casts me a quick glance.

While that didn't really answer my question, it does tell me a lot about her. "Maybe you should take some time to find out."

"What if..." She shakes her head, and plucks an imaginary piece of lint off her sleeve. "Never mind."

"Hey," I say, in a soft voice, not wanting her to hold any punches with me. "What is it?" She scrunches up her nose, and I get it. It's not easy to confront your fears, but I want honesty with her. "No judgment, Haven."

"I've never been this honest with anyone, Tyler. Not even myself. It's not easy." Her eyes search mine, and I reach out and smooth my hand down her hair, giving her time to formulate her thoughts. "This might sound strange, but people associate me with a character. That's how they see me," she says, her voice tight, like she's been scraped a little raw inside. "They don't see me for who I am, and honestly, Tyler, I don't know who I am." She puts her hand on her heart. "In here."

I close my hand over hers. "In here you're a good person."

"You don't really know that, and well.... what if I figure out who I really am and no one likes that person?"

I nod, and my heart pinches as understanding sweeps through me. I haven't known her for very long, but what I do know, I like. When she's with me, she's been honest and open, like she is now. She hasn't been hiding behind a character, and I'm glad she feels safe enough to be herself around me.

"Have you been honest and open with me?"

"Yes."

"Good. Do you like who you are with me?"

"Yes."

"For what it's worth, Haven, I like who you are with me too. I like who I am with you."

She goes quiet for a long time, and we sit in silence until she asks, "Do you miss fighting?"

I roll one shoulder. "At first, sure, but my life and priorities were changing. It was time for me to come back, and I knew it." She stares at me, waiting for me to elaborate so I add, "After Dad passed away, Sean called us all home."

"And everyone just dropped what they were doing and came, no questions asked?"

"He needed us, and we all needed each other. We'd all been away long enough." She shakes her head like she can't wrap her brain around that, and I get it. Who drops everything and returns to their childhood town because they were summoned?

Those carrying a shit ton of guilt, that's who.

The truth of the matter is, we were all stupid kids, and when Dad got tough, we all turned our backs on him. "None of us were here when Dad died," I say around a lump in my throat. As my insides squeeze tight, I shake my head and choke out, "I have no idea why I just told you that."

"Because we're supposed to be honest with each other."

"Okay." I say, but that's not it. No, I'm a little raw inside. Being back at the cabin is opening old wounds, just like everyone knew they would. "Tell me more about this apiary."

"Nothing really to tell. It's never going to happen. I'm not in one place long enough, and I honestly know nothing about bees." Her eyes go wide, like she just had an epiphany. "Maybe you could start one instead of me. Right here." She casts a quick glance around, her long curls swinging around her shoulders. "What a perfect spot."

"Fuck that." I give a hard, definitive shake of my head. "I take it you've never been stung?"

She shrugs. "I left them alone, they left me alone. That was the deal."

I chuckle. "What are you, the bee whisperer?"

She whacks me and I let loose an oomph. "Smart ass. Seriously though, there is a lot of land and foliage here. It'd be a good spot for one. You know the bee population is declining, right? It's our duty to help."

"Then you should definitely set up an apiary, because I'm not. I've been stung at least a dozen times."

"Well then, at least we know you're not allergic."

"Maybe not, but it still hurt like a bitch." A breeze blows in off the lake and I push to my feet and hold my hand out to her. She accepts it and I pull her up with me. Her body collides with mine, aligns perfectly and her softness wraps around me. I like this girl. Maybe on some level she's just as damaged as I am. Maybe that's why there's an odd bond between us. Or maybe there's no bond at all, and I'm just a hot mess inside because I'm stepping back into my pained childhood. I don't know, but I can't deny there's a strange new intimacy between us, a closeness I've never really felt before.

"Let's go inside." I try the door and find it locked, even though most don't lock up in Blue Bay. But the cabin is isolated and whoever was here last likely didn't want the locals sneaking in and causing mischief. The only ones who would have done that back in my day, was an Owens boy. I lift the planter, and find the key, thinking more about the apiary as I open the door. It helps me keep my mind off the last time I was here.

I step inside. Okay, so much for the bee conversation staving off old memories. The second I set eyes on the old recliner, propped up in the corner and yellowed from sun and age, I can see my father sitting in it, lecturing one of us boys about something or another. I blink hard and open my eyes again, but the vision is gone.

Haven's hand on my arm helps me pull myself together. "Tyler?"

"Yeah?" I ask and needing a reprieve, I step back outside to grab our bags. I set them on the old wooden floor, and they land with a thud. I turn to her, and worry lingers in her eyes.

"What is it?" she asks.

"I don't know. I guess for a minute there, I could almost see my father sitting in that chair."

She nods, moves a little closer, until her body is touching mine in a gesture meant to comfort and asks, "You guys were close, huh?"

My trip down memory lane comes to an abrupt halt and I step back, close and lock the door behind us. "Come on, let's air the place out," I say, even though it smells fresh and clean. My abrupt change takes her by surprise, judging by her wide-eyed stare, but she just shakes it off and follows me through the place, opening the windows to let the fresh night air inside.

"How many bedrooms does this place have?" she asks as she moves around the small kitchen island and into the living room. She puts her hands on the back of the sofa, her gaze moving over the recliners and the wall-mounted television, coming to stop on the bookshelf with my mom's old romance books—I guess no one could bring themselves to throw them out—and all our childhood games.

"Two bedrooms down here and one loft." I point up.

She taps her chin and glances over her shoulder as I pull the curtains back on the last window in the living room and release the latch. "Which bedroom should I take?"

I spin around and find her grinning at me. "You'll take the one I'm in."

"So bossy." She laughs. "Seriously though, eight boys." She pushes from the sofa and heads back to the kitchen, where she pulls back the curtains over the sink, the placid lake in full view, and slides the window open.

As she goes up on her tiptoes, breathing in the fresh air, my gaze drops to her sweet ass. My cock instantly hardens.

How I managed to get out of Winchester's without taking her in that bathroom, stripping her of all worries and taking her to a place where nothing exists but pleasure, is a mystery.

"Did you ever all stay overnight at once?" she asks.

"Yeah, we did a lot of bunking together when we crashed here as kids. Carter snored back then, too."

"I love that," she says, the longing in her voice wrapping around me and tugging tight. I step up to her, take her soft hands in mine. "I never had a big sleepover before," she says, with a snort. "I only ever had sleepovers on the set and that was because we had to get up early."

I dip my head, and my heart aches for her lost childhood as her sweet floral scent washes over me. "You've got to be kidding me?" She shakes her head and averts her gaze, likes she might have said too much. "You've never had s'mores around a bonfire, or told ghost stories?"

"Do people really do that, or is that just something you see on television?"

"Jesus, girl. You haven't lived until you've roasted a marshmallow and stuffed it between chocolate and graham crackers." I hold my hands out and mimic the actions.

"Sounds so nutritious." She glances at me. "I see the healthy way you eat. I can't believe you'd put something like that into your mouth."

"There's lots of things I like putting into my mouth," I say with a suggestive grin. "S'mores is close to the top of the list."

"Oh, what's the first?"

"How about I show you later."

She grins. "I'd like that." She glances around the room again, and my heart hurts for the lonely little girl who missed out on so much. I put my thumb under her chin and lift it until those big blue eyes, so full of warmth, and love—and no one to give it to—land on me. "How about this. While you're here, my family is your family. You can count on any one of us, Haven."

"You're sweet."

"And you need to stop saying that," I warn in a teasing voice.

Dark lashes fall and open slowly over those gorgeous blue eyes of hers. "Why is that?"

"If you don't, I'm going to take you into that bedroom and show you just how not sweet I am."

"You're sweet," she says again, to taunt me.

Her grin is shy, demure almost when I answer with, "I was hoping you'd say that."

10

HAVEN

Catching me by surprise, Tyler effortlessly scoops me up, wrapping his arms securely around me. I love the way he holds my body to his, carrying me like I'm something to be treasured, protected. With a strength that sends heat and need charging through me, he heads toward the stairs leading to the loft, and he takes them quickly. We reach the top and he sets me on the bed, and I instantly miss his warmth when he steps back. My God, it's crazy how quickly I could get used to being with this man. I've never been so wide open and vulnerable in my entire life. It's something I avoid, but strangely enough, it's not so scary with him.

Jutting my chest out, I lean back, brace my hands behind me, and he stands back, his powerful body hard and ready, like a predator ready to take down its prey. His gaze rakes over me and my heart beats a little faster when I catch the hungry and honest way he's looking at me. I love how there are no games with him, how he holds nothing back. Just like when we stepped foot in the cabin, he didn't try to hide the pain on his face—couldn't. Men like Tyler, men with complicated layers that run deep, well, they don't cry. Having watched my brother over the years, I know that firsthand. But I have no doubt tears were pounding behind his eyes, his insides raked raw.

He touches me with his fighter hands. He's no longer in the cage, but everything in my gut tells me he's still fighting—some invisible enemy, a demon only he can see. But there is no time to give that further consideration. Not when he's dropping to his knees and wedging his big, hard body between my legs.

Air from the open windows downstairs wafts over my body like a hot caress, carrying his scent of fresh soap and briny sea. I breathe deeply, hold it in my lungs, as he leans in and presses a soft kiss to my mouth. With our lips fused, our tongues tangle as we indulge in one another. The exchange is a soft one, less hurried then before, and I melt into him, revel in the taste of his mouth, knowing I could stay exactly like this all night.

He breaks the kiss, obviously having other plans, and inches back. As I take in the heat in his eyes, searing need pools deep in my belly. Without words, he takes his shirt off, and I let my gaze drop to take in his beautiful and battered body. I stare at him, my skin tight as I try to soothe those deep wounds with my eyes. But it's not those raised purple welts that are hurting him.

"Haven," he says, his voice a low deep rumble of simmering need.

My head lifts, and when I take in the intensity in this man, meet gleaming green eyes that are hard and dangerous, I can barely breathe. But I'm not afraid of him. Nothing about him frightens me, and maybe that in itself should be enough to scare me off.

"Yeah?" I finally manage to get out past a tight throat.

He takes my hand and puts it on his body, and his muscles

jump beneath my palms. "Touch me," he commands in a soft voice, like he needs the connection more than life itself and I get it. Tonight, he doesn't want to think. Whatever happened in this place he wants to forget, for a little while anyway, and dammit I want to be the one to help him. But as he presents this gentler version of himself, my chest squeezes, presses against my thundering heart, and turns my world a little upside down.

Careful, Haven.

I spread my fingers and he sucks in a breath as I slowly explore him, my hand moving over his hills and valleys, tracing his scars and wounds that all come with their own story. I push him back a little, and drop to my knees before him. My hand goes to his throat, and he angles his head. I run my fingers down, over his tight flesh and full veins, until I reach his shoulders. With the utmost care, I lean in to press soft kisses to each angry scar, wishing I could go deeper to chase away whatever it is that haunts him. His hands go to my hair and my name is simply a whisper on his tongue as he tugs. The man is brutal in the cage, his body scarred from hammering fists, but right now he wants soft hands on his body. My soft hands.

I slide my palms lower, and tug on his jeans. My breathing grows harsher, matching his, and heat floods my sex. He puts his hand between my legs, slides up my thighs until he reaches my damp panties and briefly closes his eyes, like he's in total agony.

"You're burning up, Haven," he says.

"I know. I'm aching for it," I say. No sense in lying. The truth is right there, between my legs. "Can you do something about that, Ty?" I rake my hand through his hair and he tugs my panties to the side.

"Something like this, you mean," he says as he strokes my clit, a light touch with brutal fingers.

Pleasure surges through me, making it almost impossible to talk. "God, yes," I say. He thrusts a finger inside me and try as I might, I can't seem to get the zipper down on his jeans. He shifts closer, shoves his thigh between my legs to widen them as he fucks me with his slick finger.

"Seems to me like you need this, too."

"Yes, but I want to see your cock." My God, I can't even believe the need in my voice. Have I ever been this needy, ever ask to see a man's cock?

"Do you now?" A grin touches the corner of his mouth as his thick finger leaves my sex. I almost grab his hand to put it back and demand he take me, but he grips the thin band on my panties and rips them clear from my hips. I gasp but he leans in, his mouth muffling the sound as he kisses me. One beautiful thick finger slides inside me again, and the needy moan of pleasure climbing out of my throat seems to do something wild to him.

"Ride me, Haven."

I move my body, rock into his finger and the needy little sound in my throat grows, expands, turns to a whimpering cry as his palm bangs against my plump clit. He gifts me with a second finger, and I twist and move and grind and cry out his name as hunger builds, claws at my insides.

"Ty," I murmur, and take my breasts into my hands as I press against him.

"Get this fucking dress off and show me your tits, Haven."

With arms that are almost too weak to move, I grip the hem of my dress and peel it over my head. His gaze drops to my breasts, and I unhook the bra, tossing it away. Breasts free of any confines, I put my thumb into my mouth and suck, getting the pad nice and wet. He watches me closely, dark anticipation dancing in his eyes as I cup my breasts and swipe my thumb over my nipple, getting it nice and plump for his mouth.

"Jesus, girl," he says, and as he continues to finger fuck me he puts his thumb into my mouth. "Suck."

I do as he asks, sucking hard, until hollows form in my cheeks, and I steal a glance downward to take in the way his cock is straining against his jeans. That just won't do. Eager to see how aroused he is, I let one breast go, and the hiss of his zipper mingles with his groans and I put my hand into his pants and wrap my palm around his cock.

He leans into me and growls in my ear. "I need my mouth on this sweet pussy, baby. I want to taste you when you come."

His hand leaves my sex, and he picks me up, manhandling me like I'm a damn ragdoll. He moves me around, positions me on the bed the way he wants me, and my God, it's insane how much I like it when he takes full control of my body. With Tyler flat on his back and my legs straddling his body, he brings me to his mouth. My hot sex hovers over his mouth, and he pulls me down until I'm sitting on his face. He swirls his tongue over my clit, licking and sucking and nibbling.

"So good," I murmur, my head going back and forth as I take my breasts back into my hands, squeezing my nipples until pain and pleasure mingle. I move, my hips gyrating shamelessly against him and the more I do it, the more of a reaction it pulls from him. He eats at me, greedy nibbles, and my body convulses. "I...I...ohmigod, Tyler," I call out. I've never orgasmed without penetration before.

He growls and I put my hands on the headboard as I shatter around his tongue, my hot cum dripping over his face, and down my thighs. He laps it up, drinking me all in, his tongue doing the most magical things to prolong my pleasure. My God, what I've been doing before wasn't sex. No man had ever given me an earth-shattering orgasm before.

The second my body stops spasming, he grips my hips

again, easily maneuvering me until my soaking sex is poised over his cock. He blows out a harsh breath, dark and needy as he pulls me down, his huge cock penetrating so deep, my entire body clenches around him.

"Yes," he cries. "You are so goddamn perfect, Haven."

He holds my hips his fingers biting into my flesh, and he moves me around, lifting me up and pulling me down hard again, and I give myself over to him, letting him control the depth, pace and rhythm. I've never felt so tiny, or so safe in anyone's arms before.

"Is this what you needed, baby?"

"It's what I needed," I say.

All strength and power, his thick smooth head disappears inside my tight channel, and his hips lift as he pistons into me. I claw at the headboard and grow wetter, hotter, my throat dry as I gasp for breath.

"Will my cock help take that ache away?"

"Yes," I cry out as he moves me faster, pulling me down on top of him until he's buried balls deep inside me. He lifts me again, higher and higher, and the sweet friction sends shards of sensations through me until my body is humming, burning with a deep need, only this man can sate. He glides into me and I soar. Skin against skin, our bodies bang in sync. Soon enough, tension peaks and my body succumbs to another full body orgasm. My sex squeezes around him, and it triggers a loud growl from him.

"Fuck yes." He pumps into me, each hard thrust for him now as my body spasms in pleasure. His grip on my hips tighten, a new kind of neediness about him as he chases his own orgasm. "Haven," he says, and pulls my mouth to his as he spurts inside me, filling me with his hot cum.

"I feel you," I murmur, something niggling in the back of my mind, but in my post-orgasm bliss, I can't quite grasp it. His tongue slides into my mouth, and I lose myself in him as he continues to pump high inside me. His groan announces his completion, and he wraps those rough, powerful arms around me, holding me to him tightly yet tenderly at the same time. My hard nipples scrape his chest as I shimmy, trying to get closer.

We cling to one another, touching, tasting, as he lifts me to slide his cock out. With my nerve endings still sensitive, I quiver around him. I shift, and put my face on his chest, loving the pounding beats against my cheek. He strokes my hair, curls it around his fingers.

"I need to dispose...oh, fuck," he says, his body going so stiff beneath me, I jackknife up to see his face.

"What?" I ask and look over my shoulders. My God, did someone sneak inside while we were having sex, completely oblivious to anyone and anything but pleasure.

"Condom. I forgot." He grips his hair and tugs.

"Oh God," I say, and slide off him, tugging the blankets up to cover my nakedness. He touches my shoulder, his eyes dark, severe...intense.

"I'm clean, Haven. You need to know that about me."

I nod. "I am too. It's been a while for me."

"Are you on the pill?"

"I take it to regulate my cycle, and you know, in case I find myself in Blue Bay with the hottest, toughest guy in town." That brings a smile to his face, like I was hoping it would. I lean down, and place a kiss on his mouth. "Don't worry, I won't make you a daddy. Neither one of us wants that."

He nods, and for a brief second I think I spot something in his eyes, something that looks a lot like disappointment, but I have to be mistaken. Not only do I barely know this man, he doesn't want kids, and especially not with a woman who is only in town for a short time. Maybe he was just disappointed in himself for forgetting. But he can't take all the blame.

"I never gave protection another thought either, Ty. This isn't just on you."

"Too hot for it?" he teases, and I laugh.

"Yeah, something like that. You have a very big..." He arches a brow, and I add, "Ego."

He tugs on my hair, his belly laugh vibrating through me. I roll toward him, so completely comfortable with him like this it's insane. It feels like I've known him my whole life when in fact, I don't know him at all, and he'd be quick to point that out.

I reach out and touch his hair, pushing it back from his forehead. I take a deep, contented breath and let it out slowly. "I love it here, Ty," I begin as he mimics my position. I take in the relaxed look on his face, so completely different from when we first arrived. "Thanks for taking me. I never thought I could find a place where the paparazzi couldn't find me. You guys are all so lucky to have each other, and this place. I just love small towns. Did you know I used to have a Norman Rockwell calendar growing up?" Lord, why am I rambling, and telling so much about myself? "I loved that calendar. I guess it gave life a sense of normalcy or something, when mine was anything but."

"You deserve normalcy, Haven," he says, his voice full of empathy and understanding.

"I don't want to pry, but what is it about this place? What is it that makes you upset?"

Darkness invades his eyes, and there's a gurgling sound in his throat as he swallows hard and rolls to his back. He puts his arm across his forehead and stares up at the ceiling, and he goes so quiet for so long, my insides clench. I shouldn't have asked. It's none of my business. We might be having sex, but that doesn't give me the right to dig into his past, and open old hurts.

"I am lucky to have my family, Haven. You're right about that. I do love Blue Bay, and I'm back because Sean called us all home. I don't hate being here, but growing up wasn't all sunshine and butterflies." I stiffen at the hardness in his voice. "Is it for anyone, though? Nothing special about me."

"I'm sorry. I didn't mean to make it out like your life was perfect because you live in a small town," I say and inch back, ready to put my clothes back on and run back to…I have no idea where, since I have no place to stay.

"Shit, no, I'm sorry," he says, and reaches for me, pulling me back against him. "I'm being an asshole."

"No, you're not," I say. "I just idealize and romanticize everything."

"There's nothing wrong with that. My brother Jamie is a dreamer like that, too. Dad tried to beat that shit right out of him." He gives a laugh that holds no humor, but since he opened the door, I decide to walk through it.

"Your father was hard on you guys, huh?" I ask, understanding that much.

"Well, at least he was around," he says, turning this back to me, showing sympathy because I might have had it worse. "I wasn't left to fend for myself on the set, Haven."

"Parents, huh?" I say, but then go serious. "You have bad memories here, in this cabin?"

He makes a noise. "They're getting better thanks to you," he says, and idly runs his finger up and down my arm, his thoughts elsewhere. Goosebumps form on my flesh as he caresses me. He goes quiet again, and I take in his body language, the internal war going on inside his head. Just when I think he's done talking, he says, "I was only ten." Pain flashes in his eyes, as his chest expands with a deep breath.

"What happened when you were only ten, Ty?" I put my

hand on his chest. His heart races beneath my palm as I offer my comfort and support, because I know he's telling me something very private, something he doesn't talk about with just anyone, and I feel very privileged and honored that he's opening up to me.

Glancing down, he snorts, like it's nothing, which clearly isn't the case. "Sean and Jamie were chasing girls, spending less and less time at home. I was used to them pairing off and the twins had each other. I had friends, but I spent a lot of time alone." He casts me a fast glance. "I was always up to no good and getting into mischief."

"Of course, you were."

"Dad didn't like my aloofness, or my reckless nature. Anyway, like I said, Sean and Jamie were tearing up the streets, and the twins were in Hope Springs with Mom, getting new clothes or haircuts or something. I can't remember, but that's not important."

I nod, and shift a little closer. "What is important?"

"That I actually thought I could make my father proud of me." He shakes his head, his eyes narrowed, pained. "Jesus listen to me. I'm a grown-ass man who has taken down bigger men in the cage, and now I sound like a goddamn kid with daddy issues."

"Between us, Rock has daddy issues too, and there is nothing wrong with that, Ty. We're all fucked up in our own ways. The thing is, we can't bury those feelings. We need to unpack them, sort through them, deal, learn and move past them." I touch his face. "You buried yours, and nothing good can come from that."

He smiles at me. "Beautiful and smart. How did I get so lucky?"

"The night is young, Ty. You can still get lucky again, but first, tell me what happened when you tried to impress your father at ten years old."

His head bobs, and that little boy lost look moves over his face once again. "We were having an overnight fishing trip. I was stoked that I had Dad all to myself. You might be right about that middle child thing," he says with a snort. "Anyway, the fish were running, and I got up extra early in the morning, before Dad. I was going to surprise him with trout for breakfast."

"I guess things didn't go as planned."

"Oh, I had a dog named Bear," he says like it's an afterthought. "It's kind of funny when you think about it."

I frown, not really understanding. "Bear is important?"

"Very," he says. "Not sure I'd be telling you this story if he wasn't by my side."

"Well I like Bear already," I say, and he smiles.

"He'd have chased off that racoon the other night. He'd done it many times, but he certainly learned the hard way to steer clear of skunks and porcupines."

I crinkle up my nose. "Oh no."

His lips twitch at the corner and he looks off in the distance, like he's remembering happy times. I watch him for a second, and put my hand on his arm. My touch brings him back to me.

"Yeah, so I went fishing that morning while Dad slept." He holds his hands out about twelve inches. "I waded out in the water and reeled in one hell of a big one."

"That big, huh?" He nods. "Your father must have been impressed by that."

"He would have been, I think, if..." I frown, and his brows knit together. He shifts, some memory making him uncomfortable. "Anyway, I was excited, and after I cleaned the fish on shore, ready to rush back here to show Dad, a big motherfucking bear decided he wanted to fight me for the fish."

"Oh my God, Tyler," I say and sit up. I cross my legs, my heart pounding. "What happened?"

He shakes his head and a hard tremble moves through him. "The thing went up on its hind legs, and Bear—my dog —got in between us. He barked and barked and barked until it woke up Dad. He came running with a shot gun, and after firing a few shots into the air, the black bear ran off."

"Thank God."

"You'd think, right?" He reaches for me and drags me back to him, and I rest my face on his chest. "That day I realized I'd rather face off against a bear than my father."

"What happened?" I ask quietly.

"I had never seen my father so mad. Well, that's not true. I'd seen him tear both Sean and Jamie new ones. I'd just never been the sole focus of his anger before that. I was fucking scared, Haven."

"Of course you were scared. You were just a little boy who'd faced off against a black bear. That's the thing nightmares were made of."

"Nope, being the recipient of my father's rage was the thing nightmares were made of. When you're ten years old and two seconds from getting mauled by a goddamn black bear, I think that's a pretty good time to show fear, and shed a few fucking tears, don't you?"

"Of course."

"My father found me shaken and trembling, but the worst part of that day, is how he left me broken and bruised. Not physically, but..." He touches his chest. "In here, you know." The rawness in his voice, the crackling thickness cuts into me, and I could weep for the little boy left battered. "He took the fish and tossed it back in the water, called me a dumb-ass, clueless kid. He said I was soft, and said he'd never be taking me fishing again." He swallows. "I tried to pretend it didn't bother me. Tried to pretend I was tough, and his words meant nothing." He shakes his head. "I wasn't very good at pretending."

"I'm so sorry, Ty," I say and put my arms around him to hug him tight. We stay like that for a long time, and his chest rises and falls as he breathes through those painful memories. After a long time, I say, "What he did was wrong. So damn wrong. Believe me when I say this, I'm not taking your father's side here, I promise, but as an outsider, I'm trying to look at it from his point of view and I wonder if he lashed out because he was scared, just like you. Scared his son was going to get hurt and said cruel things to keep you safe. You said you were always a little reckless. Maybe that really frightened him, and he said and did things to break you of that."

He shrugs like he's not sure. "When we got home, he told Mom, and I remember being embarrassed and ashamed by the whole thing."

"You never should have been made to feel that way. That was wrong."

His brow furrows. "Mom wanted to hug me, but Dad wouldn't let her. He wouldn't fucking let her, Haven." He takes a gulping breath. "She wanted to so badly, and she fought so hard not to cry, and I didn't want her to cry. It gutted me. My throat hurt so bad, trying to hold back my own tears, and I wanted to make it easier on her, so I pretended I was tough and I was fine."

"You weren't fine."

"No, I wasn't." A deep breath and then, "Sean and Jamie hugged me though, in the privacy of my bedroom so Dad couldn't see. He wouldn't have liked that. I swear to fuck if I ever have a kid, Haven, I'd hug the shit out of them, no matter what."

"I've seen you with Devon. You'll be an amazing father, Ty, and I mean that." He takes my hand and holds it tight, and I sit there quietly as he processes. After a long while, he leans into me and drops a soft kiss onto my head.

"It's crazy, but I miss him, you know. I miss him so fucking much."

"No matter what, he was still your father. I bet he's up there looking down, so proud of the man you became."

He snorts like he doesn't believe that.

"You were the middle-weight champion for many years, Ty."

"Until your fucking brother took it away," he says with a snarl that reminds me my brother would lose his mind if he knew I was here, in bed with a man he hates.

"Yeah, well, you didn't make it easy for him, and you were the reigning champ for years. That's quite the accomplishment and something any parent would be proud of."

"I don't think he even knew." His hand moves down my back, and he lightly traces my spine. "I never stayed in contact when I left. None of us did. Poor Gram had to put up with him all by herself."

"I'm pretty sure Gram could handle your father." I put my hand over my heart. "In here, I totally believe he was proud of you." He makes a sound, a half laugh, half snort, and I can almost feel the tension and pain leaching from his bones. "Thank you for sharing that painful story with me. I know it couldn't have been easy."

His head lifts and he glances around the room. "This is the first time I've been back here."

"I'm glad it was with me, Tyler. I'm glad you chose me to bring here, to create happier memories for you." He doesn't say anything, so I continue with, "Now what was that you said about being so lucky?"

11

TYLER

Birds chirping pull me awake, and I peel one eye open. The second I realize I'm in the fishing cabin, I jack-knife up, my stomach tight, every muscle taut as old memories bombard me. The shifting on the bed beside me pulls my attention, and the pain of the past eases, making room for warmth and need as I take in the gorgeous woman stirring awake.

"Morning," Haven says as she stretches her arms over her head, the sheet slipping a little lower on her breasts.

"How did you sleep?" I ask, falling back down beside her.

"I slept like a baby. I think all this fresh air is good for me," she says.

You're good for me.

I bite my tongue to keep those words to myself, even though they're true. She is good for me. She made facing the past easier, and I think on some level I knew she would, which is why I chose now to visit the cabin. I've been home two whole years and avoided it like the plague, yet the second she came into my life, all sweet, and vulnerable, it brought out a different side of me.

No need to go soft here and tell her it's possible I might want more. We're just having a good time while I protect her from a stalker. No need to scare her away sooner rather than later. As if reading my mind, she reaches out and puts her hand on my chest.

"For the record, Tyler. There is nothing wrong with being soft. I like that side of you."

I snort. "There's not much soft on me when I'm with you, Haven."

She grins at that, and the truth is, I like who I am when I'm with her. Does she like who she is with me? She spreads her hands over my heart. "In here. I like you soft."

"Listen, can we keep that between us? I sort of have a reputation to uphold."

That pulls a laugh from her, so light and carefree, I can't help but smile. I like seeing her happy like this. It's pretty much the first real laugh I've heard from her.

"Do you have to hit the gym?" she asks

"Yeah, the kids will be waiting. Come with?" I can't protect her if she's not with me, but I think I want her to come for other reasons—selfish ones.

She checks the clock. "Actually, it's still early. I don't have to be at the set for an hour, so yes, I'd love to."

I lean over her, my body wanting more which is insane. After numerous rounds of sex last night and very little sleep, I want her again. I press my lips to hers for a good morning kiss. I kind of like being the last one to kiss her before she goes to bed, and the first one to kiss her when she wakes.

My stomach takes that moment to grumble, and she chuckles into my mouth. "Uh oh, it's past feeding time. Should I be worried you're going to get hangry on me?"

"Nah, you're good. Come on, let's go see if there's any food in this place."

I pull her blankets down to expose her gorgeous naked body, and note the marks from my mouth on her skin. A grumble rumbles in my throat. I lightly touch her skin. "I'm going to kiss these all better tonight," I say.

"I'm going to hold you to that, but they don't hurt."

I stand, circle the bed and pull her to me. She wraps her arms around me, and I slide my hands down her back until I'm cupping her gorgeous backside. My cock thickens more, and she chuckles and squirms away.

"I will not be responsible for your class being late today, so go." She points to the stairs and scoops her clothes off the floor.

I tug on my hair. "You're right. You go ahead and jump in the shower and I'll find us some food. I'm going to shower after class."

I tug on my jeans from last night and head to the main level. As I rummage around in the cupboards and fridge, I notice that it's all been recently stocked. Thanks Gram. I know she wants this for me, and for herself, and I hope she's not too disappointed when Haven leaves at the end of the shoot.

I pull out some eggs, and bacon and put the coffee on as Haven jumps in the shower. Down by the dock, the boat rocks gently, and I glance out over the calm water. Maybe tonight Haven would like to go for a starlit tour of the lake.

The shower turns off and I plate our food. She comes out fully dressed, towel drying her hair. "Look at you, all domesticated," she says. She takes a sip of coffee and drops down into the chair. "Did Gram teach you to cook?"

"I lived alone for many years, and I like food, so I learned." She cuts into her bacon and takes a bite. As the fork slides into her mouth, and she moans around it, my dick thickens.

"This is delicious. I don't cook very much. I'm not great at it."

"I can teach you a few things."

"You know I'm a fast learner."

I grin at her, and dig into my food. After we eat, we set the dishes into the sink for later and jump into the truck. Her eyes are on me as I make my way out to the road.

"Thanks, Ty," she says so softly, so quietly, I almost miss it.

I reach across the seat and capture her hand. "You okay?"

She looks away, glancing out the passenger window. "It's just so peaceful here. It's sad that you missed out on so many years coming here."

"Maybe we can make up for that. I was actually thinking you might like to go out on the boat later. If it's not too late, we can even do some fishing."

Her smile wraps around my heart. "I would love that. I've never been fishing before."

"It's settled then."

We drive in comfortable silence, our fingers linked together, and I pull up in front of the gym.

"How long have you been coaching the kids?"

"About a year now. There were a couple of local boys up to no good. Messing around with the shop signs, and spray-painting things. I thought maybe they could put all that energy to better use."

"That's sweet."

"Shh," I say and put a finger to my lips. "Have to keep these kids a bit afraid of me."

The sun is higher in the sky as we exit the truck and cars pull up to the curb behind me, parents dropping their kids off. Liam Becker comes skateboarding down the road, and comes to an abrupt stop when he sees who I'm with. He hops off his board, and stares at Haven, completely starstruck.

"You better close your mouth, Liam. You're two seconds from eating that fly buzzing around your head."

Ignoring me, he stares at the beautiful woman beside me. "You're...you're..."

"Haven Roberts," Haven says and reaches out to shake his hand. "Nice to meet you, Liam."

His eyes go wide. "You know my name?"

She gives him a little wink. "Tyler just called you Liam."

"Right, shit." He glances down, his cheeks red from embarrassment.

"Language," I say and shake my head. Haven grins at me, because yeah, I drop the F-bomb a lot, just not in front of the kids. Or at least I try not to. "Get inside and get warmed up," I tell him. As the kids all shuffle in, I can still feel Haven's eyes on me. "What?" I finally ask.

"Coach Owens, it suits you."

I laugh. "Who would have thought?"

"I would have."

I nod, and say, "These kids actually mean a lot to me. They're all good inside, you know?" I put a fist against my chest. "They just need to be molded and shaped by the right person." I take a breath. "It took a trainer to mold me into the man I am today." My stomach squeezes, and my throat grows a little raw when I add, "But there's a part of me that thinks my dad had a part in that, too. I want to think that. I *need* to think that. He was a hard-ass man and our relationship was fractured, to say the least, but maybe..."

"The way he treated you boys taught you all what you wanted to be and what you didn't want to be, Tyler. There is always something to take from every relationship, family or not, good or bad."

"Like I said, beautiful and smart." I laugh and add, "Your brother always said that about you, do you know that? I love that you could always count on him, Haven. We all need that."

"I have parents, but he's the only one I consider family."

"And mine, remember." I give her a little nudge. "They're yours while you're here."

She smiles and her knuckles brush mine. It sends a jolt of heat through me. "You do realize you have your own little family right here, don't you?"

I consider that for a moment. I do spend an awful lot of time with these kids, and try to be a good role model. "In a way, I guess I do."

She puts her hand on my face. "That's so nice."

"Let's see how nice you think it is after I put you through some moves." She chuckles as we head toward the door and she glances at the exterior. "What was this place before you turned it into a gym?"

"It's the old fire station, actually. A new one was built a couple years back, and the town donated this to me to use. It's mine until someone decides they want it, which is why I am saving to build my own gym and fill it with state-of-the-art equipment. I realize the kids don't need that, but business is picking up and I'd like to grow, get a cage and maybe even host a few MMA fights in the future. I'm hoping to have a new facility before I lose this one."

"Nice of the town to let you use the space."

"Everyone at the town council meeting was in agreement. They want the kids off the street."

"How did you get into MMA anyway?" she asks as I pull the heavy door open.

"Started in jiu jitsu when I was twelve. Right here in Blue Bay. I had a great coach. Got my black belt when I was twenty."

"Impressive, and now that you mention it, I remember grappling is what you were good at."

"What can I say, I like working off my back." That brings a huge smile to her face.

"You're quite good at that, in and out of the cage."

I laugh. "You watched one of my fights?" I ask, my mind oddly going back to my old man. Was Haven right? Would he have been proud of my UFC title? Maybe, but he sure as hell wouldn't have told me. Then again, did I give him a chance? I only came back after he was gone. I guess I'll never know.

"I caught a fight or two of yours." She smiles. "I love what you're doing here, Ty."

"Being in the gym kept me out of trouble." I give her a wink. "Mostly. Now I want to give back by teaching these kids about grappling, wrestling, jiu jitsu. Lots of different techniques and lots of exercises for strength building. I tell them to find what they do best, then that will grow into what they do most, and that's when they develop a passion."

"That's a great philosophy," she says, and then laughs. "Oh my God, the fire pole is still here."

"Yeah, it's great for core strength exercises. I'm probably going to have one installed in my new place."

"You're right. It's great for core strength. Remember the movie where I played the stripper?"

"Ah, no, not really, but now I'm going to go find it and watch it."

She laughs. "Maybe instead I'll give you and up close and personal view of my moves."

I put my mouth near her ear. "You can't say things like that to me in public," I tell her. She laughs and pushes me away as the kids keep casting glances our way, the buzz of excitement in the air.

"Hey kids, this is Haven Roberts. She's going to be joining us this morning for a few lessons." I take in the freshly scrubbed face of the kids, six boys and four girls, varying in age from fourteen to seventeen, Liam being the oldest. The kid is strong, and has great potential. I'm super proud of his commitment to the sport.

The kids all excitedly say hello, and some of the older boys puff out their chests as she takes a spot on the mats. We spend the next half hour doing some exercise and stretches and because Haven is here today, we do some self-defense moves. I watch her carefully, and like how she lets her guard down with me. I've seen her different roles before, but I have to say, I like her best when she's just being herself.

By the time we're done, I'm a hot sweaty mess and in need of a shower. Haven however, looks refreshed, a soft pink tinge in her cheeks.

"Will you be coming back, Haven?" Cora asks as she stares up at Haven hopefully.

"You bet," Haven says.

"I want to be a movie star like you when I grow up," Cora tells her.

Haven smiles. "I think you'd be a wonderful actress," she tells Cora, and Cora beams. "Why don't you come by the set, and I can show you around?"

"Really?" Cora says. "That would be amazing."

I gather up the skipping ropes as the kids surround her, and Liam gives me a hand to put the mats away. "Are you two...you know," he says with a grin.

I shake my head. "We're friends and I'm helping her with something."

Liam lets loose a laugh. "I just bet you are."

"Hey," I say. "Respect, all the time, for women and for yourself, remember."

"Right, Coach," he says and nods.

I glance over his shoulder to see Amber. "Can I come too?" she asks. Haven laughs as all the kids all chime in, asking if they too can join the tour.

She holds her hands up. "How about this? I find a time

when we're not shooting, and I can bring you all for a visit. You can even all see the sets that Tyler and his family are building."

As I hear her talking about family and watch the kids bounce in excitement, an idea forms in the back of my mind. These kids are all like family to me, so maybe I can give Haven a piece of her childhood that she missed out on.

12

HAVEN

After a long day on the set, with Tyler staying close by as he and his brothers work on erecting a make-shift bakery, things have shut down for the night, and everyone is headed to Winchester's for a bite to eat. My trailer arrived late this afternoon, and while I'm happy to have some of my things, what I've realized in the last couple of days since arriving in Blue Bay is that I don't need much to take me from day to day. A warm bed, and a hotter man in it beside me will suffice, thank you very much.

Tyler almost seems like a different person today. Last night, walking back into that cabin brought a lot of painful memories. While we might not really know each other, I'm just glad I was by his side, able to help him move forward. I hate that he spent so many years with that tearing him up inside. He had a complicated relationship with his dad, seems all the guys did, and it shaped him into who he is today. That's not a bad thing. Gram was right, underneath it all, he's a sweet boy, and I love a man with a soft heart. Probably because I grew up with one. Rock is all muscles and strength on the outside, but inside he'd do anything for me. It's no wonder I gravitated toward a guy like Tyler. I just wish he and my brother liked each other. If we ever moved past a fling...

Whoa!

I quickly shut that thought down. Tyler and I do not have a future. He belongs here in Blue Bay surrounded by friends and family, and I belong... God, I really don't know where I belong anymore. Do I belong in Hollywood? I guess my next movie is going to determine that, but dammit, I hate that I have such little control over my future. I want to have hopes and dreams like Tyler. I love that he's setting goals, and wanting to build his own gym for the kids.

I make my way toward my trailer to gather up a few of my possessions, and when I enter, the hairs on the back of my neck tingle. I glance around. Nothing seems out of the ordinary, yet I can't shake the strange feeling that I'm not alone. Knuckles rap on the door behind me, and I gasp and jump ten feet in the air. The door flings open, and Tyler comes inside. After a fast glance around, he puts his hands on my shoulders.

"Haven, what is it?"

"It's nothing, really. I just had a strange feeling. I think I'm just spooked." His head dips, those green eyes murderous and intense.

"Sit here," he says and lowers me onto the sofa. He disappears down the narrow hall, checking the back-bedroom area. "All clear," he calls out. "Did something happen?"

"No, I promise." I roll my eyes at my own foolish behavior. "It's just...have you ever had the feeling that when things were going good, you just know something bad is going to follow? It's happened to me my entire life. I'm afraid to revel in the good, you know?"

He crouches down in front of me, his eyes hard, his hair a tumbled mess from working in the heat all day. "Yeah, I know what you're talking about, but there are no strings attached here. Things can be good for no other reason than they are. Sounds to me like you had a lot of selfish people in your life, people who might have gone out of their way to ruin good things for you. You're safe in here, and you're safe with me. Maybe we really did scare off whoever was sending those letters. Maybe someone was just fucking with you and moved on."

"Yeah, you're probably right." I force a smile, and my stupid brain races. Is this his way of saying we don't have to be together? Like other men, has he gotten what he wanted and is tossing me away like I'm a disposable coffee cup? Then again, I'm so closed off, expecting the worst in everyone, I never really open myself up. No wonder men leave. "That means we don't have to pretend anymore."

He briefly closes his eyes and exhales. When they open again, and lock on mine, I almost forget how to breathe. Beautiful is a word most used for a woman, but I can't think of anything else to describe Tyler.

"That doesn't mean I'm going anywhere, Haven. I hope I'm right and whoever was sending the letters backed the fuck off and is no longer getting his kicks from it, but that doesn't mean I'm going to let you out from under my thumb. Unless that's what you want?"

"No," I say quickly, probably a little too quickly. I don't want to give myself away here, showing that I'm beginning to really like him. He smiles at my enthusiasm, and it puts me at ease.

"Good, now that settles it." He brushes my hair back and places a tender kiss on my forehead. It melts the chill in my bones, and my God, I really wish my heart didn't love that quite so much. "Do you still want to go fishing?"

I smile, a new lightness inside me as he offers me up something fun to do tonight. "I don't know if I'll like it or not," I say, being completely honest. "The thought of putting a worm on a hook." I quiver and he laughs quietly.

"We don't use worms, we use flies."

My face drops. "Like a house fly? How on earth do you put a hook through a fly? And yuck, that is disgusting."

This time he laughs out loud. I sit there staring at him. What the hell did I say that was so amusing? He presses his forehead to mine, and says, "Babe, you're killing me. Not real flies, fake flies. I can even show you how to make them if you want."

"Oh," I say, feeling a little dense. "I can't believe I'm twenty-seven years old and thought you used real flies. Good God." I bury my face in my hands to hide my embarrassment.

"Don't," he says, taking my hands in his. "You didn't know. There is a lot I don't know. I remember when I was a kid, and Dad said he was going fly fishing, I thought he was trying to catch flies." I laugh hard at that. "Like I pictured him casting, trying to snatch a fly right out of midair." He puts his hand on his forehead and shakes his head.

I pull his hand away and his fingers tangle with mine. I try hard not to think about how much I love his touch, especially the tender ones like this. "Tyler, that is hilarious."

"Yeah, it is now." He makes a face like he's in agony. "Back then my brothers teased the shit out of me. Make one mistake, say one thing wrong, and you never live it down with my family." His big smile lets me know how much he loves that. "The point is, you've never been fishing, so why should you know? Put me on a movie set and I wouldn't know the first thing. You're simply out of your comfort zone."

I smile at him, loving the way he always tries to make things a little easier for me. "Thank you, but if I'm supposed to be a part of your family while I'm here, maybe you should have made fun." I smile as my insides tighten, a reminder that while he offered me himself and his family, I'm not and never

will be a real part of the Owens clan. This is all for show. I'm
fine with that. Or not. God, I am so pathetic.

"Tell me something, Haven. What is it you like to do for
fun?" I laugh to cover the sudden uncomfortableness inside
me, but he's dead serious when he says, "You really don't
know, do you?"

I give up the pretense with him. What's the point? I told
him straight up I didn't know who I was, and besides, he can
see through me anyway. While I'm here with him, maybe I
can discover a few things about myself. "This is all I know,
Ty." I shrug and glance around my trailer, one of many over
the years. "I don't know what I like."

"Maybe we need to fix that. Maybe while you're here, we
do a shit ton of stuff and see what you like. Just don't ask me
to put on a tux and hit a Broadway show in New York. I
mean, I will if you want, but I can already tell you I won't
like it."

I cup his face, my heart swelling at his thoughtfulness. I
work hard not to ask why, to consider his motives. It's just so
in my nature to consider someone's motive, to look for their
angle, figure out why they're working with me. God, this
business has messed me up, and left me broken. Tyler isn't in
the business, though. He told me he was trustworthy, and
despite everything, I do trust him. What angle could he
possibly have anyway? With this guy what you see is what
you get.

"I've been to numerous Broadway shows," I tell him. "And
while I'd like to see you in a tux—"

"You would?"

"Maybe just once. In the romantic fantasy world where I
go to lose myself, all heroes where tuxes. You'd only be in it
for a minute though if you know what I mean."

He laughs at that. "A minute I might be able to handle."

"But don't worry, no Broadway and I will never ask you to

put on a tux for me." I might fantasize a lot, but happily-ever-after doesn't exist in real life.

Don't start thinking it does.

As that inner voice warns me, a shiver races down my spine.

Tyler runs his hands up and down my arms to smooth out my goosebumps. "Are you cold?"

"No, I'm excited to go fishing to see if I'll like it."

He stands and pulls me up. "Do you have to go with the others to eat? Is that part of the process here on the set or something? Everyone seems to hang out together all the time."

"It's not a written rule or anything, and usually I would—"

"Because you always follow the rules, right?"

"Yup, pretty much. I don't rock the boat."

"It's okay to rock the boat every now and then, Haven. Sometimes good things can happen when you do."

I laugh. "This coming from the guy with authority issues."

His chuckle curls around me. "And that, my friend, is how I know sometimes it's a good thing. I'll prove it to you later."

"Um, let's just go fishing," I say, and pull myself together. "Just let me grab a couple things from the back." I gather a few toiletries from the suitcase and drop them into my purse. I don't really need much at the cabin.

"You feel better?" he asks when I come back down the hallway and I swear to God, my ovaries just did the macarena when I find him leaning against the door, boots crossed, jeans low on his hips. I will never tire of this image. In fact, I'm going to imprint it on my brain to call on later, when he's no longer in my life. But I'm not going to think about that right now. I'm just going to bask in the moment and enjoy trying new things with this man who fills me with a sense of comfort and safety.

I go up on my toes and kiss him. His big hand slides to

the small of my back and he kisses me with heat and need. A car engine starts outside, and he breaks the kiss. "Before we go back to the cabin, there someone you have to meet," he says.

I arch a brow. What is he up to now? "Yeah?"

"Kytee. She's going to put my nuts in a vice if I don't bring you by. Her words not mine."

"She sounds feisty," I say, already liking her.

"She's a fan, let me just tell you that. She's going to feed us too, so we don't have to cook or go to Winchester's."

I laugh. "I can buy us dinner at Winchester's." Heck, I have a good amount of cash socked away.

"I can buy us dinner too, but I'm saving."

I nod, understanding he's saving money for his gym. I love his enthusiasm when he talks about it, and all his big ideas. It sounds like the kind of gym my brother would love to train in, not that he'd step foot in Tyler's facility.

"Besides," he says, bringing my thoughts back. "They like to feed me, so really, I'm doing this for them."

I shake my head. The man is too adorable for his own good, or for mine. "You're selling, pal, but I'm not buying."

"Come on. you might as well meet her before you have to go to Sunday dinner. Gram is not going to let me off the hook again, and besides, I really do enjoy them."

My steps slow as we leave my trailer and head toward his truck. "I think it's wonderful that you guys all get together around a big table once a week." I glance at my shoes, my heart squeezing tight in my chest. Maybe I shouldn't go, maybe it will simply show me what I've always wanted, but won't ever have. "I don't know if I should go, Tyler. We don't want—" His laugh cuts me off and my gaze jerks to his. "What?"

"You think you have a say in the matter? No way in hell

will Gram let you get out of that. Beside she's an amazing cook, so you should come."

He opens the passenger side door to his truck and waves his hand for me to enter. Okay, it's true I'm a people pleaser but... "Didn't you just say I should rock the boat?"

"Not that boat," he says. "And the one we're getting into tonight, I'm going to rock that one for you." He braces his hands above my door, and his scent carries on a breeze. As I breathe him in, his gaze moves over my face, a small grin playing at the corners. Is it possible that he wants me there, wants me to be a part of his family, because...we take care of our own? Does Tyler think of me as his own? Wanting to be wanted for me, and to belong to a big family is rooted in my childhood, but it's absolutely insane how much I want that to be true. Despite the fact that we have no future. Right?

I take a shaky breath and he gives a quick shake of his head. "Look. I have to be there," he begins, his voice lacking the warmth from a second ago. "Since I can't let you out of my sight, you have to be there too."

Alrighty then. Guess he doesn't think of me as his own, and I need to get my head out of the clouds. This is not a fairy tale for cripes sakes. Someone left threatening letters and he's watching over me, protecting me and his family from danger, the way any of the Owens boys would.

"Wait, does Kylee know we're coming for dinner?"

He glances at his watch. "She will in about five minutes."

I shake my head. "Things are done so differently in Blue Bay. If I ever showed up at my parents' place..."

"They wouldn't welcome you?" He frowns like he can't wrap his brain around that.

"It's not that, so much. It's just we always call first, make appointments, that sort of thing."

"Well, that's fucking sad."

I nod. I guess it kind of is. "If you think it's okay if we just stop in, I'm okay, but can we stop at Benny's and grab a pie or something?"

"Yeah, sure," he says with a shrug and drives the short distance to the center of town. The streets are filled with locals and vacationers, who all begin to point and chatter as I exit the car. Normally I wear glasses, a hat and scarf, but I don't know, for some reason, with Tyler by my side, I don't mind being recognized.

"I bet they'd love some autographs," Tyler says.

"You think?" I ask, always feeling a bit awkward about that.

"Yes, but it's up to you, Haven. If you don't want to, you don't have to. You're entitled to your privacy, and don't always have to please others."

I make a face. "Are you sure? That doesn't sound right."

He takes my hands in his. "Tell me, what it is you want to do?"

"I would, but I believe you told me I couldn't say dirty things to you in public."

His grin is wicked. "You're going to pay for that."

"God, I hope so." I take a breath, and for the first time in a long time, think about what it is I want to do. "I'd love to sign for everyone."

He holds his hands up to wave everyone over. "Come meet Haven, everyone. She'd love to sign an autograph for you if you'd like." Soon enough people are surrounding us, and I catch Tyler's eye, the way he's standing back, arms crossed, scanning the crowd. My shoulders relax, everything about the way he's in charge, cocoons me in a blanket of safety as I meet and greet the locals. Soon enough, the crowd dies down and Tyler captures my hand in his. "Come on. Let's go say hello to Kylee and Jamie, and then you're mine for the rest of the night."

13

TYLER

Two hours later, after visiting with Kylee and Jamie, we're back at the cabin, and with the sun setting, we walk to the dock with all our fishing supplies in hand, and Haven glances at the lake. She takes a deep breath and her shoulders relax as she lets the air out. I take in her contentment, and love seeing her like this. Christ, when I first met her, her shoulders were hugging her ears, and every nerve in her body was firing. Over the last little while, the tension has slowly been draining from her body.

She enjoyed meeting my family tonight, but she's never quite herself around them—never really lets her guard down. I'm hoping that's going to change soon, especially after our big Sunday dinner. After years spent acting and pretending to be someone else, it's hard for her, and deep inside, she's this innocent girl who just wants to be liked. When she's with me, however, she's exactly who she's meant to be, and I'm glad I can bring that out in her.

"It's so beautiful here," she says softly, her voice carrying in the quiet night.

"Beautiful being the key word," I say, and she turns my way and smiles.

"I can't believe you have this lake all to yourself."

It's not a huge lake, but big enough that we could clear the land and put a few cottages around it. The truth is, we've all been busy getting Dad's business in the black, and none of us guys have wanted to take the job on, or maybe it's just that none of us have wanted to come back here. I don't think any of us have had good memories, but it's time to change all that, I think.

I drop the fishing gear into the boat, and hold my hand out to her and she takes it. "Easy," I say as she steps into the boat and sits. I untie the boat, and hop in. I stand and rock it teasingly, and she grips the sides.

"Tyler, stop. I don't want to land in the water."

I drop down next to her. "You're safe with me, Haven. I promise."

She smiles at me and it fucks me over a bit. I turn my attention to the engine. I put gas in it earlier, and gave it a good going over and even though it hasn't been used in a while, it's still in working order. Haven picks up one of the fishing rods and looks it over, examining it like it's a bug under a microscope. It amazes me how few experiences she's had. Now that she's under my care, that's all going to change. I plan to give her all kinds of new experiences, inside the bedroom and out.

I start the engine and take us to the middle of the lake. I power down, and silence surrounds us as I settle in next to her again. She lifts her head to the stars, and takes in the dark night. "You don't see these kinds of stars in L.A."

I put my arm around her as I look upward. "See that right there," I say and point. "That's the big dipper. Right beside it is the little dipper."

"Really?" she says and wraps her arms around herself. "Are you just making that up?"

"No, look." I trace it out and her eyes light up.

"I've never seen that before." She casts me a glance, child-like enthusiasm on her face as I reach for the blanket I brought. The night air can get cold in Blue Bay, so I wrap it around her and she snuggles in to it.

Once she's comfortable, I say, "The big dipper is known as the Ursa Major, the big bear. The little dipper is known as the Ursa Minor, the little bear. They have seven stars each." I smile at her and wait to see if she's impressed with my knowledge.

"Wow, pretty and smart," she teases.

I chuckle. "I remember all this from school because of the big bear that nearly mauled me, and my dog Bear who saved me. It's not because I was a good student." She shifts closer and I want to know everything about this woman. "I know you were schooled on the set, but did you enjoy school?"

"I actually did. I was a good student."

"What was your favorite subject?"

Her mouth twists. "Hmm, if I had to choose, I think I'd say history."

"No way."

She arches a brow. "You seem surprised."

"I hated history. All we ever did was study boring old men."

She laughs, and kisses my cheek playfully. "Maybe I like old men."

"Hey, I resemble that comment."

"You're far from old, Tyler." She glances at the stars again. "I guess I like learning about different civilizations, different times. I always thought if I could understand my past, I could figure out my future."

"How's that working for you?" I ask, not to sound like an asshole, but I'm really curious.

"Not so great. I've learned more about myself this last week than I have in the last twenty-seven years."

My heart tightens, knowing I'm a big part of the reason why. Goddammit, I want everything for this woman. She might have had a shitty past, but I want her to live her best life.

Are you living your best life, Tyler?

"I'm glad you're enjoying your time here." I pull her in close, needing her pressed against me.

"You really didn't like school?" she asks as I breathe in her sweet-smelling hair.

"None of us Owens boys did, except for maybe Jacob. He was always good at math and great with numbers. My favorite class was detention."

She laughs at that. "Detention? Are you kidding me?"

"Nope. I spent a lot of time in detention." I poke my finger into my chest. "Authority issues, remember."

She gives me a look like I just sprouted a second head. "Why on earth would you like it?"

"Well," I begin. "First, there was hardly any supervision. Mr. Harding hated staying after school and spent more time outside smoking than watching us. That was to my advantage because there was this sweet girl with the curliest red hair. Her name was Carly Hopkins."

"Oh, I think I can see where this is going."

I tug on the blanket so I'm under it with her. "She was a good girl. Like you."

"You think I'm a good girl, do you?"

Frogs croak nearby, and I nudge her chin. "Well, you used to be."

She whacks my chest, and I capture her hand and bring it to my mouth. "I still am. Mostly." She laughs. "It's been fun being bad with you, but go on. Tell me how you corrupted Carly."

"I was in grade seven."

"Of course you were."

"I tugged her ponytail and she threw her backpack at me. We both landed in detention. She was so pissed. Man, that girl hated me."

"What did you do to change that?" She blinks up at me, like she senses a fun story coming on.

"See," I say, wanting to entertain her. "I knew she had the hots for Jayden Barkhouse."

"Okay..."

"I told her, if she had a boyfriend like me, a guy a good girl like her probably shouldn't be seen with, that would make Jayden take notice of her."

"Did it?"

"Yup."

"So, circle back for me. How did you end up with her if you were just pretending to be her boyfriend?"

"Pretending was the best part, Haven. We got to kiss and touch in public, and in detention, we did a whole lot more than that. She started getting into trouble more and more, so we could hang out together in detention." I wink at her. "Fun times."

"Oh my God, Tyler. You are so bad."

"Hey, I had a service to offer."

She laughs, hard. "Yeah, you're a real entrepreneur."

"Lucky for you, right? I started understanding this pretend relationship thing at a very early age."

She rolls her eyes playfully. "Yeah, lucky for me is right, and what a hardship for you, huh?"

"Not a hardship at all," I say and kiss her hand.

"What ever happened to Carly?"

"She married Jayden." I can't help but laugh when I blow

on my knuckles and say, "I'd like to believe it had something to do with all the things I taught her."

"You should hire yourself out."

"Hey, I'm not a gigolo. My actions were purely altruistic. I like helping others, for no other reason than the fulfilment it gives me."

"Yeah, you do and while you might not have been a great student, you're one hell of a teacher."

"You mean in bed, right?" I tease.

She laughs. "Ah, I realize you wanted to take me fishing, I didn't know it was for compliments," she teases and takes my face into her hands. "But yes, Tyler. You're a great teacher and not just in bed. Those kids in your class adore you."

For no reason, other than the need for the connection, I lean into her and plant a soft kiss onto her mouth. Our lips linger, and warmth and intimacy arc between us, a strange new shift in the air. My heart beats that much faster, and my blood pumps a little quicker as a peculiar need tugs at something deep inside me.

"All right, let's get fishing, but there's one more thing I have to show you." I point. "Look over at that cluster of stars."

She follows my gaze. "I see it."

"Any idea what it is?"

"Nope," she says.

"That's called Solomon's Pentagram," I tell her. As she follows the cluster of stars with her finger, I add, "That protects you from danger."

She puts her hand on my stomach. "I thought you were the one who was going to protect me from danger."

"You're right," I say with a laugh, and we both look up again in time to see a shooting star.

"Oh my God, Tyler, did you just see that?"

"A shooting star. Quick, make a wish," I say and slam my

eyes shut. Haven goes quiet beside me and I can't help but wonder what it is she's wishing for. Me? Well, I know what I want. I'm ready to settle down with a family of my own. The wish I made was that it was with the one person who was made for me. My heart misses a beat when I inch one eye open and see that Haven's lids are still pinched shut. They finally open and a wide smile lights up her face.

"You should always wish on a shooting star," I tell her. "Gram always told us that since we were little."

"Did your wishes ever come true?" she asks.

"I did get that bicycle I wanted when I was seven." We both laugh at that, and I run a soft strand of her hair around my finger.

She exhales a contented sigh. "Are we supposed to keep our wishes a secret?"

"Yeah, we are," I say, even though I'd like to know what's going through that beautiful head of hers. I could probably guess. Haven wants to discover who she really is, but she doesn't need a shooting star for that. No, I'm the man she needs for that because she might be a famous movie star, but things aren't all sunshine and roses for her. It can't be easy walking through life not knowing who you are or what you really want.

"When I was little, I used to see quite a few shooting stars out here on the lake," I tell her.

"I don't think I've ever seen one before." She blinks dark lashes over blue eyes that glisten in the moonlight. "Do they have a special meaning?"

I nod. "It's an omen that you're on a good path."

She goes quiet for a moment, her lips quirked at the corner. "I like that, Ty."

"Do you think you're on a good path?" I ask her.

Her head drops, and she toys with the line on the fishing rod. "I hope so."

"Do you want to just stay like this or try fishing?"

She sits up. "Fishing, of course. I can't wait to reel in a big one."

"Didn't you already do that?" I ask with a wink.

"My God, that ego of yours!" She laughs. "I'm so glad you can back it up."

Laughing, I remove our blanket and grab our gear. I open the toolbox and pull out some spinning bait.

"They don't look like flies."

"That's because tonight we're just going to cast. We're not fly fishing." Her mouth twists, and as I get our rods ready, I take a minute to explain the differences and the different techniques. "So you see, there's quite a bit of skill involved in fly fishing, and we can't really do it from this boat. Another time though, if you're really interested in learning."

"I'm interested in trying everything at least once."

"Okay," I say, and flick my rod to release the line. "Did you see how that was done?"

She nods eagerly, and releases her line. "Perfect, fast learner." She beams at the compliment, and we both go quiet for a very long time, lost in our thoughts as a comfortable quiet surrounds us.

We listen to the sounds of nature as the sun's long rays glisten on the lake. She shuffles beside me, breaking the quiet. "Tyler?"

"Yeah."

"Tonight was perfect. The best night ever."

Everything I feel for this woman comes crashing over me and I take an unsteady breath. "It's about to get better?"

"Yeah, why?"

I gesture with a nod to the tight line on her rod. "You just caught a fish."

I'm pretty sure I've never seen Haven so relaxed as she helps herself to a big scoop of potatoes, and tries to listen in to all the conversations going on around the table. This is the second Sunday night dinner she's had at our place, and she's growing more and more comfortable with my family. She says something to Kylee, and gives baby Jesse a smile as he sits on Kylee lap as she feeds him purred carrots. He spits it out, and Haven just laughs as it lands on her blouse.

She wipes it away like it's nothing and I'm glad that she's not upset by it. For the last few days, we've been both working on the set, and at night back at the cabin, we've been going on the boat, which she loves, and falling into bed together every night. Tonight, however, I have something different planned for us.

Oh yeah, since things don't get started until later in the day for her, tonight we're doing something fun, something she missed out on during her childhood and I can't wait to surprise her. Later this week, I have other things planned. We're still discovering all her likes and dislikes, inside and outside of the bedroom, and I'm having fun watching her blossom. It's a goddamn tragedy that she has no idea who she really is inside. All I know is I like this girl when she's with me. I like how she trusts me, puts herself in my hands, understanding I don't want anything from her, and this is not about tit for tat.

The best part in all this is that Haven has not received one single threat since she's been here with me for this couple of weeks, and I haven't noticed any strangers lurking about, or following her around.

"How are you feeling, Summer?" Haven asks my sister-in-law as she pushes away from the table and puts her hand on her stomach.

"Indigestion," she says, and Sean jumps up and grabs the diaper bag. He roots around inside and pulls out some meds for Summer. "Thank you," she says.

"When you have kids," Kylee says to Haven. "Let's hope you don't get it as bad as Summer does."

"The Owens boys give everyone indigestion," Summer says with a smirk as she chews on some tablets.

"Hey, I resemble that comment," Jared says and takes a big bite of roast beef. Haven laughs, and under the table she puts her hand on my lap, like it's the most natural thing in the world.

"Oh, Tyler, when your mom was pregnant with you, she suffered dearly," Gram says.

"Yeah?" I say. "I didn't know that."

"That's the middle child for you," Carter says with a smirk. "Causing trouble just to get attention, even before birth."

I glare at my cousin as he sits there with a smirk on his face. "Um, weren't you the middle child too, Carter?" I ask.

He throws his hands out. "Right, so what I mean is it takes one to know one."

I just shake my head, and put my hand over Haven's to give it a little squeeze. "Dude, you're the one with issues," I say, and while I'm right, I can't deny that we have all been facing our own demons since coming home, some sooner, some later, but with Dad's presence all around us, it's hard to bury the past. On the road and in the cage, it was a hell of a lot easier.

As Carter mumbles something under his breath, an insult to me no doubt, Gram passes around a basket full of rolls fresh out of the oven.

"So delicious," Haven says. "Jace, if you gave cooking lessons, I'd take them," she says and a ridiculous bolt of jealousy that I really wish I didn't feel zaps through me.

Jace smiles at the compliment. "I've actually been thinking about opening my own restaurant. Blue Bay could use some fine dining. Been looking at space downtown, actually. The old fire station would be a perfect location for me, but I haven't approached town council about it. I'm not about to take it out from underneath Tyler."

Shit, I didn't know that. "I'm hoping to find a new place, a space better suited for a gym," I say, a sudden, new sense of urgency about me. With Jace wanting it, I need to find something sooner rather than later. I don't exactly need to be downtown, but I don't want to be too far out either. Some of the kids walk, bike and skateboard to the gym. A few months back, an old fish processing plant was torn down. The land went up for sale, and before I could even think about putting in an offer—I would have had to take a substantial loan, something I've been trying to avoid—someone snagged it. I'm not sure what's going up there. I think the owner is renovating himself, considering we're the biggest construction business in town and weren't approached.

Gram beams at him. "Jace, I think that's a wonderful idea." She turns to Haven. "Did you know Jace has his own cookbook?" She jumps up and disappears into the other room as I consider the new space I want, and how much it would cost to properly fit it for a competitive club. The guys would help put it up, and costs wouldn't be that high. It's the land and the equipment holding me back.

"This is the second Sunday dinner you've cooked for me and I didn't even know that," Haven says, and stares wide-eyed at my cousin. Her gaze jerks to me and pulls my thoughts back. "Why didn't you tell me that, Tyler?"

"Look at that." I shake my head and laugh. "We were just talking about Carter and me being the middle child, and somehow conversation shifted to Jace's accomplishments." I feign insult and cross my arms over my chest. "Talk about being ignored."

"Right, buddy," Carter says with a grin. "Summer, you'd better stop at two. We don't need any more middle children."

"Oh, poor Ty," Haven says. "Doesn't get enough attention." As everyone laughs, she gives me a wink that lets me know she'll be making up for that later. We continue to talk, and eat, and joke around the table, and I don't miss the way Carter keeps glancing at me, like he has something on his mind.

After our meal, Jace presents us all with apple crisp, and Haven is definitely going to pay for all the moans of pleasure she keeps making. She turns her attention to Jamie, and asks about his tattoo business. She listens intently as he tells her all about it, and she asks about his tattoos and the meanings. I love how she's interested in my family, and how they have all brought her into our circle, treating her like she's one of us. I did tell her that my family was hers for while she was here, but it's clear how much she loves this, craves this kind of normalcy.

Once the dessert has been devoured, Haven helps Summer with Devon, and I find Carter. We both step outside and crickets chirp around us and we sit on the front porch.

"Something on your mind?" I ask.

"Yeah, actually," he says and scrubs his chin. "You asked me to keep my eyes open for anything or anyone strange, and there was this guy I didn't recognize him from the cast. He looked like he was in his late teens, baggy jeans, black ball cap. Anyway, he was scoping out Haven's trailer."

My stomach squeezes. "You got a good look at him?"

"Pretty good. I don't think he's a local. I went to approach him, but when he saw me coming, he took off."

"On foot?"

"Yeah, through the trees, and down to the ocean. He was fucking fast, and it was obvious I frightened him, which tells me he was up to no good. I was about to chase him, but Mason flagged me down. Needed some design changes made." He puts his hand on my tense shoulder. "Sorry I let you down, cuz."

I look at the long driveway. I still have an hour or so before I have to bring Haven to the cabin for her surprise, and dammit, I want to talk to this kid. It could be nothing more than some punk wanting a glimpse at the gorgeous movie star, or it could be more. "Want to hit Winchester's, ask around?"

"Is this something you should talk to Officer Walker about?"

I glance over my shoulder to make sure we're alone. "If I have to, I will." I know I promised Haven I wouldn't go to the cops, but if this guy was trespassing, Walker should know about it. Christ, Summer almost ended up dead from her secrets. I'm not going to let anything like that happen to Haven.

"Let's ride our bikes. Scare the little motherfucker straight if we find him."

Carter grins. "People should know better than to fuck with any middle child."

As his bark of laughter curls around me, I push to my feet. "I'll let the others know we're taking a quick ride."

Inside the house, I walk through the rooms until I find Haven. She has baby Jesse in her arms and he's drooling all over her. She has a huge smile on her face, and my throat squeezes. That baby looks good on her. She said kids didn't fit into her lifestyle, but what if she changed that lifestyle?

What the fuck am I saying?

Haven is here for the shoot, and deep down has no idea who she is or what she wants. Why I'm suddenly envisioning a future together here in Blue Bay is beyond me, and fucking ridiculous. As if feeling my eyes on her, her head lifts, and the warmth and softness in her eyes messes with my ability to think. I stand there a beat longer, just staring at her, until Summer clears her throat.

"Are you just going to stand there looking like the village idiot, Tyler," she teases, with an-all knowing smirk on her face. I really wish my sisters-in-law couldn't read me so well.

"Carter and I are just taking a quick ride. Are you okay here until I get back?" I ask Haven.

"She's perfectly fine," Kylee says. "Now go. We have some more girl bonding to do, and I haven't finished telling her all the stories from your childhood."

I shake my head. "Don't believe anything they say," I warn Haven, who is looking at me with concern in her eyes. It's not like me to leave her alone, and I can just imagine what's going through her head right now. "Just a quick ride," I say to assure her. "You're in good hands."

"Of course, she is," Summer and Kylee blurt out, and even though there are eight guys, and two male kids in this family, there isn't enough testosterone to go up against either of those women. I laugh, thinking what it would be like if we added Haven to the mix. The three of them would be a force, that's for sure.

I turn to go, and Summer says, "You can kiss her goodbye, Tyler. We won't look."

I shake my head. Summer and Kylee are as bad as Gram, always trying to marry me off. My boots scuff the floor as I cross the room, bend down and place a kiss on Haven's mouth, and not because they told me to, but because I want to. Little Jesse makes a fist and whacks me on the head, then grabs a fistful of my hair, like he's trying to shove me away.

"Jesus," I say.

"No swearing around the kids," Kylee warns.

"Right, shit, sorry." Kylee rolls her eyes as I try to remove Jesse's sticky fingers from my hair. "I guess he wants you all to himself." I give Haven a wink. "Smart boy."

A warm pink flush moves into her cheeks. My God, she looks so damn adorable it's all I can do to keep myself from hoisting her over my shoulder and dragging her upstairs, caveman style.

I put my mouth close to her ear. "See you soon."

The girls all go back to chatting, but I don't need to turn around to know Haven's eyes are on me, watching me until I'm out of her line of vision, and I like that. I like how she focuses in on me, like I'm the only one in the room.

Outside I find my cousin on his bike waiting for me and I hop on mine. It's a nice night for a quick ride. I follow him down our long driveway, and we pass the movie set, and head toward Main Street, not so busy this time of night. Most of the vacationers are at their barbecues, or enjoying the cool ocean. We head toward the cottages and glance around. When we fail to find the kid, we stop at Winchester's.

Officer Walker comes sauntering out of the place, and he stops before us. "Boys," he says. "Shouldn't you be home enjoying Sunday dinner?"

"Just finished," I say. "Out stretching our legs."

"Is that what you're doing?" he asks. I nod, and he says, "This movie is bringing a lot of folks to town for a glimpse. Good for the economy. Winchester's is busier than usual on a Sunday night."

"Yeah, much busier than usual," I say, and add, "Maybe we should bring in extra security too."

Walker, the sly son of a bitch with a grudge against the Owens boys, says, "You think that's necessary?"

I give a casual shrug of indifference. "I'm just thinking you wouldn't want any trouble in your town, Officer." That seems to get his attention.

"You expecting trouble, Tyler?"

"Just saying. If this goes well, other production companies might want to film here. Like you said, it's good for the economy."

He scrubs his chin, and before he walks away, he says, "Have you noticed anything unusual lately?"

"No, but we should all be diligent and keep our eyes open," I say, and he stares at me for a second before walking away. I didn't straight up tell him about the stalker, but at least I put a bug in his ear, and since he prides himself on keeping crime low in Blue Bay, he won't want any kind of trouble.

We head inside, and at the door, all eyes turn to us as my cousin scans the establishment looking for the kid. I consider what everyone sees. Two tough-ass bikers looking for trouble. A few eyes shy away, and we head to the bar. Our buddy Beck, who owns the place, comes from the back.

"What's up, guys? Not used to seeing you here on a Sunday night. Looking for trouble?" he asks, only half teasing.

"Just looking for a guy, about this tall, shaggy brown hair, thin, and kind of strung out."

Beck snorts and leans toward us. "You just described half

the kids who summer here with their wealthy parents. Bored, buying drugs, trying to get lucky with the local girls."

"Yeah, you're right," I say, and spin on my stool. I crack my knuckles, anxious to introduce my fist to whoever is harassing my girl.

My girl?

Fuck yeah, she's my girl, and I'd love to put a call into her brother to fill him in on what's going on. Not with me sleeping with her, but that someone, maybe even one of his enemies, could be after her. Again, that would be breaking trust, and I can't do that.

I check the clock on the wall. "I have to go," I tell my cousin, and we both head back outside. In less than half an hour, Haven is going to get the surprise of a lifetime. Before that happens, I have to make a quick trip to Benny's to pick up the one thing that will make tonight extra special for her. I can't wait to see her face when she sees her big surprise.

● **15**

____

HAVEN

____

While I'm having a great time chatting with Summer, Kylee and Gram, my gaze keeps roaming to the hallway leading to the front door, not that I can see who's coming and going from my seat on the sofa. But I'm anxious, having no idea what Tyler is up to or where he's gone, and while he was trying to play it cool earlier when he kissed me goodbye, he looked a little edgy, like he was itching for a fight. The others might not have noticed it—or maybe they did. They are, after all, family. For me, while I'm only pretending to be his girlfriend, after spending so much time with him, I've learned a few things about Tyler and have come to understand his body language a little bit better.

Honestly, I've never considered myself a good judge of character. I usually just err on the side of caution and assume everyone has their own best interests at heart. Tyler, however, is proving to be so much more, a man of character and integrity. Solid and dependable. I've let my guard down with him more than any other man. Which is probably why I have a string of bad relationships behind me, and no, they weren't all with my leading man. That's just a stupid rumor.

The front door opens and closes with a thud, and my heart slams right along with it, hoping, praying it's Tyler, and he's okay—that nothing bad happened to him. I mean, he's a big guy, a dangerous looking man who could frighten anyone, but a stalker? They're unpredictable. Irrational.

I listen for the sound of his boots on the floor and when I hear his heavy, assured footsteps—easily able to pick them out now—relief rolls through me. Tyler constantly says I don't know him, and he was right, at first. The more time we're together, the more I realize he really is one of the good guys. I wish my brother could have seen this side of the man he hates. Not that it matters, really. They don't need to be friends. Not for my sake anyway. I'll probably never set eyes on Tyler once we're done filming. God, I wish that thought didn't leave me with a sour taste in my mouth.

"Looks like the guys are back," Gram says, pulling my thoughts back as her all-knowing eyes stray to me. I force a smile as she pushes to her feet and smooths her hands over her dress. I have a feeling nothing gets by her, but I'm not about to drag her into my troubles. I shouldn't have involved Tyler, but was vulnerable when he asked me what was wrong. He was just so open and honest, so easy to talk to, I ended up spilling my secrets.

Gram snickers. "That boy is probably hungry again." She shuffles off to the kitchen, and muffled voices reach my ears as she speaks to Tyler.

"I guess I should get going." I lean in to give Devon, and a sleeping Jesse, a kiss goodnight.

Kylee smiles up at me when I stand. "Don't forget, Friday night, my place."

"I won't, and I'm bringing a homemade dessert." I pull a face and consider my talent in the kitchen. Not that there is anything to consider. But I want to bring something nice to the barbecue. I love the way they've all brought me into their circle, the way they're treating me like family. It's insane how much I want to be a part of this loving clan, but Tyler and I aren't a real couple. My smile falls as another thought hits. Could I be putting this family in danger? My God, if anything happened to anyone of them, I'd never forgive myself. Maybe I should just forget this movie and get out of Dodge.

"Are you okay?"

Tyler's voice comes from behind, and his hands land on my arms, rubbing away the sudden chills racing along my flesh. I turn to face him, and my heart goes a little wild. His eyes narrow in on me, his gaze dark and probing as he assesses my face.

"Fine, just tired," I fib. I also forgot my purse in my trailer. Can we swing by."

"Sure. You ready to get out of here?"

I nod. "If you are."

He puts his hand on the small of my back, and the sun is low on the horizon as we say our goodnights and walk to his truck. As that uneasy feeling creeps back, I glance around to see if anything is out of the ordinary. I'm not sure what I expect to see. It's just that I have no idea where Tyler was, and it's making me a bit anxious. Inside the truck, I buckle up and glance at him. He doesn't say much, just starts the truck and buckles himself in.

"Is everything okay with you?" I finally ask. Obviously, he's not about to tell me anything.

He grips the steering wheel and stares straight ahead for a second. "Carter saw some punk hanging around your trailer today."

I stiffen. "You went looking for him?"

"I did, but I didn't find him."

His hands tighten on the steering wheel until his knuckles

turn white. I link my fingers together on my lap and peer into the night. With my gaze straight ahead, a blur of trees in my vision, I concentrate on my breathing.

"It might be nothing, but it could be something," he says.

"You told Carter," I state, my throat tight, accusation clear in my tone.

A beat of silence and then, "No. Carter and Jared are on the set, so I just asked them to keep their eyes out for anything suspicious." I turn when I hear the disappointment in his voice, and his gaze is dark and hard as it meets mine. He glares at me, and I can't help but think a sucker punch would have less impact on my gut. "They don't know about the letters. I'd never tell them that, Haven. I wouldn't betray your trust like that."

My stomach clenches, and I hate myself for accusing him. "Sorry, Ty," I say quickly, wishing I could take my words back. "I always go straight for the worst."

"Why do you do that?" he asks, the hardness gone from his voice. He peels his hands from the steering wheel, and shakes them, like he's trying to loosen the tightness and tension.

"The environment I grew up in, I guess. It's pretty cutthroat. No one is really your friend. Everyone wants something from you, and if you don't give it, they find a way to take it." As the words leave my mouth, I shake my head. Why on Earth am I still in that kind of environment? Oh, probably because it's the only way of life I know. Being here with Tyler though, learning about his way of life, is something this girl could get used to.

What's between you two isn't real, Haven.

Tyler blows out a breath, his features softening as he captures my hand. "Things are done differently here. I told you before, and I'll tell you again. You can trust me."

I nod, hating that I jumped to conclusions like that. Tyler

is just trying to protect me, and it's sweet that he asked his family to help without really involving them.

"Okay," I say, and close my hand over his.

He puts the truck into gear, and gravel crunches beneath the tires as we make our way to the main road. He drives me to the trailer, and I'm about to jump from the vehicle, and rush inside but he comes with me. His strength and presence calms me. I grab my purse and he guides me back to the passenger side. Once I'm buckled in, he circles the truck, climbs in and starts it. As we head to the cabin, I turn to him.

"Tell me more about your gym, and how you want it designed," I say.

"Look in there," he says and gestures to the glove box. I pull it open and find a notebook filled with ideas and designs and equipment, and the names of the distributors and prices associated with it.

"You have it all figured out," I say. "I'm impressed."

"I hate that I'm taking up space at the old fire station when Jace wants it. It's the perfect location for him. I really need to find a place so he can buy the place."

I put the notebook full of his dreams and aspirations back into the glove box, safe and sound. I hope he does get to fulfil it. I've seen him with the kids, and he's a natural. The respect and adoration on their faces filled my heart with warmth. "I really love how you guys all care for each other so much. You'd all sacrifice to make the other one happy, wouldn't you?"

"Isn't that what family does?"

I nod, thinking of my brother as I stare out the window. A comfortable silence surrounds us as he drives. After a few minutes, he turns down the road leading to the cabin. Our little home for the time being. I smile as I consider the way we're playing house, our evenings fishing on the lake, and nights falling in bed together, our mornings around the small breakfast table. It's straight out of a Norman Rockwell calendar, and everything I expected in this small town. I angle my head and take in Tyler's handsome features in the dashboard light.

He glances at me. "I hope you're not too tired."

Assuming he has sex on the brain, I say, "Never too tired for you, Ty."

His soft chuckle warms me from the inside out, and I look forward when we drive past an abandoned car along the gravel road. "Whose car is that?" I ask.

He doesn't speak, instead he looks straight ahead and I sit up a bit straighter. What the heck is going on and why isn't he answering me. As we approach the cabin, I spot two more vehicles. My nerves leap, and Tyler reaches for my hand again.

"It's okay, Haven. This is just your surprise."

My gaze jerks to him. "What are you talking about? What surprise? You never said anything about a surprise."

"If I did, then it wouldn't be a surprise, now would it?" He stops the truck and puts it in park. He rests his hand on the back of my seat, and lightly runs his fingers through my hair. "Remember you said you never had a sleepover as a child, no s'mores over the fire." He reaches behind the seat and produces a paper bag. I glance in and see a s'mores kit.

"Tyler," I say, my heart crashing against my ribs, and when I hear my name being called and turn to see the kids from his gym all standing by the cabin waiting for us, tears pound behind my eyes. He did this for me? He set up this surprise because I missed out on it as a child. I resist the urge to pinch myself because guys like Tyler, they're too good to be true, right? Once again, I wait for the ball to drop, for something bad to happen. It's in my nature to worry when things are going too well.

"Hey, I thought this would be fun," he says, misreading my reactions for the very first time. "But if you don't want to it's fine...I mean, the kids love you, and like you said, they're sort of my family, and since my family is your family when you're here—"

I hold my hand up to stop his worried ramblings. "I love this." I sniff and shake my head. "I just can't believe you arranged this. I'm just a little overwhelmed here. No one has ever done anything like this for me before. You're the sweetest guy."

"There you go again," he says, to lighten my mood, no doubt.

"Don't worry, I won't tell anyone."

His grin is wide, but there is loving concern in his tone when he asks. "You ready or do you need a minute?"

I swipe the tears about to spill and take a breath. "I'm ready."

I grab my purse and when we exit the vehicle, and the kids come running over. "Haven, come sit by me," Amber says as Tyler hands her the s'mores kit. "I have this soft blanket we can sit on."

"Just give me a minute to get changed," I say and under the guise of slipping into something more comfortable, I disappear inside to gather myself, while Tyler takes a moment to chat with the parents who've dropped them off. I'm being rude. I should be out there making an appearance, saying hello to the people trusting me enough to hang out with their kids, but I just need a second.

I hurry to the loft, and open my purse, in search of a bit of lipstick and blush. When I do, and my gaze lands on another note, I suck in a fast breath. Who the hell was in my trailer, rifling through my personal belongings? Anger and fear present at the same time, and adrenaline begins to flood my body. I take a few more fast breaths, my heart crashing in my ears.

Coming for you soon.

I grab the paper, and my first instinct is to tear it up, but I can't. I need to keep them in case we need them for evidence after...after someone hurts me, or someone close. My God, I can't let my thoughts go there. Could the guy who'd been lurking earlier don't this? I crush it up, and toss it onto the bed, and work to slow my racing heart and get control over my emotions and tears. I don't want to look like I'd just come from the rinse cycle when I see Tyler. He's gone to great lengths to set tonight up and I don't want to ruin it.

I slip into my yoga pants and hoodie, and my heart nearly stops when another thought hits. What if whoever put this in my purse is close by? What if the kids are in danger?

"Haven?" I spin at the sound of Tyler's voice, and his gaze drops, takes in the paper crunched up on the bed. "Fuck," he says. He crosses the room. "Let me see."

He smooths out the paper, and as he reads it, I say, "Do you think that guy lurking did this?"

"I'll find him."

"Do you think...the kids are safe?"

"You know what, Carter and Jared have always enjoyed a bonfire. How about they join us?" I shake my head and he cups my face. "I'm not worried about tonight. Whoever did this, whoever is trying to scare you, I doubt they even know where we are, or that they'll try anything with so many people. I want you to feel safe though, so let me call the guys."

"I don't want to put them out."

"S'mores, Haven. They're not going to say no to s'mores and really, we could use a few more adults here, just to make sure there is no tent swapping later on."

That pulls a smile from me. "Yeah, Liam looked like he had a thing for Jessica the other day."

He laughs. "Liam has a thing for you, but yeah, we need more supervision for the overnight hours." Backing up to allow me to change, he pulls his phone from his pocket. I assume he's asking those two because I've been around them on the set, and those are the guys he's asked to watch out for something suspicious. I hurry into my comfy clothes, and Tyler ends the call.

"They're on their way."

"Are you sure they won't mind?"

"It's how it's done, Haven."

I put my arms around him, go up on my toes and press my mouth to his. "Thank you, Tyler."

"Go on," he says, giving my backside a slap. "They're all waiting for you."

"You coming?"

"Yup, lead the way."

We hurry outside, and a new sense of lightness washes over me when I take in all the big smiles, and the fire already started in the pit. A few parents linger, and I make my way over to introduce myself before I settle in next to the kids. After I say hello to the three parents, two women and one man, who'd obviously brought all the kids, a pretty woman who looks like she might be in her early forties gives me a warm, motherly smile. She sort of reminds me of Shannon.

"It's so nice of you and Tyler to do this," she says. "I hope it's not too much for you. They can be a handful."

"This was all on Tyler," I say. "A surprise for the kids and me." I give her a wink, and say, "I think Tyler has everything under control." I glance over my shoulder to see him interacting with the kids. Honest to God, that man needs kids of his own.

"Our Cora is so excited," the man next to the pretty woman says and I turn to him, and take in the way he glances at his daughter. I love that look of adoration on his face. "She wants to be an actress, you know."

"She told me, and I'm so glad she's excited."

"Okay, we should go," the pretty brunette says. "No child for the night, I'm hitting Winchester's," she teases.

I laugh as they all head to their vehicles, and make my way over to the fire. Amber points to the blanket and I drop down next to her and sit cross-legged.

Liam hands me a stick, and I just look at it. He laughs. "For the marshmallows. When Tyler said you'd never been to a bonfire before, I didn't believe him. I do now."

All the kids laugh and I soak up the excitement in the air. "Just please tell me no ghost stories."

"Nope, can't tell you that," Cora says, and I can't help but smile as I gaze at Tyler. This was just supposed to be about sex. Damn my heart for not minding its own business.

16

TYLER

The smile gracing Haven's face over the course of the night was more than I ever could have asked for. Every time I glanced at her, laughing, having fun with the kids and eating a ton of s'mores, it did something weird to my insides. The truth is, I love seeing her this happy, would love to make her this happy every day. She's kind, giving and nurturing, and she deserves to be given those things in return. With shitty parents, it's clear she can only count on her brother, and now of course, she can on me too.

Speaking of brothers. Christ, if mine could hear my thoughts, I'd have to cash in my man card. I don't give a shit, though, I loved seeing her in her element with these kids, even when they were telling ghost stories. A small chuckle rises in my throat as I turn on the hose and extinguish the bonfire.

The kids are all in their tents, boys in one, girls in the other, and Haven is inside the cabin with my brother and cousin. They're talking low, and for some weird reason, I sense it's because they don't want me to hear what they're saying. Earlier, she went to my truck. I asked her what it was she needed, and she just brushed it off, saying she wanted to stretch her legs. I'm not sure why she's suddenly being secretive. Is she up to something? Maybe the better question is, when the hell did I get so paranoid?

Oh, since you've started falling for Haven.

Shit.

I can't go there. She's not sticking around, and when it comes right down to it, I'm her bodyguard, not her boyfriend. Even though I'm played out, I'm not the kind of guy a girl brings home. Then again, maybe I am. I'm no longer in the cage, no longer on the road going from one fight to another, one girl to another.

I'm settled here in Blue Bay, ready to put my playboy ways behind me and start something real. Do I want that with Haven? Hell yeah, I do. Problem is, she doesn't even know who she is, or what it is she wants in life. She's as lost as I used to be. Maybe by the time the film shoot is over, she'll know herself a little better, see how good we are together, and go after things that make her happy. I'm just not sure that's me, or Blue Bay. I'm a guy who never taps out or goes down without a fight, so I plan to do my best to show her all the things she'd be giving up if she leaves here.

Smoke clouds the air as the fire dies, and I turn off the hose and reel it back up. I do a perimeter check to make sure everyone is in bed safe and sound, and glance at my own tent, which is set up between the boys and girls. I'd like to be snuggled in bed with Haven tonight, but staying outside is the responsible thing to do. Plus, I don't plan to sleep much, not after Haven showed me the letter. Carter and Jared are inside with her, so I know she's safe and I'm not a bit jealous that she's deep in conversation with them, about God knows what. Nope, not jealous at all. Much. I mean, I know my family and they'd never break bro code, but a part of me doesn't like the seriousness of their conversation.

I head inside to get ready for bed, and Haven grabs her phone from the table and shoves it into her back pocket as my brothers go silent. I cast them a quick glance. "What's up?" I ask causally, even though my insides are tight. What the fuck is going on here?

"Nothing," Haven says quickly, a big smile on her face as Carter and Jared just shrug.

"Telling stories about me?" I ask as I grab a water bottle from the fridge. The guys laugh.

"What's to tell? You're boring as fuck," Jared says. "Before Haven arrive you were moping around Winchesters like a goddamn Saint Bernard in a heat wave."

I arch a brow and eye him. "Did you just compare me to a Saint Bernard?"

"Yeah, except a Saint Bernard is probably better groomed."

I run my hand through my hair as he snickers. Okay, I probably could do with a cut. I turn my attention to Haven. "Can I talk to you for a minute?" I gesture with a nod to the loft upstairs, where she'll be sleeping tonight, alone.

"I'm calling it a night, anyway," Carter says and pushes from the table. "Early morning tomorrow."

"Yeah me too," Jared says.

"It was nice chatting with you guys tonight," Haven says. "I appreciate you coming over."

"Anytime," they both say, and go off to different bedrooms. I gesture toward the loft and Haven climbs the stairs. Once we reach the top, she turns my way. My heart melts a little when I see the chocolate on her face.

"You're kind of a mess," I say and wet my thumb. I brush it over her cheek and she laughs.

"You mean to tell me I sat there talking to Carter and Jared and neither bothered to tell me I had food on my face."

"Maybe they thought it was adorable too," I say.

"Hardly." She puts her arms around me like it's the most natural thing in the world.

"You had fun tonight?" I ask, even though I already know the answer. I guess the needy part of me wants to hear her say it.

"The best," she says and gives me a kiss. Our lips linger for a moment, and I slide my hands around her back to hold her to me. Her nipples brush up against me and I give a groan of want.

"Shh," she chuckles, and it's so nice to see her fear from earlier gone. She actually sounds drunk on happiness tonight. "We don't want to wake the kids."

As soon as those words leave her mouth, my heart misses a beat, imagining she's saying that about our own family. What the fuck is wrong with me? I shake my head. "You're right. You okay in here without me?"

She nuzzles close, and I almost forget about my tent and crawl in with her, but that wouldn't be the responsible thing to do. I laugh at that. When the hell did I become the responsible one?

"I'll be okay, but that doesn't mean I'll be happy about it," she murmurs.

I kiss her forehead and tuck her hair behind her ears. "What time do you have to be on set tomorrow?"

"Around eight. Not so bad."

"Tomorrow I have to work on the fight scene. Later in the day though, so that gives me time with the kids in the morning. If you feel okay traveling in with Carter and Jared, that is. As much as I don't want you out of my sight, I should stay here to make sure the kids all get picked up, plus I thought it would be fun to do some exercises in the lake with them."

"They're going to love that," she says and stifles a yawn. "Hey, maybe before their parents take them home, they can stop by the set. If I'm not too busy, I can show them around, their parents too."

"I'll check and see, but I'm sure it can be arranged."

She exhales, contentment all over her face. "Tonight was so much fun, Ty."

My throat squeezes tight at the pleasure in her voice and I give her a soft smack on her ass. "Okay, get to sleep." She makes a mewling sound as I make a move to go, but instead turn back to her. "What were you and the guys talking about?"

She grins and angles her head. "You sound like you're jealous?"

"No," I say quickly, and her grin falls. What? Did she want me to be jealous? "If I'm going to be your bodyguard, I should probably know if you told them about the letters."

"No, I didn't," she says. "And they didn't ask. I love that they just show up because you asked them to, and don't need to know the details." I stand there for a second, and note the way she hedged the question. I guess whatever they talked about, privately and intimately, is none of my business. I don't have to fucking like it, though.

"Goodnight," I say. I make a quick trip to the bathroom to get ready for bed and ten minutes later, after checking the perimeter again, I crawl into my tent. Crickets chirp and animals scurry in the forest as I close my eyes to rest them. It's strange how coming back here isn't quite so hard anymore. Haven and I have been making good memories, happy ones, and tonight, neither of us are going to forget it in a hurry.

Minutes tick by and sleep pulls at me, but I'm reluctant to let it take me over. I take a deep breath, and when I hear rustling that sounds like footsteps, my senses go on high alert. I unzip my tent and spot a figure moving toward me. I'm about to take whoever it is to the ground, and ask questions later, until I realize it's Haven.

"Hey," she says, her voice a low, sleepy murmur.

"Are you okay?" I ask, and glance around the woods. Has something spooked her? Other than crickets chirping, my ears meet with silence.

"I couldn't sleep." Her warm scent reaches my nostrils as she comes closer, and I breathe her in. "I didn't mean to wake you."

"You didn't. Get in here." I open the tent and she crawls in. "What are you doing wandering around?"

"I wasn't. I wanted to crawl in here and sleep with you. I wasn't going to wake you."

I open my sleeping bag, liking that she wants to be close to me. "Crawl in," I say. She does and I move in beside her, thankful that I have an oversized bag that easily sleeps two.

"I'll sneak out before the kids wake up," she says, her voice a soft whisper.

She turns to her side, and I drag her to me. She gives a contented sigh, and her hair tickles my nose as she drifts off. I doze beside her, the warmth of her body pulling me under. The next thing I know, birds are chirping in the distance, and I open one eye, and then another. A smile touches the corners of my mouth as I take in the sleeping woman beside me. Neither one of us moved in our sleep.

I inch back, and she moans. Since I don't have the heart to wake her, I unzip the tent and leave her to sleep. I'll let the kids know she decided she wanted the tent and I hung out inside with Carter and Jared.

Inside, I find the guys stirring, and I head straight to the coffee maker. "What the hell are you guys doing up so early?"

"Busy day," they both say, and I stare at them. "You both have two hours before you have to check in on the set."

"I've taken up jogging," Carter says with a grin. I look him over. The guy is in great shape, and clearly lying through his teeth.

"Yeah, same," Jared says and sticks out his gut, which is nothing but rows and rows of muscles.

"Fine, don't tell me then." Come to think of it, even before Haven arrived, the guys have been getting up early and leaving the old homestead. There are no secrets between us, so maybe they really have taken up jogging. "I suppose you're not going to tell me what you three were talking so quietly about last night either."

"If you have to know, we were telling Haven that you're a boring old man, and she'd be better off with one of us."

They both snicker as I pour them each a cup. I hand them over and as they swill the coffee, I brush off last night, chalking up their conversation to nothing other than the guys getting to know her. She is, after all a movie star, and they were probably just interested in meeting some of her friends—not that she really has any. She said so herself.

"Thanks for coming last night," I say.

"When I'm out on my run this morning," Carter says. "I'll keep my eye out for that kid."

"I appreciate that," I say. "Would you guys be back from your jog around eight, to take Haven to the set? I need to stay back and see to it that the kids get home okay."

"Yeah, no problem." He sets his mug on the table with a clunk. "I get that Haven is in some kind of trouble," Jared says. "I don't need to know what it is, but we've got her back."

I nod, gratitude filling my soul. Honestly, it's good to be back, good to be around my family. I can't even imagine what it's like for Haven to only have her brother, who isn't around much, thanks to his training and fights. "I know you do."

Jared goes serious for a second. "It's been a long time since you've been here."

What he's really asking is how I'm doing, but not wanting to do it in a way that brings back hard memories. "Yeah, long time." I smile. "Haven tried to talk me into putting in an apiary. Apparently, she's very worried about the bee population."

They both chuckle. "Not a bad idea," Jared says.

"Hey, maybe you might want to make this your permanent place," Carter says. "Christ knows I'm done sharing a bed with you when Gram opens her place up to strangers, or anyone passing by on the street." I shrug. The thought had gone through my mind.

"I'm sure no one would mind. Maybe we could even open up the lots around the lake. It might be time I left Gram's place too," Carter says.

"I'm trying to move away from you, Carter," I tease, although I think it's a good idea and about time we did it. "Let's talk to Sean," I say. My big brother has a good head on his shoulders. He'll probably want a family meeting, and I'm sure Gram would be happy to have her house back. We all invaded two years ago when Sean called us home. She's happy to have us, but she'd like to see us all settled down, and opening lots around the lake would allow us to be close if she needs us. She's not getting any younger. That thought sits uneasy with me. I'd love to see us all married and with kids, and my God, one of us should be able to give her a great-granddaughter, for Christ's sake.

I take a sip of coffee and look outside as ideas on how to take this place from a cabin to a home form in my brain. Then again, if Haven leaves, leaving me with nothing but good memories of the place, it might take me another twenty years before I step foot in the place. I can't imagine being here without her.

"I haven't seen that look in your eyes in a long time, brother," Jared says, as he puts his hand on my shoulder.

"What's that supposed to mean? What look?"

"The look that tells me there's something worth fighting for."

17

HAVEN

"We could have asked Jace to help," Tyler says, as I repeatedly read the chocolate cake recipe on my phone. Thank God for Pinterest and all their yummy recipes, because I'm sort of lost in the kitchen.

"I am not going to ask Jace to bake me a cake for Kylee's barbecue. I'm doing it myself." I glance at him, my chin lifted in defiance as I take in his sexy stance. My gaze rakes the long length of him as he casually leans against the counter, his feet crossed at the ankles—testosterone coming off him in waves. I swear I can't get enough of him. Singlehandedly—or could it be singledickedly, yeah, not a word, I know—this man might have ruined me for every other.

Working to get myself together, I really want to make a great dessert, I nod toward the fridge. "Now if you could make yourself useful, get me the eggs, that would be a big help."

"I prefer to be useful in other ways."

"While I prefer that too," I say with a grin. "I need those eggs."

He laughs as he grabs the eggs and sets the full carton

beside me. "I can cook, but I'm not much in the baking department." He glances at the flour all over the counter, my clothes and my cheeks. "Doesn't look like you are either."

"Hey," I say and toss some flour at his face. He coughs and blinks, and looks completely adorable as he tries to brush it away. My heart does a little dance in my chest, and a sigh I have no control over escapes my lips as everything inside me melts a little. I turn my face toward him and lift my chin, needing him close, needing his intimacy. "Kiss me, Ty."

He steps closer, and cups my face. I love that I don't have to ask him twice. I let go of the bowl and wooden spoon and turn into him, our bodies aligned. I will never tire of this man's touch or kisses. His warm lips move over mine, and a little moan catches in my throat as I sag against his hard body

"You know," he says and glances at the clock. "Benny's sells amazing baked goods. We could get a cake, toss away the package and pretend you made it."

I chuckle as his cock thickens against my body, and deep between my legs I grow needy. "I could never do something like that. Besides, we've all eaten Benny's sweets." I snap my fingers. "They'd know in a heartbeat it wasn't mine."

He shrugs. "Maybe, maybe not, but it would free up some time and I could bend you over this counter and put my cock in you," he says, pushing my hair from my shoulders so he can place hot, open-mouthed kisses to the sensitive spot on my neck. While I love that idea as much as I love how Tyler seems to have made it his mission to discover all my likes and dislikes, and in the process, teach me more about myself, about who I really am, I'm not a girl to pass someone's cake off as my own. I don't think Tyler would do that either.

"Tyler, you're making this hard," I say, my body warm and wanting, and craving all he's offering.

"*Hard* being the key word here, Haven." His big fingers bite into my hips as he bangs his thick cock against my sex.

I steal a glance at the clock. "What if we're fast?" I say, my brain shutting down as need rushes through me. I spent all week on the set with him close, watching him as he worked through a fight scene with my leading man, and the supporting actor, Zander, who fights with Jonah. He was shirtless for the most part, his skin glistening under the summer sun, and it was all I could do to keep my mind on my lines. Fortunately, there have been no more threatening letters.

"If you want to keep mixing, I can do all the work," he says.

He turns me toward the counter, and nestles in behind me. His big hands slip under my T-shirt and cup my breasts. I arch into his touch. "I'm...not sure that's possible."

"Sure it is," he says. "Just keep stirring, I'll just be back here having my way with you."

I grab the wooden spoon as he unhooks my bra. "Is this even sanitary?" I say with a laugh, even though I don't really care. Maybe I will buy something at Benny's. Honest to God, I'm insatiable around Tyler. I want everything he has to give.

Everything he's not willing to give.

I shut down that thought as he chuckles against my neck and the sound vibrates all the way to my sex. His mouth leaves my flesh as he drops to his knees and the next thing I know, he's dragging my pants down my legs. I lift my legs to help him out, and a fine shiver goes through me when his hot breath curls around my thighs.

His rough hands slide up my legs, parting them a little. He reaches my outer thighs, and slides his hands inward until they're inches from my aching clit.

"How's the cake coming?"

"Not," I say. The only thing that's going to be coming is me. I try to stir, try to read the instructions, but they blur before my eyes as arousal grips me hard. "Ty," I murmurer as he shifts between my legs, his back to the counter, his mouth on my sex. Holy hot. I glance down, and move my hips to rub my sex against his face. He growls and I swear to God, I have never done anything hotter.

He slides his tongue along the length of me, and my legs tremble. I try to concentrate on the cake, toss a bit of baking powder in. Damn was that the right amount? I really don't know, but how's a girl to bake when a man is gifting her with his tongue, doing magic between her legs like it was his God-given mission in life?

I groan and he inserts a finger as he takes my clit between his teeth, nibbling until pain and pleasure mingle—until the four walls close in on me, nothing mattering but this man between my legs and what he's doing to both my body and my heart.

He works his thick finger inside me, and I toss the bowl to the side and claw at the counter. My breathing grows rough, heavy pants that sends the flour on the counter into the air.

"Tyler," I cry out, the dual pleasure centered between my legs taking me higher and higher.

"That's it, Haven," he says, his voice a low, rough murmur. "Come all over my face."

I move my hips harder, and I buck against the blade of his tongue as he fucks me with his finger. This time I'm control-ling the pace and rhythm, grinding on his mouth and finger as he holds completely still for me. Pleasure centers between my legs, and the world fades to black as I let go, my hot cum spilling all over his fingers and face.

I gasp for breath and he stays between my legs, not moving as I ride out each hard wave of bliss. When did I become so free and open, just taking what I want? I don't know but I sure do love how Tyler brings that out in me.

My body stops spasming, and Tyler slides out from

between my legs. He climbs to his feet, his hands all over my body. "I'm going to put my cock in you now," he murmurs into my ear. The hiss of his zipper sends heat down my spine, and his hands go behind my neck, easing me onto the counter. Through my T-shirt, my nipples score the countertop as he positions his cock at my opening, and in one fast thrust, slams into me, driving me harder against the counter.

I gasp and as I reach for the other edge of the island, trying to find purchase as he fucks me, I knock the entire carton of eggs onto the floor. They smash, but that doesn't slow either of us down. He pounds into me. Hard fast thrusts, like something inside him broke, like he can't get deep enough. I steal a fast glance at him over my shoulder, and my heart speeds up as intense green eyes meet mine. He's beautiful. The most beautiful man I'd ever set eyes on. My gaze leaves his to take in the clench of his jaw, the rippling of his muscles. He fucks me like he wants more, needs...something.

My body jerks as he changes the rhythm, long, agonizing slow strokes, where he pulls almost all the way out, only to drive back in again, his crown hitting my cervix and arousing me all over again. That's when I get it. He wants me to come with him. I reach down, and put my hand over my clit.

"Fuck yeah," he growls as I stroke myself and arch a bit more to get him in just a little deeper. "Haven..." I barely recognize his feral voice as I offer every part of me up to him, heart and soul, even though it's only my body he's after.

He plunges in and out of my hot, wet pussy, driving the air from my lungs in a whoosh and I wouldn't want it any other way. I love the way he fills me, the way he holds nothing back. A hard shudder moves through me, matching his perfect rhythm as his cock hits places so deep I'm sure I've died and gone to heaven. Delirious with need to orgasm again, I roll my hips and rear back to meet each brutally perfect thrust. I close my eyes and just like that I come again, a glorious rush of heat that covers his pumping cock.

"Haven." His voice is a deep, raspy growl as he stills deep inside of me.

"Yes, I feel you."

Pleasure rolls through me as he fills me with his hot cum, and my body shakes, almost violently as he pulses and throbs high in my sex. There is no doubt that Tyler has left his mark on me and in me, and I want that. I want all I can get from this man before I leave, and leave I must. As much as I like Blue Bay, this isn't where I belong, and I can't forget Tyler is just lending his family to me. This is pretend—he's not talking long term and I don't know if that's something I could do even if I wanted. One thing I do know however, is if I'm not careful when I leave here, it might be without my heart.

Ty lightly touches my shoulder, and I shudder as he trails his hand down my back. He leans over me and presses kisses to my back. "I think we ruined all the eggs," he says and for some reason, and I have no idea why, I burst out laughing. I guess it's better than crying. He laughs with me and adds, "But the good thing is, I was fast, and can run to the store to get you more."

His cock slides from my body, and he exhales sharply. "Stay put."

"Can't move anyway." I take a deep breath, and realize I must look a mess with flour in my hair and on my face. Don't even get me started on my clothes. I chuckle, because I really don't care. My world is so superficial, and one always has to look their best or risk the worst pictures ever landing on the front page. With Ty, I can be dressed in a sack, with food all over my face and he'd still want me. Is that because he's a guy, or because he might see this, us as something more. "Rubber knees," I add.

He gives my backside a little squeeze and his laugh curls

around me as he dashes to the bathroom. He comes back with a cloth to wash me up, and the gesture tugs at my heart, far too tightly. I cough to hide the mess of emotions pinging around inside me. Tyler finishes cleaning me, and slowly lifts me until I'm standing upright. He has a huge smile on his face as he spins me to face him.

"My God, Haven, you are gorgeous," he says as he smooths down my hair and brushes the flour from my face. I smile up at him as he grabs my panties and hands them to me. I tug them on, and shimmy into my pants, and stand back as he zippers himself back up.

"You're not so bad yourself."

"I think you might need to get out of these clothes."

"So soon?" I tease, as I glance downward to take in his cock. "Or do you need a minute?"

"Funny girl." His eyes narrow in on me as he places his hands on my face. "I kind of feel bad for distracting you." He glances at the mess on the counter. "You really wanted to make a homemade dessert and I think we blew it."

"I didn't blow anything," I say with a chuckle, suddenly giddy again. He laughs and I put my hand on his chest, loving his strong heartbeat beneath my palm. "I think we can still do this, though." I wink at him. "You know, since you were fast and all."

"Hey, don't go spreading that around town. Reputation, remember."

"You don't want the girls to think you're fast?" The sudden thoughts of him with other girls doesn't sit well with me, but he can sleep with whoever he wants. Sure, we're doing the monogamous thing while I'm here, but then he's free to bed whomever he wants, and judging from the girls who stare at him, he could keep his bed warm with a different woman for a month straight.

He wraps his arms around me, and drops a tender kiss

onto my mouth. So tender, it feels like this is about a whole lot more than sex. "No, and I'm not normally that fast. It's your fault."

"Oh, you're blaming your insufficiencies on me now, are you?"

"Insufficiencies?"

I laugh. "Kidding. Let's check the eggs, maybe two survived."

He holds me a moment longer, like he's not ready to let go, then glances at the clock. "I can run to the store if they're not. It's the least I can do." He gives me a sheepish look, and I put my hand on his face.

"The least," I tease.

He steps away and crouches. Strong hands that just pleasured me thoroughly sort through the broken shells. "Three survived, somehow."

"Perfect," I say and turn the tap on to wash my hands.

"I'll get this mess cleaned up if you want to keep going." He grabs paper towels and begins soaking up the eggs.

I pick up the plastic bowl. "I have to start over. I don't think I put the right amouth of baking powder in. I was kind of distracted, in the best possible way, of course."

"We can still do Benny's."

"Do you know how many times I've been invited to barbecues?"

"A lot."

"No. Never. It's always fancy cocktails and fancy dinners at fancy restaurants."

"Ah, sorry you have to slum it here."

I laugh. "Are you kidding me? I love it, which is why I want to be a good guest and bring something special. Maybe I'll get invited back."

"I'm sure you will."

He goes to work on cleaning the eggs, and I dump the

bowl of flour and start again. As he cleans, I glance at him. I hadn't meant to grow close to him, and I probably shouldn't get in any deeper, but I can't help but want to know more, everything, about him.

"Ty."

"Yeah?"

"Have you ever been serious with a woman?" His head lifts and eyes that carry a measure of hurt meet mine. Dammit, I must have hit a sore spot. "I'm sorry, it's none of my business. You don't have to tell me."

He climbs to his feet, and dumps the shells into the garbage. "No," he says. "I've never been serious. I was always on the road, and fighting was my life. Hard to have a wife and family with that kind of lifestyle."

"True. My brother is still living that kind of life."

"You?" he asks and peels off more paper towel. "I mean, we can't always believe what we read in the papers right?"

"I've been in relationships, and I thought things with my last boyfriend were serious." I give a very unladylike snort. "Until I learned he was sleeping with a couple other women. I like that you're a one-woman kind of guy."

"I'm not a cheater." He bends and wipes up the rest of the mess and I take that moment to admire his wide back and broad shoulders.

"That's music to any woman's ears."

He stands and dumps the waste into the trash. "Was he your co-star?"

I cringe as he washes his hands. "I don't just date co-stars you know."

He turns back to me, "I know, you can't believe everything. I mean, have you seen the shit written about me?"

"I have, and I might have believed it, until I met the real you. I like the real you, Ty."

"I like the real you too, Haven."

I smile at that. He's been helping me discover the real me, and I think she's a pretty great person.

"To answer your question, Brett was a co-star and one of the girls he was sleeping with had a hatred for me, and sold some very intimate pictures of Brett and me to the press." I shake my head, disgusted at the level some people will stoop to. "Revenge and quick cash. I hope it was all worth it for her."

His eyes narrow. "You don't think she could be the one behind the letters?"

"My first reaction to that is no. She fell off the grid, and she got what she wanted, right? But I guess anything is possible."

"Probably a long shot then."

I measure the baking powder and dump a teaspoon into the bowl. "Now that you're here in Blue Bay, do you think about that? I mean I saw you with Devon, and Jesse, and you were great. Summer said you didn't want kids, but you're so good with them."

"I do like kids. I just don't want to mess them up."

"I don't think you would."

"Thanks for the vote of confidence, and for what it's worth, I think you'd be a great mother. My nephews already love you. They'll miss you when you leave, you know," he says, and I turn when I hear something odd in his voice, something that sounds like he's asking a question, rather than making a statement.

His eyes meet mine and my heart leaps in my chest. My God, is he feeling me out, trying to see if I'm leaving here? And when he says the kids will miss me, is it possible he really means *he'll* miss me? Is there more going on here, or am I just being a stupid romantic again, seeing things that aren't there and confusing sex with love?

We pull up in front of Jamie and Kylee's place, and Haven carefully reaches for the door with one hand as she balances the chocolate cake in the other. It might not look like the world's prettiest chocolate cake, but I'm betting it tastes good, since Haven poured her heart and soul into it.

"You got it?" I ask.

"Got it," she says, and beams at me, so proud of her accomplishments.

"Shit, stay put," I say when I spot a news van pulling up behind us. Haven glances over her shoulder. I reach for the door handle and she stops me.

"I know you don't like dealing with them anymore than I do. Let's just go inside and ignore them. We're supposed to be a couple anyway, right?" She offers me a smile but it's a bit shaky.

"They'll make shit up, Haven." She goes quiet for a moment, thoughtful. "Give me a second, I'll go talk to them," I say.

"Okay," she agrees, rather reluctantly.

I slide from the car and make my way to the news van. The driver rolls down his window. "Well, if it isn't Tyler Owens," he says.

"What do you want?"

He glances out the window. "Are you with Haven Roberts?"

I lean into him, an intimidation factor. "Who I'm with is none of your business. Don't make me prove that the hard way." His smile falters. "Look, I'm just going to my brother's for a barbecue." As much as I hate the media and the way they distort everything, I realize the guy is just trying to do his job. "How about this. Leave me alone, and maybe I can get you a pass onto the set or something?"

He pulls a card from his pocket and hands it to me. "Thanks, man."

I glance at Haven, and catch her eyes in the rearview mirror as I put the card into my pocket. "Now take off."

I back up as he leaves and when he's out of my line of vision, I walk to the passenger side door and open it. "Taken care of," I say.

"Thank you." Balancing the cake, she carefully exits the car, and I put my hand on the small of her back. "Did you take his card?"

"Yeah," is all I say. I don't want to bother her with the details, or worry her. I'll talk to Mason tomorrow about the media. I wasn't a total prick to the guy, so hopefully he'll do a nice spin.

She nods like she doesn't really understand why I'd do that, and I go silent as the ocean breeze catches the hem of her summery dress, lifting it to expose her sleek legs. Her gaze leaves mine, and the lines around her frowning mouth smooth out as she takes in my brother's place.

"Wow, so gorgeous," she says. "Right on the beach. What a dream house."

"You'd like a place on the beach?"

"I prefer the cabin. I like the privacy, and I like having you all to myself out there."

I grin as we enter without knocking; no one ever expects me to knock. We step inside and I give more thought to turning the cabin into my permanent place. Maybe it really is time one of us puts the old place to use. Only problem is, I want to put it to use with Haven.

"We're here," I say in my outdoor voice and Kylee comes racing around the corner, her finger to her lip. "Oops, sorry," I say with a grin as she cocks her head, listening for Jesse's cries.

"Whew," she says, and points a finger at me. "You're lucky. We just got the boys down. They're both super cranky and if you wake one of them, you're on duty."

I give her a salute. "On it."

"I baked," Haven says in a low voice and holds the cake out.

Kylee's eyes go wide. "You didn't have to do that."

"I know." She gives a casual shrug. "I wanted to."

"Come on out back, Summer and Sean are already here."

"Who else is coming?" I ask.

"Just us, when the other Owens boys get steady girl-friends, they'll get an invite too. Until then, they don't get Jamie's awesome barbecue."

"All the more reason to stay single," I whisper and nudge Haven.

Kylee turns around. "I heard that."

"I'm kidding. Jamie is a master chef."

Outside we find Jamie at the barbecue and Sean and Summer sitting at the table, my brother nursing a beer, as Summer drinks what looks like lemonade.

"Hey so good to see you," Summer stands—okay, more like moans and groans as she pushes to her feet—and gives Haven a hug.

"Um, hello," I say. "Over here." Summer rolls her eyes, and I crook my finger. "Bring it in sister," I say, and she throws her arms around me.

"Bro," I say as we all sit and Kylee sets a wine glass in front of Haven. "Red or white," she says. "I'm not pregnant and I miss having a wine buddy." She gives Haven a wide grin.

"Please be her wine buddy," Summer says and Haven laughs. "So I can live vicariously through you until this little one is born."

"You don't have to twist my arm. I'll have red."

"I think you mean we'll start with red," Kylee says. "It's been a long day with Jesse. Those teeth had better come in soon."

Sean stands and grabs a beer from the cooler. He untwists it and hands it to me.

"Thanks, bro." I step up to Jamie at the barbecue to see what's cooking.

He glances over his shoulder as the girls all talk. "Things good?" he asks, in that big brotherly way that says he knows something isn't right.

"Yup."

"Heard Carter and Jared were at the cabin with you last Sunday night."

"We had the kids from the club overnight," I say, even though I'm sure he already knows that. "Could use the extra hands with so many kids."

He nods. "Okay, good," he says, and I get it. He's letting me know he's got my back. I glance down the beach and spot a guy walking by, pants baggy, a black ball cap, his gaze latched on us.

"Do you know who that kid is?" I ask and Jamie turns. I

have no idea if he's the punk who was hanging out at Haven's trailer, but he fits the description. Then again, lots of kids who summer here with their parents fit the description, but this punk is watching us a little too closely. Which is pretty stupid, considering any one of us could and would snap him like a twig if he tried to hurt Haven.

"That's Tucker Miller. He's with his folks in the gray and white cottage down the road. I did some work on their deck last year. Why?"

"Right, I remember. Good kid?"

He glances at Tucker again and flips the steak on the grill. Smoke rises as he sizzles the other sides "I haven't had any problems with him, why?"

I shrug. "Carter said some punk was hanging around Haven's trailer."

He cocks his head, his brow furrowed. "Want to go ask him?"

"Just keep an eye on him for me," I say. Christ, I don't want to scare the kid if he's innocent. Officer Walker would be all over my ass for harassing the rich folk who summer here. I take a sip of beer and turn to find Haven and the others all leaning in, their voices low. I catch Sean's eye and he leans back, ending the conversation. Why the hell is she always in deep conversation with my brothers?

"What's up?" I ask, and drop down next to Haven. I put my hand on her thigh and give it a light squeeze.

"Oh, just telling everyone here about last Sunday's bonfire," she says and I stare at her. Why the hell is she lying to me?

"Really?" I ask, giving her a chance to tell me the truth.

"Why don't you help me with the salads," Kylee says, and Haven rises. I'm not sure what's going on, but I definitely plan to get to the bottom of things later.

Summer makes a move to get up and Kylee points a finger at her. "Stay. We got this."

They disappear inside, and Sean stands to grab a plate for Jamie.

"I like her," Summer says. "Don't fuck this up, Ty."

I laugh. "Why don't you tell me what you really think?"

She leans into me. "I know you, Tyler. When you build something, you build it to last."

"Ah, okay." What the hell is she getting at?

She runs her finger around the rim of her glass, her chin up a notch and I know a lecture is coming on. "Did you enjoy putting that temporary structure up for the movie set?"

"Not really."

"That's what I mean." She takes a sip of her lemonade, and I tug at the peel on my bottle. "When you build something, you don't want to see it torn down. I have never seen you build something with a woman before, but you are here, whether you realize it or not."

I nod, totally understanding what she's getting at. I've never built anything with a woman. Never wanted to. Things are different with Haven, but she's here only temporarily and I can't forget she's with me because she needed a protector. Will she ever see me as something more or am I simply setting myself up for disaster? "You don't really know what's going on, Summer. Things aren't quite as they seem."

"Maybe not, but I have eyes. I see the way you look at her."

Haven comes from inside, a big salad in her hand. "This all looks de—" Her voice falls off when she glances at Summer and me. I'm not sure what she sees on our faces, but her steps slow. "Everything okay?" she asks, her face paling a little. She glances up, searches the beach.

Shit, I hate seeing her so worried. "Everything is fine.

Summer is just getting hangry," I say and Haven's shoulders relax.

"This one is going to be just like his uncle," she teases. "Needing food all the time."

Haven drops down next to me, and Sean puts a plate of steaks in the middle of the table. "Dig in," he says and Haven glances at me. I give her a smile to let her know she is safe, and we weren't talking about her stalker. For the next hour, we eat, and laugh and my family is kind enough to tell Haven stories about me from our childhood. I don't mind, though. I love the smile on her face. In fact, I love an awful lot about this woman.

We clear the dishes and Kylee brings out the chocolate cake, and Haven says, "I'm sure it tastes better than it looks."

"It looks amazing," Summer says, and we hear a cry from inside the house. Sean disappears and comes back with two bundles in his hands. He passes Jesse to Kylee, and sits Devon on his lap. Devon instantly grabs a fistful of cake and shoves it into his mouth.

"I think it's good," I say. "Devon's eyes just lit up."

We all laugh and moan in appreciation as we devour the cake and before we know it the sun is low on the horizon. Perfect for what I have planned. After a round of hugs, I toss my arm around Haven and lead her to my truck. The night air is warm, and I've never seen Haven look more content than right now—outside of bed, that is.

"Want to go for a ride?"

"Sure, it's still early."

We jump into the truck and I head for the old homestead. "I thought we were going for a ride," she says when I park.

"We are. On my bike."

"Oh," she says her eyes wide.

"You up for that?"

She nods eagerly and I love the trust she has in me. "I am, but I'm in a dress."

"Just keep your legs wrapped around me."

"That shouldn't be a problem," she says and my dick twitches, liking the idea of that too.

I grab my spare helmet from my truck and put it on her head, fastening it tight. "It's a bit big, but it will do for tonight." I make a mental note to pick up a smaller helmet for her tomorrow.

I put my own helmet on, jump on my bike and balance it for her. She slides in behind me, and tightly wraps her legs around my body. Her warmth seeps into my skin as I start the bike and head out onto the winding road that follows the shoreline. Her hands hug me tight as she settles against me. I take my one hand off the bike and lightly rub her hands to make sure she's warm.

We ride a little longer and when the sun disappears in the horizon and the stars dot the black canvas overhead, I make my way back to town. I find a parking spot on Main Street. I help her off the bike and remove her helmet. I grin as I look at her.

"What's so funny?"

"Nothing, you look adorable."

"God, I have helmet hair, don't I?" she asks and starts to smooth her hands over her mess of curls. I capture her hands and tug them away.

"Leave it. You always look great."

She eyes me like she's not sure she believes me. "Fine, what are we doing here?"

I gesture with a nod to Sugar's. "Ice cream."

"Oh, God, one dessert tonight was enough. I won't fit into my clothes."

"You'll thank me for that. Sugar's has the best ice cream in the world."

"That's a big claim, Ty." I laugh and take her hand. The bell chimes overhead as we enter the ice cream shop and ten minutes later, as we're strolling down Main Street and her moans reach my ears, I grin and turn to her.

"Am I right, or am I right?"

"You're right. Best ice cream I've ever had." She casts me a quick glance. "Best night I've ever had."

"I thought the night we went fishing was the best night ever."

She gives a noncommittal shrug. "I'm a woman, and it's my right to change my mind," she teases. "Seriously though, every night just keeps getting better and better."

"What do you normally do on a Friday night?"

"Dinner with 'friends', but most nights I'm home alone." She does air quotes around friends, and my heart squeezes. Everyone needs someone to count on. She has her brother, but he's busy with his career, and I hate the thoughts of her home alone on a Friday night. "What about you?" she asks.

"Well, the guys and I normally go to Winchester's and—"

She holds her ice cream free hand up to stop me. "Say no more," she says with a laugh.

"For the record, this is much better."

She smiles at me. "I think so too," she says and slides her hand into mine. We walk in comfortable silence, and I point out the shops, giving her a little history lesson on the town, and once we finish our cones, we head back to my bike. We take off for the cabin, and once there, I help her remove her helmet, and she goes up on her toes to give me a kiss.

"Tonight was perfect," she says, her gorgeous eyes sparkling under the moonlight. Fuck, I love seeing her this happy. I put my hand on her face, and brush my thumb over her soft cheek.

"It's not over yet, Haven."

"Oh?" she says with a grin. "You have something else planned?"

"Yeah, I do." I take her hand and lead her to the water. I drop down onto the dock and pat it. "Sit with me."

She sits, and kicks her legs out as the moonlight glistens on the dark water. We sit like that for a long moment, a comfortable silence surrounding us. She breaks it and says, "Have you given any more thought to opening a gym, especially now knowing Jace wants your place for a restaurant?"

"I've been thinking about it non-stop. I just wanted to have enough saved so I could open with a bang, and not have to add pieces once I've saved up enough. There was a perfect location, but I was too slow to react. I didn't have enough of a down payment at the time."

"Oh, that's too bad," she says. "Where was it?"

"An old fish plant on the water. Great spot."

She puts her hand on my thigh, and gives a reassuring squeeze. "Something will come up, I'm sure."

I nod. "I could always clear lots around the lake and put something up there. It's not the ideal location, but it's a location. What are your thoughts?" I ask, wanting her opinion.

Instead of answering, she says, "How on Earth am I going to go back to city living after this?"

Crickets chirp and bull frogs croak as I take her hand in mine, not really understanding her change in subject. She's the one who brought it up, but I don't press. I have more important matters at hand, like trying to get her to fall in love with Blue Bay—with me. I shake my head, hardly able to believe how fast and how hard I've fallen for this woman, but the truth is, I am building something with her and I don't want to see it destroyed. Rock is probably going to lose his mind when he finds out, but I'll deal with him when the time comes.

I stand and peel my shirt off. "Let's go for a swim."

"I don't have a suit."

"You think you need one?"

"What if someone comes?"

"Someone is going to come," I tease and pull her to her feet. I look over her face. "Don't tell me you've never been skinny dipping."

"I've never been skinny dipping," she says with a laugh. "Seriously, though, what if someone sees us?"

"The only ones who are going to see us are the frogs and crickets, and I have it on good authority that they're pervs anyway." She laughs out loud, and I reach for the hem of her sundress. "Is that a yes?"

"That's a yes," she says, and I lift her dress over her head. She raises her arms to help and once I have her partially naked, I stand back and admire her lush body. I scrub my face, anxious to get my mouth on her. "You are so gorgeous."

My dick thickens as I appreciate her curves, and I tear into my pants to release the pressure. She wiggles out of her panties and darts a glance around. "This is kind of fun." I take my dick into my hand and stroke and her gaze drops to watch as she unhooks her bra. "What was that you said about coming?" she teases. I growl and reach for her, but she backs up and jumps into the water.

When she resurfaces, I say, "You're going to pay for that."

"You'll have to catch me first." She swims away, her laughter echoing in the still night.

"I'll catch you," I say and dive in. Fuck, that's cold. I come up and shake the water from my face, but can't seem to find her. "Marco," I call out, feeling like a kid again and loving the new memories we're making here.

"Polo," she responds, and I turn toward her voice. I swim after her, and she's laughing so hard, it doesn't take much time for me to reach her. I wrap my arms around her. "Caught you."

"Yeah, you did. Now what are you going to do with me?"

I find her mouth with mine, and we sink below the water as we kiss. Her legs wrap around my waist, and I swim us to the dock. With a little boost, I help her up, and climb up behind her. Her body is cool from the water and I wrap my arms around her.

In no time at all, her skin is warm, hot from my touch, and I gather our clothes and make a little pillow for her. "I need to be inside you, Haven."

My cock pulses, eager to feel her softness wrapped around it. I lower her onto the deck, and she puts hers arms around me as her legs widen for me, and invitation that tugs at my pounding heart.

I reach between our bodies and slide a finger inside her, and a growl rips from my throat when my finger meets with hot wetness. I love how she's so ready for me. I pump her for a minute, my slick finger brushing that sensitive bundle of nerves inside her until she's writhing and moaning beneath me. My mouth finds hers and she whimpers as I remove my hand and place my bare cock between her legs.

"This what you need, Haven?" I ask and press my crown inside. Her body tightens around me, and when she answers with a needy moan, I piston forward, driving high and deep inside her, wanting to stay just like this...forever.

"Haven," I murmur into her mouth. Her tongue tangles with mine, her nails scoring my back as I completely fill her. "So good."

"Yes, so good," she agrees and moves her hips. Her tight channel fucks my thick cock, and I let her work my dick for a minute longer. I take her hands, put them over her head, and pull almost all the way out. My turn to take over. Her nipples tighten against my chest as I jerk my hips forward and slide into her. She's so goddam drenched I easily glide in, our bodies fitting together so perfectly. She was made for me. I fucking know it.

Her legs hold me tight, her soft thighs around my hips, and my heart beats an unsteady rhythm as I fall just a little more for her.

"Tyler," she whispers, her heat searing my dick as we make love. Intense heat zaps my balls as I go up on my hands and push inside, rocking hard against her body. Her hips lift, meet and welcome my every thrust. Her hands go to my chest and she splays her fingers, like she wants to touch every inch of me, inside and out. I revel in the feel of her soft palms, the way she circles my tight nipples.

Sensations batter my body, and I slow the pace a little, not wanting this to be over just yet. I push my pelvis against her clit, each time I fill her, and her eyes close as a hard tremor wracks her body and strokes my aching cock.

She moans a low, aching sound that lets me know she's right there. "I'm...oh God, Tyler." She takes a gulping breath as the heat of her release scorches my dick. She comes around my cock, each hard pulse taunting my release.

"I love when you come like that," I say, and give her a second to catch her breath. Her eyes meet mine, and my world tilts on its axis. Jesus, I've never wanted anyone the way I want her. Her sweet pussy hugs me tight and I power into her, chasing my own orgasm now. I bury my face in the hollow of her neck, and taste her sweet skin as my dick throbs. Lost to everything but her, I give myself over to the pleasure and fill her with my seed.

She cups my head and brings my mouth to hers, and we kiss. Slowly this time, each savoring the taste and moment as I deplete myself in her. I push her hair back, and take in her eyes glistening, post-orgasm contentment all over her face. I free her mouth and she inhales and lets it out slowly.

"I'm so glad you caught me," she says with a smile.

"You like what I did with you huh?"

She's about to answer, but instead her smile falls and she turns her head quickly. "Did you hear that?"

I follow her gaze, and peer into the dark woods. "What did you hear?"

"I thought I heard a noise, like a click or something."

My insides tighten, as I pull out of her and sit up. "Chances are it was just a twig breaking. Probably a racoon or something. I'm sure it's nothing," I say to reassure her, but what if I'm wrong? What if there is something or someone out there, and I was so lost in her I missed it. Fuck, I shouldn't have taken her out here like this. She put her body in my hands and I don't take that lightly.

"What if it's a bear?"

I help her sit up, and she reaches for her dress. "Want me to go check?"

"No," she says quickly. "One encounter with a bear is more than enough." She puts her hands on my face, and there's real worry in her eyes when she adds, "I am not going to sit here and watch a bear eat you alive."

"Eat me alive, huh?"

"You know what I mean."

"Worried about me, Haven? Afraid an injury will keep me from protecting you?" I ask, a ridiculous ploy to hear her say I'm more than simply a bodyguard to her.

She opens her mouth, then shuts it again as she frowns. Her head drops for a second, and there's a storm in her eyes when she makes a fist and holds it up. "Something like that, but know this, I'll kill you if you get hurt."

"That's a little counterintuitive, don't you think?" I say, but her words trigger something in me and my mind races back to all those years ago. Is it possible that Haven was right? That my father acted out of fear? Sure, he was a hard-assed son of a bitch, on all of us, but maybe it was because he only wanted what was best, raising us and making good men out of us the only way he knew how. Did he react and say cruel things because he was so scared? Is it possible Haven is doing the same? Does her worry for my safety imply she's feeling more here too? Or am I really just getting ahead of myself, and conjuring up things that aren't real?

19

HAVEN

The warm afternoon sun shines down on me as Jonah and I stand outside the exterior of the newly constructed bar front and share an intimate moment. All eyes are on us, as I go up on my toes and kiss him. His hands slide around my back, and while he might be a good kisser, his lips on mine do nothing for me.

Honest to God, after Tyler, I'll never be able to look at another man, and I'm sure there is no one out there who can take my body to the heights of pleasure like Tyler has. Yeah, okay, it's true. I asked him to be my bodyguard, but over the last few weeks, he's become so much more. Just yesterday, my brother called me and for the first time in my life, I've not called him back. I fired him off a quick text to let him know I'm okay, but how can I talk to him and act normally? I might be an actress, but I'm not good at lying and to me, an omission is the same as lying.

We break the kiss and I spend the next few seconds gazing up at Jonah, letting the camera capture the adoration in my eyes. Right now, the only way I can portray those emotions is by pretending I'm staring up at Tyler. My God, I am in so much trouble here. We'd only met a month ago. How could I have fallen so fast and so hard? How could I not? Tyler is...everything.

I loop my arm through Jonah's, ready to walk to the gazebo and finish our scene, but when I take a step, he remains perfectly still, jerking me backward.

"What's going on?" I ask.

"Mason called cut."

Shit.

I was lost in thought; I hadn't even heard him end the scene before we finish it. I stand there, and Jonah frowns at me. I blink to pull myself together, and my heart speeds up.

Jonah puts his hands on my arms, and gives a gentle squeeze. "Hey, where'd you go?"

"What? I..." I glance around, and everyone is walking off for a break, and I give a little laugh. "Sorry, I was so into the scene I didn't hear Mason."

A beat passes between us. "You sure that was it?" he asks, and looks over my head. I slowly turn, and find Tyler standing on the road talking to the same reporter who showed up in the van at Kylee's house last week.

"Everything is fine," I tell him as his warning once again circles my brain.

He fights dirty, will do whatever it takes to get what he wants.

Tyler hasn't asked anything of me. In fact, he's the one who jumped in to protect me. I didn't ask him to. He did it of his own volition. We've been having fun, getting to know each other—getting to know myself. The rumors are wrong. I know it deep in my heart. Tyler is a good guy, one of the best guys I know. Besides, I know all about rumors and the validity behind them. I've been the victim of many myself. Untruths printed about me to drum up business for television and magazines.

When I first met Tyler, all I knew was what was said

about him, the fight between him and my brother that fueled sales. But he can no longer say I don't know anything about him, because I do. He's shared a side of himself with me that had to be difficult, a side, I suspect, he's never shared with another.

"I need a quick break," I say and step away. I smooth my damp hands over my jeans as I walk to my trailer. The second I lift my head, I spot movement, and from the corner of my eye, I see a young man dart into the woods. My heart jumps into my throat and I glance around, but Tyler is still talking to that reporter. I swallow the lump in my throat, and open the door to my trailer, stepping inside and locking it behind me. I lean against it and glance around. Nothing is out of the ordinary and from first glance it doesn't look like anything's been taken.

I scan the counters, searching for a note, and I take a fast, relieved breath when my search comes up empty. I push off the door, and quietly walk down the hall, to check the other rooms. I drop down onto the sofa and that's when I notice something written on the mirror of my makeup table.

Coming for you.

My heart seizes, and my hands fly to my mouth at the same time my door rattles. I stiffen, and stand quietly to peer out the small window. Relief rolls through me when I find Shannon standing outside, glancing over her shoulder. She looks like she's about to dart off when I unlock the door and open it.

"Shannon," I say. We don't normally lock our trailer doors, but its courtesy to knock first. "What's going on?"

Instead of answering, she says, "Haven, what is it? You look like you've seen a ghost."

I don't want to tell her. I can't let anyone know what's going on, but I'm so shaken up, it's hard to hedge right now.

She does a fast glance around and when she sees the mirror, she gasps and takes my hand in hers.

"What is going on?"

"I don't know," I say, as she looks at me with motherly concern. It's true, I've never been a great judge of character, but Shannon has always been nice to me. She's the one person I like and trust. "Just some strange letters." I swallow down my fear and add, "I'm sure it's just someone playing a joke."

She shakes her head. "You have to go to the police, Haven. You have to report this."

"No, you know as well as I do that if I report this I might never work again. I've been bringing nothing but trouble to the set." The thoughts of never working again suddenly isn't so scary. Being here with Tyler, I've come to discover so much about myself, so much about my wants and likes outside of show business. My heart squeezes a little at that knowledge. He's taken me to so many places, shared so much of his life with me, and even brought me into his family. How the hell can I walk away from that? I'm not sure, but I do have an obligation to the cast and crew to finish this movie, and I can't let anything interfere. Maybe I should call my brother to see if he has any enemies—outside of Tyler that is.

A knock sounds on my door, and I jump up. "Haven, it's me," Tyler says, announcing himself before he opens the door. His eyes go wide when he sees us both sitting there. "What's going on?"

I gesture with a nod toward my mirror. He steps in and scrubs his chin as he reads it. "Fuck," he grumbles under his breath.

"I think she should go to the police," Shannon says. "Her safety is more important than this movie."

"I happen to agree," Tyler says.

"Ty, no." I jump up. "You know I need to finish this." He

takes me into his arms. "If they have to recast now, it will cost big time."

"I should go," Shannon says and hurries outside.

"Shannon, wait, what did you want?"

She hesitates for a second. "Oh, I just wanted to see if you wanted to go over lines for our scene tomorrow."

"Oh, okay," I say. "Let's do that next break." She leaves and I frown, watching her go.

"What?"

"I don't know. It's odd. She was supposed to be running lines with Olivia. I saw them go into Olivia's trailer, and why would she come to my trailer looking for me, when I'm supposed to be in the middle of a scene. Then again, maybe she knew Mason cut it short."

"You don't think—"

"No, she's an innocent middle-aged lady, and probably just looked out her window and saw me walking here."

"Mind if I talk to her?"

"It's not her, Ty. I saw a young guy running from here. It must have been him."

"What did he look like?"

I give the details and Tyler curses. "Yeah, that sounds like the same guy Carter saw. I'm going to go find him."

I nod. "Okay. I'm safe here with everyone around, and Carter and Jared are right outside."

"I'm taking Carter with me. You stay around the others, okay. I don't want you alone."

"Okay," I say, my nerves settling a little. He gives me a kiss on the forehead and a comforting hug and disappears outside. I take a fueling breath and a few minutes later, after pulling myself together, I step outside. I run into Olivia, who's sipping a coffee and reading over her lines. "Hey," I say.

She smiles up at me, and I grin, instantly knowing that

look on her face. She's been hooking up with Jared. I turn my head and find Jared watching us both.

"So Jared, huh?" I say with a laugh. "Has his grandmother been matchmaking with you guys? I suppose you'll be at the next Sunday dinner."

She frowns. "What are you talking about?"

"Oh, Grandma Nellie, she's always trying to marry the guys off. She wants a great-granddaughter."

Olivia stands there looking at me like I've just been released from some asylum. "Are you okay?" she asks.

Okay, so apparently it's only Tyler and me she's trying to marry off. Does that mean she doesn't think Olivia is right for Jared, yet I'm right for Tyler? There's no doubt that we do fit well together.

"Nothing." I give a dismissive wave. "I just haven't been getting much sleep." Olivia gives me a knowing grin, and I ask. "Were you and Shannon running lines earlier?"

"Yeah, why?"

"Oh, no reason. She just showed up at my trailer and wanted to run lines with me."

"Weird. She took a quick break to grab a coffee but didn't come back with any." She points to her head. "I think she must be going through menopause or something. She can't seem to remember anything these days."

I shake my head, because that's not a nice thing to say at all. As Olivia takes a sip of her coffee, my phone rings. Thinking it might be Tyler with news on the boy, I excuse myself and tug my phone from my back pocket. The call display informs me it's Rock, and I hesitate for a second. My phone keeps ringing, so I slide my finger across the screen.

"Hey, big brother," I say and stifle a yawn. "How's it going?"

"I'm the one who should be asking you that question?" I

hear something bang in the background. He must be at the gym.

"Why do you say that?"

"You haven't returned my call."

"Just busy."

A beat of silence and then, "How's the shoot?"

I inject a measure of enthusiasm into my voice when I say, "It's great. Going really well. It's so pretty here on the East Coast." I try not to ramble. Rock always knows I ramble when I'm nervous about something. "How's training?" I ask, redirecting the conversation.

"Good."

"Ready for the big fight in Vegas next month?"

"Yeah."

"You're going to win, right?" I ask.

"Of course I am," he says with a chuckle.

"You must make a lot of enemies, winning all the time."

He goes quiet and I curse under my breath. Dammit, does he know I'm fishing for information?

"Yeah, so I was thinking about coming to see you on set. I haven't been to the East Coast in ages."

Christ, he knows something is wrong, and I can't have him coming here, seeing Tyler and me together.

"While I love the idea of that, we're shooting day and night." Okay, it's true, we do shoot late, and some scenes are at night, but I'm still bending the truth.

"Is everything okay?" he asks, and I cringe at the sound of his knuckles cracking.

"I'll be back before you know it, Rock. Then we can celebrate your upcoming win and have some quality time together." I love my brother and miss him dearly, but the thoughts of leaving here doesn't sit well in my gut. In the background, someone calls out to him, and his voice is muffled on the phone as he answers. "I have to go, but I look forward to seeing you."

"You too," I say and end the call. I shove my phone back into my back pocket. Emotionally and physically exhausted, I stand there for a second and draw in some deep, rejuvenating breaths to wake myself up, and I toss up a silent prayer of thanks when I spot Gram bringing trays of hot coffee to everyone.

"You look like you could use a cup or ten," she says.

I chuckle. "Thank you," I say and graciously accept the paper cup. I don't even care if it has sugar or milk. I'm after the caffeine fix. I take a big drink and find her green eyes locked on mine.

"Are you sleeping well at the cabin?" she asks, and warmth moves into my cheeks. Despite an hour in the makeup chair earlier, I still have dark smudges under my eyes, a sign of late nights in Tyler's arms.

"It's so gorgeous there. All the fresh air makes me sleep well." It's not a lie when I finally do fall asleep, I sleep soundly.

She gives a smile and looks off into the distance, like she's remembering a happy time. "Tyler's grandfather and I built that home."

"I heard."

"I have all my special movies stored there. Have you had a chance to watch any yet?"

"No, not yet. Long nights on the set," I tell her.

She takes my hand in hers and pats it. "Why don't you and Tyler look through them? I'm sure you'll find the selection most interesting."

She walks away, and as I watch her go, an odd feeling pulses through me.

What is she up to?

20

____

TYLER

I glance over at Haven, who is resting her head against the seat, her eyes barely open. I reach out and take her hand in mine and give it a little squeeze. Obviously, I've been keeping her up too late at night when she has to get up at the crack of dawn and work long into the night.

"You okay?" I ask.

Her head turns my way and she gives me a soft smile so steeped in sweetness and gratitude, my heart misses a beat. "Perfect."

"I'll find him tomorrow," I say, knowing everything won't be perfect until I catch the bastard who's threatening her. Fuck, I hate that Carter and I couldn't find the punk who'd been hanging around her place. I'm pretty sure it's Tucker, the kid we saw on the beach. We went straight to his cottage, and his folks said they hadn't seen him all day. I figure a knock on his door first thing tomorrow should do the trick. I don't care if I wake him up. In fact, I hope I do. I want to catch him off guard and tired. Maybe then he'll tell me what he's been up to and why.

"Thanks Ty," she says. She goes quiet for a long time, her

head down, in thought. "He must be the one behind it, but what I still don't understand is how he would have slipped me a note at the airport bathroom. It doesn't really add up, does it?"

"You're right. It doesn't. All the more reason I need to talk to him, and either find out if he's up to something, or rule him out." I turn down the road leading to the cabin, and she lets out a soft sigh, sleep pulling at her. "Are you hungry, or do you just want to go to sleep?" I ask.

"I could use a bite. We have some leftovers from the other night. I can heat them up."

"Or I can heat them up and you can veg on the sofa, and watch TV."

She sits up a bit straighter. "That reminds me. Gram said something strange to me today."

Not at all surprised—I realize Gram has been match-making—I cast a quick glance her way, and note the line in her forehead as she frowns. "What's that?"

"She asked if we've been watching any movies. She thought we might like something in her collection."

I frown, and grip the wheel a bit tighter. "Yeah, that is strange."

"Then you don't have any idea what she's talking about, do you?"

"None." Gravel crunches beneath my tires as the cabin comes into view, and my stomach no longer clenches when I look at it rising up in the distance. But it does tighten as memories of my dad, of that early summer morning, trespass on the happy times Haven and I have been creating here. I miss him. I miss him so fucking much, despite how much of a hard-ass he was, not to mention how infuriating and unyielding he was to every single one of us. It was his way or no way and yet there was only one thing in this world I ever wanted, and it was to make that man proud. I could never do anything right, and now that he's gone, any chance I had of putting a smile on his face, or receiving a stupid slap on the back for a job well done, died with him. I know my brothers and cousins are all fighting the same losing battle.

I ease into the driveway, and kill the ignition. I slide from my seat, circle the vehicle and put my arm around Haven's waist as she steps from the truck and stretches out fatigued arms. Bullfrogs croak, crickets chirp and a fresh floral scent fills the air as we head inside. The more time I spend here the more it grows on me.

I point to the sofa. "Sit, I'll reheat the leftovers."

"Not going to argue, bossy pants." She heads toward the sofa, and I chuckle as I open the fridge, pulling out the leftovers. I toss the pasta into the microwave and turn to find Haven rooting through the old DVDs and videos from an era gone by.

"Find anything good?"

"Gram sure has an eclectic taste in movies." She holds up some old romantic comedy and I groan as I glance at the cover.

"Tell me you're not going to make me watch that."

"Maybe," she says with a grin. "Wait, what are these ones?"

She pulls a black case free and opens it. Inside there are a bunch of DVDs. "No clue." I step closer. "Not labeled?"

"Yeah, it says...Tyler, and numbers next to it." Her eyes are narrowed when they meet mine. "Do you know what this is?"

"That's my father's handwriting. Maybe it's something he recorded, although I don't really remember Gram or Dad having a video recorder when we were kids. Some of our friends' parents did though, for birthday parties and things like that. Maybe that's what it is."

"Should we put one in and see?"

"Sure."

She pries one DVD from the case and I make my way back to the kitchen, pulling our food from the microwave. I'm not sure why, but as I divide the pasta and carry our plates to the sofa, an uneasy knot twists my stomach. Haven reaches for the remote and flicks the DVD on and settles herself against me on the sofa. I shift closer and put my feet on the coffee table as I stab a piece of pasta and slide it into my mouth.

"Mmm, good," Haven says as she bites into the creamy penne I made a couple nights ago. She helped with the preparations of course, and I love how she loves learning new things, never afraid of backing down from a challenge.

I wait for something to flash on the screen as I stare at it. "I hope it's not anything embarrassing."

"I hope it's from when you were little. I bet you were a cute kid."

"Modesty prevents me from correcting you."

She laughs and whacks me. "My God, you guys must have been a handful." She rolls her eyes. "Wait, what am I saying. You all still are. Gram probably went gray well before her time."

Just then the DVD starts playing, and the pasta I'd just swallowed, rises in my throat. "What the fuck?" I croak out, and I and tug my feet from the coffee table and plant them hard on the floor. I sit up a bit straighter, my heart somewhere in the vicinity of my throat.

"Tyler," Haven says, her voice a bit shaky. Clearly, she's as confused and surprised as I am. "Is that..." She leans closer to the TV, and I look at the image through her eyes. I was leaner then, tougher, my face harder, with more angles, but make no mistake about it, that's me on the screen, entering the cage for my very first fight.

I set my plate onto the coffee table and brace my elbows on my knees. "Yeah, that's me." My insides twist and my throat squeezes so tight, breathing becomes near impossible.

"Ty," Haven says and puts her hand on my arm, clearly picking up on my confusion as I try to catch a breath to refill my lungs. Restless, and antsy, I stand on shaky legs and rake my hand through my hair, tugging hard enough to cause pain —an effort to distract myself and keep the tears at bay.

"What the fuck am I looking at?" I say, even though I already know, and pick up the case with the rest of the DVDs inside. I tug them out, and flip through them. They all have my name and dates. Lungs seized, I drop back down beside Haven, put my elbows on my knees, and cover my face with my hand.

"Holy fuck," I say my words mumbled behind my palms. Haven goes perfectly still. I'm not even sure if she's breathing. Fuck, I'm not sure I am either. My stomach clenches, like I'd just been sucker punched. I guess in a way I have been. Standing back up, I grab another DVD, and shove it into the machine. I stand there, and when my face fills the screen, as I prepare for another fight, every muscle in my body tenses, each cord so taut, I'm sure something is going to snap. I toss in a third DVD, a fourth and a fifth, and every single one has my father's writing on it.

"He...recorded..." I choke on my words, try to get them out, but they're stuck deep in my throat. I grab a fistful of hair and tug again as I try to wrap my brain around this.

My father recorded my fights?

A deep tortured sound I have no control over crawls out of my throat, and Haven is right there, her arms around me, holding me tight as I sort through this unexpected discovery. I just stand there, wrapped in her arms, adrenaline flooding my body like I'm going into fight or flight mode. I swallow, a little less unstable on my feet. Grief and shock work their way through my body, and suddenly I'm exhausted. Too exhausted to stand—to think with any sort of clarity. As my brain and body shut down, it leaves room for a barrage of emotions to tear through me.

I back up, and Haven comes with me. Unceremoniously, I plunk back down on the sofa and she reaches for the remote to lower the volume. Acid burns up my esophagus, my insides raked raw as my world tilts on its axis.

"Haven," I say, my voice rough, like someone took a cheese grater to my throat.

"I'm here." I tug her to me, cradle her head in my arms.

"I never knew," I say, my voice low and hollow.

She shifts and puts her arms around me. "He was proud of you, Ty."

As soon as those words leave her mouth, my chest squeezes tight and tears pound behind my eyes. I pinch the bridge of my nose. Real men don't cry, right? That's what dear old Dad always told us. Despite it all, I am who I am because of him, and to be honest, I like who I am. I especially like who I am with Haven.

"It's okay to cry, Ty."

I swallow hard and take a sobbing breath as the overflow of tears falls down my cheeks. I swipe at them, and take a deep, hard breath. Dad wouldn't want to see me cry. But he's not here to see me, just like he wasn't at any of my fights. That doesn't mean he hadn't seen them, though.

"Un-fucking-believable." Never, ever in my life did I expect to find DVDs with my fights, and judging by how many there are, he recorded every single one. I snort and shake my head.

Haven cups my face, her touch like a healing balm to the open wounds I never thought would heal. She gives me a soft smile. "He was proud of you," she says again, and that's when I understand the depths of pain I'd been carrying around with me. My father died alone, none of us boys there to help him.

He was clearly a man who had no idea how to give love, how to show it to his boys. But this...this here, these DVDs, say so much. They say everything.

"I wish I'd known." I glance at Haven. "If I'd known, maybe I wouldn't have stayed away so long. Maybe he wouldn't have died alone and sad." I press my palms to my eyes. "We all fucking abandoned him."

"From everything you'd told me about your father, I don't think he ever would have told you anyway, Ty."

"You're right, he wouldn't have, but Haven, my God, when I have kids, they're going to know their old man is proud of them. I'll tell them every goddamn day."

She pulls my hands from my face, and offers me a soft smile. "Yeah, you will. You'll be a great dad," she says, and my heart fills with everything I feel for her. I need to tell her. I need to tell her I went ahead and fell for her despite the rules we put into place. How could I not? She's everything, and while neither of us are perfect, we're definitely perfect for each other. Knowing my Dad did this, and that I wasn't here for him, makes me want to speak up, take chances—never miss an opportunity to tell someone how much they mean to you. Fuck, I don't want to lose anyone else I love.

"Haven," I say. I take in her tired eyes as she watches me carefully.

"Yeah?"

I open my mouth, about to lay my heart on the line, when a crashing sound from outside cuts me off. Haven stiffens, and I put my hands on her shoulders. "I'm sure it's nothing. Probably a racoon."

"Damn racoons," she says, her lids blinking rapidly. The noise obviously frightened her.

"You stay here. I'll go check."

I make a move to stand and she stops me. "Ty."

"Yeah?"

"Are you okay?"

I exhale, and nod. "I don't think I've ever been this okay." I let my gaze fall to the stack of DVDs. "He was a lot of things, but he loved us. I know that now."

"Yes, he did. He was proud of you all. His generation, they didn't always know how to say the words, you know."

"I know."

She stifles a yawn, and I reach for her hand and pull her up. "Why don't you go crawl into bed? You're exhausted. I'll be up in a few minutes. I just want to check on the boat, and do a perimeter check and find out what that noise was. I'll lock the door, so don't open it for any reason."

"I won't."

I eye her. "Do you feel safe?"

She leans into me, her breath warm on my skin. "I always feel safe when I'm with you, Ty."

Her words wrap around my heart and give a gentle squeeze. "Okay," I say and drop a kiss onto her forehead. "Head on up and I'll be there in a few minutes." I give her ass a light smack and she yelps and heads up to the loft. Once she's secure, I go outside, lock the door behind me, and spend the next fifteen minutes walking the property and checking on the shed and boat. Nothing seems out of the ordinary, other than a trash can tipped over. I have a new lightness about me, and I know Haven and I need to talk. I need to tell her how I feel before it's too late, and she goes back to L.A. I'm not sure what will come of it, but it's a chance I have to take. I've lost so much time with my father, years of being away and being resentful. I am not going to lose those years with Haven.

I unlock the door, and the place is quiet when I step inside. I head to the loft, my heart beating double time. I spot her beneath the covers. I'm about to call out to her, but stop when I hear her soft breathing noises. While I need to talk to her, I'm glad she's asleep. She's been exhausted. Deciding to wait until tomorrow, I undress and crawl in beside her. With a stupid smile on my face, I spoon her. As though needing my comfort and touch, even in sleep, she snuggles against me. I've been inside this woman numerous times, yet holding her like this, accepting my feelings for her, and all I want is something far more intimate.

I just pray to God she wants the same things.

21

HAVEN

"Oh my God," I say and jackknife up in bed.

"What's going on?" Tyler asks from beside me.

"We slept in. I was so tired last night I forgot to set the alarm." I toss the covers off and stand.

"Okay, you go shower, and I'll get your breakfast ready."

"I don't have time for breakfast."

"You can eat it in the truck," he says. "You need food in your stomach, Haven."

I shake my head, but love the way he cares about me like that. "Okay, thanks. I'll grab a fast shower." I hurry to the bathroom, and take the world's fastest shower. I don't bother with my hair, or makeup, that will be done on set, so I climb into a pair of shorts and a T-shirt. Filming has been going great the last few days, and we'll be wrapping up sooner than I ever thought we would be. My stomach sinks. While I'm glad everything is going well, and I'm proving to be the drama-free professional that I am, I wish things were going to drag on a little longer. I'm not quite ready to leave Tyler.

In the kitchen, I find Tyler putting my food in a plastic container, and filling a Thermos mug with coffee.

"You are my knight in shining armor," I tell him.

He grins. "I didn't think you believed in fairy tales, Haven."

I shrug. "I shouldn't, but there is a part of me that's a hopeless romantic, living in that Norman Rockwell calendar."

He chuckles and gives my ass a light slap. "Let's move it."

We hurry to his car, and I casts him a quick glance. "Sorry for falling asleep last night."

"While I wanted to ravish you, I like that you felt safe enough to fall asleep, and just so you know, it was likely a racoon we heard. The garbage can was tipped over."

I nod and take a sip of my hot coffee, needing the caffeine fix. "I was so tired."

He puts his hand on my lap, something I've grown accustomed to, and love, and he gives it a squeeze. "You needed the sleep."

"Tonight we'll talk about that ravishing part."

His face drops, goes serious, and he looks ahead. "Was it something I said?"

"Yeah. Tonight, we do need to talk."

My entire body stiffens at the seriousness in his voice. "We can talk now," I say, worry gripping my stomach. I know we're pretending, playing house, and we set rules. He's pretty good at reading me, which means he could very well tell that I'm getting in deeper than I should.

He casts me a fast glance and the green in his eyes is darker. He hesitates, and my heart misses a beat. Whatever he has to say to me, isn't coming easy to him, which leads me to believe I'm not going to like what I hear. "No, you need to concentrate on work, and your lines."

"Okay," I say for lack of anything else. Is he ending this thing between us? I get men wanting something from me and discarding me after they've gotten it, but Tyler isn't like any of those other men. Maybe I'm reading this all wrong. Maybe he's not ending it at all. Maybe he wants more from me, the same way I want more from him.

Do I dare hope?

We both go silent, lost in thought, and I dig into the toast and scrambled eggs. "Did you eat?" I ask.

"I'll grab something later."

My heart warms, loving the way he puts me first and worries about the little things, like eating. "I appreciate this," I tell him.

He simply smiles and the next thing I know, we're at the set. He seems a bit different this morning, distracted maybe, like he has something weighing him down. He catches Carter's eye as I make my way to outfitting and make up. Normally he gives me a kiss before he leaves, but this time he's walking away like a man on a mission. What is going on with him? Something is clearly bothering him.

I try to put that out of my mind as I prepare for my next scene, and after makeup and outfitting, I spend the morning and the better part of the afternoon working. By the time I see Tyler again, he has a very strange, very worried look on his face as he and Carter stand near his truck and chat.

Since I'm on a thirty-minute break, I begin to head toward them, but my phone rings. The special chime informs me it's Rock calling, but I'm not really in the mood to talk to him. I glance around the set, and notice everyone on their phones. Whatever they're looking at must be shocking, judging by the looks on their faces.

My phone continues to ring. Rock is clearly on a mission. My throat tightens. Maybe I better answer. Perhaps he's in some kind of trouble.

I pull my phone from my back pocket, and as I slide my finger across the screen, I note the way Tyler's watching me, his heavy-lidded eyes locked on mine, worry all over his face.

"Hey Rock, what's up."

"Are you kidding me?" he fires back. "You don't know?"

Okay, I'm not sure what's going on, but Rock had a deep voice. Never in my life have I heard this kind of high-pitched hysteria coming from him. I sink down onto the closest bench, and that's when I spot Jonah coming my way, his steps fast, purposeful. I have no idea what is going on. I only know it has something to do with me and it's really, really bad.

"I've been working all day. I don't know what's going on."

"I'll send you a link. You need to check it out, but make sure you're sitting down first."

My heart jumps into my throat and air is almost impossible to get as I click on the link and pictures of Tyler and me, in a very compromising position on the dock, come into view.

"Oh, God, no," I say and bend forward, as my stomach twists and turns. That night after our swim, I heard noises. Tyler reassured me everything was fine, but nothing was fine. Some reporter must have been in the woods, taking pictures of us. As the world fades to black around me, Jonah drops down onto the bench next to me. His worried eyes are narrowed, agitated. No doubt he's worried I've fucked up this shoot.

He shakes his head at me. "Jesus Christ, Haven. What have you done? After everything, I thought you'd be more careful not to bring trouble to the set. Now this. I warned you."

I put the phone back to my ear and hear my brother say, "Wait, is that...Tyler Owens you're with. Jesus, Haven, you're with Tyler."

"Rock, I'll call you back." I end the call before he can say anything, and take a couple fast breaths.

"We were careful. No one should have known how to get to that place. Not without directions."

"What do you mean by that?"

"I mean it's in the middle of the woods, down a road that

doesn't even look like a road. Tyler assured me we could never be followed and how no one could find the place without a map, especially if they didn't live around here."

"You know what that means, then?"

My head jerks his way and I wrap my hands around my stomach. From the corner of my eye I catch Tyler and Carter talking to the director. I can't hear what they're saying, but it's obviously a very serious conversation about me, judging by the way their glances keep landing on Jonah and me.

"No, I don't," I say, my thoughts coming in fragmented bursts as tears threaten. My God, is this going to ruin my career, this movie. How the hell did this happen?

"Tyler is obviously the one behind it," he says.

"He would never do that," I blurt out, instantly defending the man I love.

"Really now. Come on, use your brain, Haven. Your brother stole his title. They're mortal enemies. What better way to get back at Rock than to ruin his sister? Plus, it probably put a big chunk of change in his pocket."

Air evacuates my lungs in a fast whoosh as his words ping around my brain. "He wouldn't do that," I say. "He wouldn't."

"Did he need money for something?"

"Yeah, but..." I begin, my words falling off as I think about the gym he wants to build and the hefty price of the equipment.

"No buts, he obviously did this. Two birds, one stone. Or should I say one Rock."

I turn to see Tyler, who's talking on his phone, and a big stupid hiccupping sob catches in my throat as old insecurities come rushing back, cutting off my air supply like I'm in one of Rock's choke holds. Could Jonah be right? Could he be the one who set this up? I mean, he and my brother are enemies, and he did suggest it might be an enemy of Rock's who was doing this. Is that why he hadn't been able to find the punk, because he wasn't really looking for him? Was that all just for show to throw me off his scent?

Oh, God, no. This can't be happening.

Tyler ends the call and starts walking toward me. I stand on shaky legs, and Jonah walks away, leaving me to deal with Tyler myself. His eyes trail Jonah for a second, and then he turns to me.

"Listen, I have to tell you something, and it's not going to be easy. Maybe you should sit."

I continue to stand, my legs ramrod straight. "Might this be what you want to tell me?" I ask and hold the phone up to show him the picture of the two of us making love—correction, having sex, there was never any love involved on his part, obviously. He scrubs his face, not at all surprised. Oh, and why is that? Because Jonah had to be right. He must have set this up for the money. I snort. My whole life men have used me and discarded me. I thought Tyler was different. I thought he didn't want anything from me.

"I guess now you can afford a new building and all the equipment for the gym."

He goes quiet, so quiet I'm sure I hear every bird chirping in a ten-mile radius. Those green eyes of his darken, turn murderous as they glare back. I wait for him to say something, do something. Deny it even. Seconds turn into minutes and I finally blurt out, "You know you didn't have to do this. Your brothers were going to surprise you with a new building and everything you needed. It was hard for me to keep quiet. All I wanted to do was tell you they bought that fish processing plant on the waterfront. Remember that night you showed me your notes and equipment specs you keep stored in your glovebox?"

"Yeah."

"Your brothers and cousins were planning a big surprise, and brought me in because I knew what you wanted." I stare at my phone, disgusted and ready to vomit when I see the picture. "I guess this was all for nothing." I give an almost hysterical laugh. "Or maybe it wasn't. I guess this was a good way to get back at Rock. Fucking his sister was the perfect revenge. Well done, Tyler." Here I thought we were building something between us, but nothing was real. Why on earth did I ever let myself hope it was. "You're a better actor than I'll ever be." I stand there another minute, waiting for him to do something. I catch Mason glaring at me. "I'll probably never work again." I take a deep breath. "Aren't you going to say anything?"

"I think you've said it all, Haven."

"I guess I did then," I say, my heart shattering into a million pieces. I guess there was a part of me that was hoping I was wrong, that past hurts had no place between Tyler and me, but yet here he is, not denying anything.

"I guess I'm no longer needed here."

"Right, I guess not." Apparently, my stalker situation is no longer an issue. He must have been using that to get close, lure me into a sense of security so he could fuck my brother over, and fuck me in the process. When will I ever learn?

He turns, and stupid tears fall down my face in a rush as I take in the slump of his shoulders, the way his muscles flex with each movement. In the distance I hear a siren, but I have no chance to consider what's happening when Mason points his finger at me, and then gestures toward his trailer. With my entire head spinning, and my heart shattered, I head toward the trailer, and swipe at the tears to try to pull myself together. A police car stops near Tyler, and Officer Walker climbs from the driver's side. I go perfectly still when he says something to Tyler, and then glances around the set. I follow his gaze, until I'm staring at a very worried looking Shannon. What the hell is going on? Shannon starts to back up, but the officer is on her in seconds flat handcuffing her hands behind her back.

I'm about to run to her rescue, but Mason grabs my arms. I spin his way. "Why are they handcuffing Shannon?"

He glares down at me. "I think the better question is, why didn't you tell me about the letters?"

I blink once, then twice, and angle my head to see Tyler watching us. "He…told you."

"He gave me the heads up about Shannon. Told me the police were on the way."

Shannon is squirming and cursing at the cop as he walks her toward us.

I try to quiet my racing mind. "Are you saying Shannon was behind it?" I mean it seemed strange when she was trying to get into my trailer, but…no, it couldn't be her, could it?

"Yes," she was behind it," Officer Walker says as he steps up to us. "She hired one of the vacationers to leave you a messages and scare you. Don't worry, he's headed to the station, and won't be bothering you again."

With my heart already broken, the shattered pieces crumble, and tears flood my eyes. Is there no one I can trust? No one who doesn't want something, or isn't out to harm me?

"Shannon?" I ask. "Why?"

She snarls at me. "Don't play innocent with me, Haven. You've been stealing roles that should have gone to my daughter. She's Hollywood elite, not you." With a nod she gestures toward Tyler as he climbs into his truck. "You're nothing but a slut, sleeping with everyone to get ahead, and causing nothing but trouble. You don't deserve any of this," she spits out.

I stand there stunned, my entire body too numb to move as the world crashes in around me. Officer Walker gives her a nudge to set her in to motion, and I turn to find Tyler driving away—leaving the set and my life forever.

"To my trailer now," Mason commands, pulling my focus.

A big stupid hiccupping sob catches in my throat as I force my legs to work and blindly follow him. Honest to God, I can't believe this is my life right now. I just lost the only man I ever truly loved, found out the one person on set I liked and trusted was out to hurt me, and now I'm about to lose this job, too.

22

TYLER

It's been nearly two full weeks since Haven accused me of doing something so ridiculous and underhanded that I've been walking around for days wanting to punch something. Hard. Is that what she thinks of me? That I'm the kind of guy who would do something like that?

When we first met, I told her she didn't know me, and she didn't. I didn't know her either. Lord knows what we read in the papers is total and utter bullshit. Christ, if you went by what was written about me and Rock, you'd think we were mortal enemies. We're not. He's a good guy and a good friend, and he was there when I was going through a tough time, just like Haven was there for me when I found the DVDs. After spending all of our time together, I'm pretty sure I saw a side of her that she never knew existed. Haven found herself in my arms, discovered her likes and dislikes, and I loved watching her blossom beneath my touch. Nothing made me happier than watching her discover who she really was, and come to realize that person was pretty damn awesome.

I guess deep down, she didn't know me, and I really didn't

know her. I never thought she'd jump to conclusions about me, and accuse me of tipping off the media for profit. That's pretty fucked up and leads me back to one question—is that the kind of guy she thought I was? While she might have been learning who she was, she clearly hadn't taken the time to get to know the real me. Maybe it just wasn't that important to her.

Despite all that, despite the knife she shoved straight into my heart, I still would have stayed on to be her bodyguard—as fucked up as that sounds. But her safety was and still is, important to me, and I'd never let her or her brother down like that. Sure, he's not going to like the idea that I was in his sister's bed, but he's going to be grateful that I watched out for her.

A noise at the door pulls my attention and my heart leaps as I spin. My gaze lands on Gram, and I have no idea why I thought—hoped—it was Haven. She's gone. After Officer Walker arrived on the set, and arrested Shannon, they finished up the shoot quickly and cleared out, leaving no traces that they'd ever been here—physical traces to be precise. Haven's presence is still imprinted on my heart.

Seriously though, who would have thought it was Shannon screwing with Haven all along. It makes sense though. She would have been at the airport, in the ladies' room with Haven after they arrived in Connecticut. It's beyond my comprehension to think she paid a local kid to leave letters, to try to scare Haven away from the set all because she was jealous that Haven landed the lead and not her own daughter. I shake my head at that. Haven really does work in a fucked-up industry. I'm just glad in the end Shannon was caught, and the boy she paid is going to be doing community service for his involvement. Haven is now safe to go back to the life she lives—one where she has no friends, and men always want something from her.

"Hello," Gram says, and I shake my head to clear it. Not that I ever think that will happen. Everywhere I look, I see Haven, which is why I need to get the fuck out of the cabin. Although I slept with her back in my bed at the old homestead, and the second I lay my head down, I expect those memories to come back in a painful flash.

"Hey Gram, what are you doing here?" I ask, and work to inject a bit of enthusiasm into my voice.

She walks around the cabin, tracing her finger over the back of the sofa. "Looks like you're packing up to come back home."

"I don't want to be here anymore. Bad memories."

Her head lifts, and her brow raises as her gaze latches on mine. "Some good ones too, don't you think?"

I glance at the loft. If I try really hard, I can still smell Haven's scent on the bedding. They need to be washed, I just haven't been able to bring myself to do it. "Yeah," I say under my breath. I really don't want to get into my love life, or lack thereof, with my grandmother.

Gram steps outside into the shade, and I follow her. Big clouds block the afternoon sun, and she lifts her face to the sky. "Did you get a chance to watch any of the movies?"

I loosely drape my arm around her and watch the waves lap the shore. "Yeah, I did." I turn to her. "Did you always know?"

"I knew," she says.

"How come you never told me?"

"There is this thing called fate." The fine lines around her eyes crinkle as she smiles up at me. "You learned the truth when it's time to learn it. Not a second before or after."

I chuckle but it holds no humor. "When did you become a philosopher?"

She taps her head. "Still got lots going on in here, Tyler."

"I know you do, Gram," I say and go quiet. She's here for a reason, and I suspect I'll be finding out why very shortly.

"Haven's gone."

Ah, and there it is, the real reason she's here.

I try to sound unbothered, but suspect she'll see right through me. "Yup, back to L.A. Not that I'm keeping tabs." It's a lie, I am.

She makes a tsking sound. "I'm sure glad your father isn't around to see any of this."

I stiffen, and my arm falls from her shoulder. I back up and sit on the porch step. "What's that supposed to mean?"

"You made him proud your whole life, Tyler. But this... let's just say I'm glad he can't see you now." She gives a slow shake of her head.

My insides twist. "Gram, what are you talking about?"

"You're a fighter, Tyler." She flexes her bicep and the corner of my mouth turns up at her attempt to show me her muscles. "Your father bragged about you so much." She smiles and her eyes light up, like she's recalling a happy memory. "He told everyone how tough you were, how nothing frightened you."

"A bear frightened me," I remind her. "He didn't like that too much. Wasn't too proud of me that day."

"You were a kid. Your father was never good with his words, but he was so scared you were going to get hurt that day, he lashed out from fright." She glances down, and her lips pinch tight. "He came to me later that night, told me what really happened, and that was the closest I've ever seen him to tears."

My heart pinches tight, and I take a deep breath to ease the pain in my throat. "Really?"

She blinks, like she's reliving the moment. "I don't think he slept for a week."

"I...I didn't know," I say and try to sound casual, like my insides aren't being filleted like a lake trout.

"You didn't suspect he lashed out from fear?"

"Not until Haven said something similar to me when I told her about the incident." God, I have to stop saying her name, have to stop thinking about her. I'm losing my damn mind as it is.

"Look at you now. All grown up and not so tough. I think you were braver when you were ten and facing that bear."

"Jesus, why don't you tell me what you really think." I never knew Gram to be cruel, but she's not being very nice to me now.

"What are you afraid of, Tyler?"

"I'm not afraid of anything."

"You're a fighter. So why aren't you fighting for her? Are you really throwing in the towel so easily? Here I thought when things got tough, you got tougher." She purses her lips, a slow shake of her head. "Guess I was wrong."

I pinch the bridge of my nose and let her words sink in. She drops down beside me, completely quiet, as wildlife sounds fill the void. "What if she doesn't want what I want?" I finally say, breaking the silence between us. "What if I was never anything more than a bodyguard to her? Women have never really seen past the MMA fighter. I've always been a guy they wanted in their bed, but not their hearts."

"Ah, there it is," she says as she nods, and puts her hand over mine. I take in her gnarled, arthritic joints, the dark spots on her skin. Gram has lived a long hard life with all us boys, and my father, and even though her hands hurt her, it doesn't stop her from knitting, baking and tending to her garden. She's the tough one in the family. The smart one too. "Tell me about Haven."

I exhale, as my mind races and unable to help myself, a smile touches my mouth. "Well, she doesn't like fishing with real worms, or flies," I say and laugh at the private joke. "She loved having a campfire with all the kids from my class." My heart squeezes as the sound of her laughter still rattles around inside my brain. "She loves kids, and I tell you, she deserves a family of her own. People might say she doesn't want kids. Well, she never said that. She said she didn't want to bring them into her world and honestly, I don't blame her. It's cutthroat."

"Tell me more," Gram says.

"She's a hard worker, one of the hardest I know. She loves learning new things, and isn't afraid of trying anything. I really love that about her."

"Is that what you love?"

"One of the things."

"Tell me what else you love."

"I love her smile, especially when she wakes up in the morning and finds me beside her." I cringe. "Sorry, maybe that was too much information."

"I'm old, son. I'm not dead. I know what sex is."

I give a very uncomfortable laugh and she pats my hand, encouraging me to continue. "I love the relationship between her and her brother, and how our family all took her in, and treated her like she was one of us. She loved that too." I swallow the lump in my throat and say, "There wasn't a single person in the world I wanted by my side except her when I found those DVDs."

"Sounds like you love just about everything about her. What do you think she loves about you?"

My stomach clenches so tight, I'm sure I'm going to vomit. "She accused me of some pretty awful things, Gram," I say through clenched teeth.

"That's not what I asked, but since you brought it up, why do you think she did that?"

I gaze out over the lake, and take in the bobbing boat. My

God, we had so much fun in the water, and I'd never seen her eyes bigger than when she reeled in that trout. "I guess she's used to seeing the worst in people. Outside of her brother, she's never been able to count on anyone." My heart crashes against my ribs when I add, "I wanted to be the guy she could trust and count on, you know? I tried to be that guy, but I guess she never saw me as anything more than a man who was out for his own best interests, just like every other guy in her life."

"You were that guy she could trust and count on, but old fears and insecurities came back to haunt her when she saw the pictures. That's understandable, don't you think? She clearly expects the worst, probably because she's only ever been shown it."

"When things are going good for her, she waits for bad to follow. She told me that."

"I think I know someone else like that."

My head rears back. "Me?"

"You fell in love, and like Haven, your old fears and insecurities rushed back to haunt you."

I take in her narrowed eyes, the fine line marring her skin. "What do you mean?"

"You just finished telling me women want you in their bed, but not their hearts. Seems like you both let the past invade on the future." She exhales slowly and glances away, giving me time to think. "Shame, really."

My mind races, spins, and I watch a bird soar overhead as I absorb her words. After a long moment, I turn to Gram, and she turns to me, watching me like she's waiting for me to have some big epiphany. I sit there and consider everything, and then suddenly, the clouds overhead clear, showcasing a blue sky as understanding dawns in small increments. My God, I'm the world's biggest asshole. Instead of reassuring Haven that I'd never do anything to hurt her, that I wasn't behind the pictures, I just stood there because I was afraid she didn't love me the way I loved her and it was easier to just walk away, keep my heart safe, and go down without a goddamn fight. Haven knows me. She knows exactly who I am, and she was just as scared as I was. She told me that when things were going well, she was always waiting for the other shoe to drop. That's because people have always let her down, and what did I do, I let her down by letting her believe the worst.

"Shit."

"There you go," Gram says, the minute my mind settles on the truth. Hell, she's so happy her dense grandson finally got a clue, she's not even calling me on my language.

"Now, answer my question," she says. "What do you think she loved about you?"

"I...I think...everything." I grab a fistful of hair and tug as bile punches into my throat and my pulse beats like I'd just downed a triple espresso. A garbled sound spills from my lips. "I really messed this up, didn't I?"

"I think you both did, actually."

"I let her say those things and didn't even defend myself. I let her believe the worst of me. She probably hates me."

"There's only one way to find out, isn't there?"

"How?"

She stands, turns toward me and puts her hands on my face. "You're a smart boy, I have faith that you'll figure it out."

She saunters off, and I shake my head. Where would I ever be without my Gram, my family? A family I want Haven to be a big part of, because there is no one in the world that deserves it more than her, and goddammit, I want to be the man she can count on, and trust so deeply that if something like this ever happened again, she'd know in a heartbeat I wasn't behind it, because I only ever have *her* best interests at heart. She comes first—in and out of the bedroom—and I need her to know that without a shadow of a doubt.

Gram climbs into her too-big truck and heads out the road. The second she's out of sight, I put a plan together. I'm not sure if it will work, but I am not going down without a fight—and what I'm about to do will likely get me a good ass kicking, but I don't care. I pull up my contacts and hit call. The phone rings three times, and then the line clicks in.

"You've got some fucking nerve calling me."

"Hello to you too, Rock."

I sit beside my brother on the private plane he chartered, and restlessly fiddle with the pages of the magazine on my lap. I didn't really want to go on this trip with him. No, with my love life and my career in the toilet, all I want is to sit home and wallow in self-pity.

"How much longer?" I ask.

He checks his watch. "We should be landing in about twenty minutes." I catch the way he's looking at me, concern written all over his face.

"I'm fine, Rock," I say. It's a lie. I'm not sure I'll ever be fine again. When I returned home, Rock was waiting for me at the airport. He didn't chastise me for not carefully guarding my private life and putting everything in jeopardy. He just put his arm around me and took me home. He's a good big brother like that, so when he asked if I'd travel to New Jersey with him for his fight, I agreed. He's always there when I need him, so I want to be there when he needs me.

I stare out the window, and the landscape comes into view as the plane descends, preparing to land. Something niggles in the back of my mind. "Wait, I thought your fight was in Vegas." Cripes, I'd been so wrapped up in myself, I never even stopped to consider anything else. I'm such a shitty sister.

"That's next week, remember."

"What day is it?"

He grins, and shakes his head. "The day doesn't matter. All that matters is seeing you happy again."

I force a smile. "I take it that means you're going to win this fight." Watching him win always makes me happy.

"Actually, you're the one who's going to win, Haven," he says, and I stare at him.

"What does that mean?"

He folds his big barrel arms across his chest. "You'll see."

"Jeez, when did you become so cryptic?"

"When did you start asking a million questions?"

I roll my eyes and stare at the magazine, but the words just blur before me. I toss it aside, and tilt my head back to rest it on the seat. Sleep hasn't been coming easy to me these days, and when I do finally drift off, my dreams are always filled with Tyler.

Sweet Tyler, who went out of his way to protect me. A man who said he wasn't interested in kids, yet is so good with them. A guy who doesn't do relationships, yet played house with me and remained monogamous the whole time. A man who said he'd only ever put my best interests first.

Stop thinking about him.

Ignoring that inner voice, I let my mind drift again, and relive the way those rough and tough fighter hands touched me with passion and tenderness. How could a guy who displayed such caring concern for everyone, turn around and do something so horrible?

Maybe he didn't.

As that thought hits like a slap to the face, my lids fly

open and I find my brother watching me carefully. "Why do you and Tyler hate each other so much? Was it just because you guys were rivals, or was it something else?" I've always been a bad judge of character and it would make me feel so much better if he just told me Tyler was a shitty guy.

"I was wondering when you were going to ask me about him."

I sit up a little straighter. "You were?"

"I'm surprised it took you so long."

"What's between you two? Did he steal your girl or something?" I joke with a snort, but really, I am curious. Being rivals is one thing, but why all the hate? The Tyler I saw and fell in love with was liked by everyone.

My brother cocks his head and stares me down, like I'm one of his opponents. "Please, Haven." He points at himself. "Have you seen this face? This is the face that has girls fighting for a piece of me, not running the other way."

I laugh at his playfulness. "Ego much," I say but as soon as the words leave my lips, I'm once again thinking of Tyler and his ego. I consider his reputation as a player, and how that first night we slept together I straight up said I wasn't looking for a future. He responded with, 'No future, I get it.'

I took that to mean he didn't want one either, but what if I was wrong? What if I was wrong about a lot of things, mainly him tipping off the reporter?

"Rock."

"Yeah."

"How come you're still single?"

He snorts out a laugh. "You really are full of questions today." He leans forward and braces his elbows on his knees. "Where is this coming from?"

"I just...I don't know. Just curious."

"I'm a fighter, the kind of guy a girl wants to get with, not marry. I train a lot, and travel a lot. I'm not what you'd call good boyfriend or husband material. I'm a notch on the bedpost, Haven. Women aren't looking for a future from me, and I've come to accept it."

My heart races a bit faster, as I wrap my brain around that. "Do you think most fighters like you feel that way?"

"I can't speak for the other guys. But if you're asking about Tyler, I'd say he has his own demons. I also think if the right girl came along, he'd fight for her. Hard."

I sink back into the chair, my throat tight as my heart aches. I guess I wasn't the right girl, considering he just let me walk. Then again, if he wasn't behind the pictures and hadn't tipped the reporter off, why would he fight for me after I said some pretty horrible things? I wrap my hands around my stomach. My thoughts sway back and forth as a storm rolls through me.

"Rock."

"Yeah?"

"You never answered my question. Why do you and Tyler hate each other?"

He grins and shakes his head. "We don't. That was all for show, our way to sell tickets."

I blink several times, sure I heard him wrong. "You *don't* hate him?"

"No, I never did. He's..." He pauses and briefly closes his eyes like he's remembering something. "He's one of the best guys I know." He cracks his knuckles. "Until he messed with my kid sister. What the hell ever happened to bro code?"

My heart jumps into my throat, and a measure of panic races through my veins. "He's...one of the best guys you know?" Did my brother just say something nice about Tyler? Am I in the twilight zone here?

"Damn straight he is."

"I...didn't know. Why didn't you ever tell me that before?"

"Why would I? You never knew Tyler. Besides, I figured you knew our antics were for showbiz, and you of all people know how stories can get twisted just to sensationalize them and sell more magazines."

The blood in my body drains to my feet, and I'm sure I must look like a ghost. "I...I should have known." How could I have been so stupid? I grip the edge of my seat, dig my nails in as I consider this new information.

He's one of the best guys I know.

"Haven, he was there for you when I couldn't be. He stepped up to protect you, and let me guess, he didn't want anything in return."

I start breathing a little faster, working to circulate my blood. "You're right," I say. "He just wanted to watch out for me. He said if he had a sister, he'd hope someone would do the same for her."

"Right, because that's the kind of guy he is."

"You don't think he was behind the leaked pictures?" I ask, sounding breathless, even to myself.

"What I think doesn't matter." He leans a little closer. "What matters is what you think."

My brain races, reliving every single second I was with Tyler. From the minute I kissed him in the bar, to our first night in his bed, right up until I accused him of using me to fund his gym. Oh God, what the hell have I done?

Only ruin the best thing that's ever happened to you.

And why is that—oh, because I lumped him in with every other man in my circle, and he's anything but. He's the leading man and real-life hero any woman would want.

"I think I might have made a big mistake."

"Yeah, you probably did. That's why we're in Connecticut," he says and waves his hand toward the window.

"What are you talking about?" I try to leap from my seat

to look out the window, but my seatbelt holds me back. "What is going on?"

"I'm not sure what's going on. I just thought I should bring you here."

"Have you talked to Tyler?" Before I can answer, I ask. "Oh my God, you did, didn't you? What did he say? Does he hate me?"

"Don't know much, Haven." He gives a casual shrug, his relaxed composure a complete contrast to the tightening of my shoulders. "Just knew you had to be here."

The plane comes to a stop and panic grips my throat. "He hates me, doesn't he? Oh God, Rock. I can't go see him."

"Too late to turn back now. We're already here and you know what I always say, anything worth having is worth fighting for."

My stomach twists and turns as I unbuckle and stand on shaky legs. "What if he doesn't want to see me? What if he tells me to just leave?"

"What if he doesn't?"

"Rock—"

Before I can get the words out, he puts his hands on my shoulders and levels me with a glare. "Do you really want to spend the rest of your life asking what if?"

"No, I don't," I say quickly. That might be worse than Tyler telling me he hates me.

"Then let's go."

I touch his arm. "Wait, you were furious with Tyler when you found out about us. You didn't come here to knock his teeth out, did you?"

"I am not going to knock his teeth out." I breathe a sigh of relief, until he adds, "A black eye however." I stare at him, certain he's kidding. Please let him be kidding. Tyler can handle himself just fine, and while Rock might have taken his title, just barely, Tyler is not a man to go to his knees easily.

That's not entirely true—he happily went to his knees for me, numerous times.

Snickering—Rock is obviously pleased with his black eye comment—he exits the plane after the door is opened and I follow him off, my carry-on bag over my shoulder. I only packed light, thinking I was staying in New Jersey for one night. I had no idea Rock had this up his sleeve, and honest to God, my legs are shaking so hard, I can barely manage the steps.

Forty-five minutes later, we're in a rental car, and my brother casts me a fast glance. "You know where we're going, I take it?"

I look out the window, watch the trees fly by. "I think we should try his cabin." A fresh wave of nerves fire inside me, and I swallow. "What did Tyler say to you?"

He grips the steering wheel tighter. "You two need to talk. That's all I know."

I fuss with the hem of my T-shirt, and try to practice my yoga breathing to calm myself down. I give Rock directions and before I know it, we're turning down the road leading to the cabin. I suck in a fast breath, and with my heart beating so fast, I'm sure I'm going to pass out. What if he's furious with me? What if he tells me to fuck right off?

What if he doesn't?

I take another breath to pull myself together. Rock is right. I can't spend the rest of my life wondering what if, and if there's one thing Rock taught me growing up, anything worth having is worth fighting for.

Tyler is worth fighting for.

Suddenly I can't wait to see him. I'm practically jumping from the rental before it comes to a complete stop, but the second I get out of the car, I go perfectly still. What the heck is going on here? I catalogue the area, note the wide open space at the back of the cabin, where the trees have all been cut and removed. Is Tyler opening the land up to sell lots? I narrow my gaze, and take in the big brood boxes at the end of the property, and the small shed going up. At least I think it's a shed. But I'm definitely looking at brood boxes—which house honeybees. Oh my God, is Tyler starting an apiary?

The deck boards squeak and I shift my attention to the cabin. As soon as I see Tyler standing there, and I take in the way he's dressed, my world goes a little fuzzy around the edges. I wobble, and I'm about to grab the car to hold on, but Tyler is right there, putting his big strong arms around me, to hold me upright.

"Hey," he says. "You okay?"

My gaze roams his handsome face, and damp hair, as I breathe in the scent of his freshly showered skin. "I..." My focus drops down to take in the tux he's wearing. "You're..." My heart leaps. I can't believe he's in a tux. I blink numerous times, thinking back to when I told him I'd love to see him in a tux. "Why..."

He laughs. "Do you always give one-word answers?" he asks. It's the same thing I asked him the first night we met when he was showing me to his room.

"Tyler," I say and pound on his chest, very aware that my brother is watching us both closely, and he's not picking a fight with the man I'm in love with.

"I'm in a tux because you said all heroes should wear one, and I want to be the hero in the story you call life, Haven."

"I..." Tears pound behind my eyes as his words sink in. How can this man not hate me? "I'm sorry, Tyler. I'm so damn sorry." This time the tears do spill and softness moves into his eyes. "I never should have accused you."

"Hey." He brushes my tears with his thumbs. "I'm sorry too. A real hero fights for his woman. He doesn't let insecurities or demons stand in his way. I wanted to be the one guy, outside of your brother, who you could trust and count on, and instead, I just let you walk away."

"After what I said, I can't blame you."

"I know where your fears were coming from, Haven. I honestly do. But you need to know that you can always trust me. I would never in a million years put my interests over yours."

I nod. "I know, you proved that to me over and over again. I just...my past..."

"My past too. It fucked me over, and made me think you could never see me as a life partner. I didn't give you enough credit, and that's my fault. I love you, Haven. I swear the second I saw you at Winchester's, I was a goner."

I laugh through the tears. "I love you, too."

"I know you have a career and will be traveling, but I want us to be together. When you're not working, I want you here with me. I want to make this cabin our new home. I don't want your dreams to be dreams, Haven. I want them to be a reality. I want you to live in that Norman Rockwell world you romanticize." He waves his hand toward the brood boxes. "I've been learning all about beekeeping."

I honestly can't believe he did this, and the way he's looking at me right now, with such love and adoration, fills my heart with all the love I have for him.

I shake my head and back up. "No, Tyler."

His face falls, and so do his shoulders. "Haven—"

"I know who you are, and I finally know who I am thanks to you. So, get out of this tux." I grin at him. "You're a beekeeper now. You need to be in a bee suit."

The corners of his lips curl. "No, you're the beekeeper, and I need to be in this tux."

"Why?"

He steps away from me and I have no idea what's going on. He walks to my brother's door, and Rock climbs out. My pulse skyrockets as the two men stare each other down. I'm about to run and put myself in between them, even though I'm sure Rock was only joking about the black eye. But the second Tyler asks my brother for permission to marry me, a big stupid hiccupping sob catches in my throat. My God, it's the most romantic thing I've ever seen in my life.

"Of course you have my permission." My brother nods and slaps Tyler on the back. "I know she'll be in good hands," he says. "But we'll be talking about the bro code later."

They both grin as they shake hands, and Tyler comes back to me, tugging on the tux like it's the most uncomfortable thing he's ever worn, and it probably is. He's not a tux guy. No, he's a jeans, T-shirt and tool belt guy and I wouldn't want him any other way.

He drops to one knee in front of me and pulls a box from his pocket. He opens it and when my gaze lands on the diamond, I gasp. "I asked Rock to bring you here. To this spot, where we fell in love. I love you, Haven. I want to give you the family you want and deserve. I want to fill this place with laughter and happiness. I want you here with me when you're not working. I want the late-night feedings, the interfering family, the dog, and the minivan. I want it all with you, and I hope you want it all with me. I let you walk away once, but not this time, this time I'm not going down without a fight."

"Ty..."

"Please say yes. Make me the happiest guy on the planet."

"I can't say yes to all that," I say, as he stares at me. "Long distance relationships never work."

"Haven—"

"Which is why it's time for me to leave Hollywood behind."

He angles his head, his worried gaze moving over my face. "Are you sure? I'd never want you to regret—"

I put my finger to his lips. "I have never been more sure of anything. For the first time in my life, I know who I am and what *I* want."

"What do you want, Haven?"

"I want you." With my insides shaking with happiness, I hold my quivering hand out, and he puts the gorgeous diamond on my finger. I turn to find Rock smiling at me. He's a real-life hero too, and someday I hope he finds his happily-ever-after. Tyler stands, wraps me in his strong arms, and places his warm lips on mine. He kisses me until I'm dizzy, until Rock clears his throat. Laughing, Tyler sets me down.

"Do you think we should go tell your family?" I ask and he shakes his head, incredulously. "What?"

"I don't think you have any idea what you're getting yourself into."

"What's that supposed to mean?" I ask when the cabin's deck boards squeak again. Tyler turns sideways and waves.

"They're all here."

Just then Summer, and Kylee, and Gram, and all the guys come from inside the house and tears of happiness well up inside me. Arms are thrown around me and kisses land on my cheek, and nose and forehead as everyone welcomes me into the family.

"Okay, enough, enough," Tyler says and pulls me into his arms. I glance into his gorgeous green eyes. Not only did I lose myself in this man, I found myself too.

"I love you, Ty."

"I love you too," he says.

"Okay, everyone," Gram says and claps her hands. "Let's leave these two lovebirds alone. They need to get to work on giving me that great-granddaughter."

Everyone laughs, and Tyler just shakes his head. "Like I said, you have no idea what you're getting yourself into."

I smile, and go up on my toes to put my mouth near his

ear, my words for him only. "Maybe not, but I know what you're getting yourself into, as soon as we get you out of the tux, that is."

"I do love a girl who knows what she wants," Tyler—my real-life hero—says and scoops me up and carries me inside, proving happily-ever-after doesn't just exist in the movies.

AFTERWORD

Thank You!

Thank you so much for reading, **Hammered**, book a in my Blue Bay Crew Series. I hope you loved this story as much as I loved writing it. Be sure to keep reading for an excerpt of **The Playmaker.**

Interested in leaving a review? Please do! Reviews help readers connect with books that work for them. I appreciate all reviews, whether positive or negative.

Happy Reading,

Cathryn

THE PLAYMAKER

Nina

Fat drops of spring rain pummel my head, wilting my curls as I dart through Seattle's busy traffic to the café on the other side of the street. My best friend, Jess, is inside waiting for me, undoubtedly hyped up on her third latté by now.

I step over a pothole and search for an opening in the traffic. I hate being late, I really do. I totally value other people's time, but when the email came through from my editor, asking me to write a hot hockey series, my priorities took a curve. I've worked with Tara for a couple years now, and I know her like—pardon the pun—a well-worn book. To her, hesitation equals disinterest. She's a mover, a tree-shaker, and it wouldn't have taken long for her to offer the opportunity to another author. She wanted a quick reply and I had to give it to her.

I got this!

Yeah, that was my response, but what did I have to lose? I've been in such a rut lately, thanks to my fickle muse, deserting me when I needed her most. I swear to God, sometimes she acts like a hormonal teenager. I need to whip her into shape so I don't lose this gig. The royalties from a series will help make a sizeable dent in the bills that are piling up high and deep.

High and deep.

I laugh. One of those self-derisive snorts that crawls out when you'd really rather cry. Yeah, that pretty much sums up the *I got this* response I emailed back. High and deep, like a big steaming pile of—

A car horn blares, jolting me from my pity party. With my heart pounding in my chest, I step in front of the Tesla and flip the guy off. I safely reach the sidewalk and once again my mind is back on my job, and off the impatient jerk in the overpriced car.

I step up on the sidewalk and lift my face to the rain, the cool water a pleasant break from this unusual spring heat wave we're having. Pressure fills my throat. The hum of traffic behind me dulls, leaving only the sound of my pulse pounding in my ears. Panic.

Why the hell did my editor think I, former figure skater turned romance novelist, would want to write a series about hot hockey players? Yeah, sure my brother is an NHL player, but that doesn't mean I'm into the game. I hate hockey. No, hate is too mild a word for what I feel. I loathe it entirely. But you know what I don't loathe? Eating. Yeah, I like eating. Oh, and a roof over my head. I really like that, too.

I draw in a semi self-satisfied breath at having rationalized my fast response.

Except my reply was total and utter bullshit. I don't *got this*. In fact, I...wait, what's the antonym of *got this*? All that comes to mind is, *you're screwed*. Yep, that pretty much describes my predicament.

Why didn't I just stick to figure skating?

Because you took a bad spill that ended your career.

Oh right. But seriously, a hockey series... Ugh. Kill me. Freaking. Now.

I reach the café, pull the glass door open and slick my rain-soaked hair from my face. I quickly catalogue the place to find Jess hitting on the barista. Ahh, now I get why she picked a place so far from home. I take in the guy behind the counter. Damn, he's hotter than the steaming latté in Jess's hand, and from the way she's flirting, it's clear he'll be in her bed later today.

I sigh inwardly. It's always so easy for her. Me? Not so much. Men rarely pay me attention. Unlike Jess, I'm plain, have the body of a twelve-year-old boy, and most times I blend into the woodwork.

I pick up a napkin from the side counter and mop the rain off my face. Doesn't matter. I'm not interested anyway. From my puck-bunny-chasing brother to all his cocky friends, I know what guys are really like, and when it comes to women, they're only after one thing, and it isn't scoring the slot. I roll my eyes. Then again, maybe it is.

And of course, I can't forget the last guy I was set up with. What he did to me was totally abusive, but I don't want to dredge up those painful memories right now.

I shake, and water beads fall right off my brand-new rain-resistance coat. At least something is going right for me today. Semi-dry, I cross the room and stand beside Jess.

"Hey, sorry I'm late."

Jess turns to me, smiles, and holds a finger up. "I'll forgive you only if you're late because you were knees deep into some nasty sex, 'cause girlfriend, it's been far too long since you've been laid."

Jesus, what ever happened to this girl's filters?

Thoroughly embarrassed, my gaze darts to the barista, who is grinning, his eyes still locked on my friend, looking at her like she's today's hot lunch special and ignoring me like I'm yesterday's cold, lumpy oatmeal.

Ugh, really?

"Non-fat latté," I say, and scowl at him until he puts his eyes back in his head. I might be an English major but I have a PhD in the death glare. Truthfully, I'm so sick of guys like him, one thing on their minds. Then again, Jess only wants one thing from him, so I really shouldn't have a problem with it. Why do I? Oh, maybe because Mr. Right, my battery-operated companion, isn't quite cutting it anymore, and it's left me a little jittery and a whole lot cranky.

Jess is right. I *do* need to get laid.

Jess's lips flatline when she takes me in, her gaze carefully accessing me. "What?" she asks, her mocha eyes narrowing.

God, sometimes I really hate how well she can read me. "Nothing."

She straightens to her full height, and I try to do the same, but she dwarfs me, even without her beloved two-inch heels. I square my shoulders, but it's always hard to pull off a high-power pose when you're only five foot two, and teased relentlessly about it.

"Come on," she says, and guides me to a corner table. I peel off my coat and plunk down. Jess sits across from me. "Spill."

I point to my forehead. "Do I have 'idiot' written here?"

She looks me over, and cautiously asks, "No, why?"

My phone chirps in my purse, and I reach for it. Great, it's my editor wanting to set turn-in dates. "How about never?" I say under my breath.

"Uh, Nina. You're talking to your phone. You better tell me what's going on."

"You're not going to believe what I just agreed to."

"Do tell," she says and leans forward, like I'm about to spill some dirty little sex secret. If only that were the case.

I grab my phone and hold it up, showing her Tara's message. "I just agreed to write a hockey series," I say, and toss my phone back into my purse, mic-drop style—without the bold confidence.

Jess pushes back in her chair, clearly disappointed. She lifts her cup, and over the rim, asks, "I don't see how that makes you an idiot."

My mouth drops open. Jess and I have been friends since childhood. She of all people knows how much I hate hockey. "Are you serious?"

She shrugs. "You're a writer."

Mr. Sexy Barista brings me my coffee and he shares a secret, let's-hook-up-later smile with Jess. "And...?" I ask when he leaves.

"Writer's write and make things up. I know you hate hockey, but what does that have to do with anything?"

"I can't come up with a plot, or write about the game, if I don't know anything about it."

She shakes her head. "And I can't believe your brother is a professional player and you never once paid attention to the game."

"I was busy pursuing a professional skating career, remember?"

She reaches across the table and gives my hand a little squeeze. "I know. I'm sorry."

My tailbone and neck take that moment to throb, a constant reminder of a career lost.

I didn't just lose my dream of skating professionally the day my feet went out from underneath me, I lost my confidence, too. A concussion will do that to you.

Good thing I majored in English in college. Once I hung up my skates, I began to blog about the sport and sold a few articles. I joined a local writers group, and after talking to a group of romance writers, I tried my hand at one. Much to my surprise, it actually sold. I went from non-fiction to fiction, in every sense of the word. Happily ever after might exist between the pages, but it certainly doesn't in real life. At least not for me.

I take a sip of my latté, and give an exaggerated huff as I set it down. Jess instantly goes into problem-solving mode when she sees that I'm really stressed about this. As a brand-new high school guidance counselor, she can't help but want to fix me.

"Okay, it's simple," she begins. "You have to learn the game."

"How am I supposed to do that?"

"Turn on the TV and watch."

"I can watch a bunch of guys chase a stupid puck around a rink all I want, I still won't be able to understand the rules."

"How dare you call my favorite sport stupid."

"Jessss..." I plead. "What am I going to do?"

She crinkles her nose. Then her eyes go wide. "I've got it. Shadow your brother."

I give a quick shake of my head. "No, he's on the road, and he won't want me hanging around."

Jess goes quiet again, and that hollowed-out spot inside me aches as I think about Cason. I miss my brother so much and wish we were closer. Cason and I grew up in a family where there were no hugs or words of affirmation. I know Mom and Dad loved us, but as busy investment bankers, work consumed their lives. Sure, they put me in figure skat-ing, and Cason in hockey when we were young, but they never shared in our passions, or really supported our pursuits.

I guess I can't expect my brother to display love, when none was ever displayed to him.

"Why don't you teach me?"

"It might be my favorite sport to watch, but I don't really know all the rules. I think you'd be better off getting your brother or..." She straightens. "Wait. I got this," she says, and I cringe when she tosses my three-word email response back at me. A warning shiver skips along my spine, and I get the sense that whatever she's about suggest, is going to take me right down the rabbit hole.

"What about Cole Cannon?"

I groan, plant my elbows on the table, and cover my face with my hands. "Never," I mumble through my fingers. "Not in a million freaking years."

Jess removes my hands from my face. "Why not? He's your brother's best friend. I'm sure he'll help you."

"Cocky Cole Cannon, aka, The Playmaker. Do I need to say any more?" I reach for my latté and take a huge gulp, burning the roof of my mouth. Damn.

"I know you hate him, Nina, but—"

"Of course I hate him. You remember the nickname he used to use when we were kids—Pretty BallerNina. I was a figure skater, not a ballerina," I could only assume he was mocking me about being pretty too, but I keep that to myself.

"At least he worked your name into the moniker, and hey, it could have been worse. He could have called you Neaner Neaner, like Cason did."

I glare at her and she holds her hands up. "Okay, okay. I get it. But Cole's been home for a month, recovering from a concussion, and his team—the Seattle Shooters, in case you don't know the league's name," she adds with a wink, "are probably going to make it to the playoffs, so you know he's watching all the games. You don't have to like him to ask him to explain a few of the plays, right?"

"I suppose."

Wait! What? Am I really thinking about asking The Playmaker to help me? I reach for my latté and blow on it before I take another big gulp.

"And if you ask me, while he's helping you learn the plays, I think you two should hate fuck."

I choke on my drink, spitting most of it on my friend as the rest dribbles down my chin.

OMFG, how embarrassing. All eyes turn to me. Mortified, I grab a napkin and start wiping my face, but Jess is laughing so hard, I start laughing with her.

"Couldn't you have waited until I swallowed?" I ask.

"That's what she said."

"Ohmigod, Jess. How are we friends?"

She waves a dismissive hand. "You know you love me because I'm hellacioulsy funny."

"I do, just stop cracking jokes when I'm drinking."

She leans towards me conspiratorially, and I brace myself. "I wasn't joking. You and Cocky Cole Cannon should hate fuck. He's as sexy today as he was when he used to hang out with Cason at your house when we were teens." I give her a look that suggests she's insane. She ignores it and wags her brows. "He's explosive on the ice, but do you know why they really call him the Cannon?"

"Because it's his last name."

"Yeah, but that's not the only reason."

Don't ask. Don't ask.

"Okay, then why?" I ask.

"'Cause he's loaded between his legs."

Yeah, okay, I totally set myself up for that.

"You don't know that," I shoot back. My mind races to my brother's best friend, and I mentally go over his form. He's athletic, tall and—as much as I hate to admit it—hot as hell. The perfect trifecta. Could he be packing too? Working with some top-notch equipment?

Jesus, what am I doing? The last thing I should be thinking about is Cole's 'cannon'.

"Come on." Jess grabs her purse. "I'll drive you there."

I flatten my hands on the table. "I'm not going to his house, especially not unannounced."

"Give him a call then."

"No."

She sits back in her chair and folds her arms, a sign she's changing tactics. "And here I thought you liked your condo and food in your cupboards."

I groan at the direct hit.

Her voice softens and she touches my hand. "But you know you always have—"

"Fine." I stop her before she brings up my trust fund. Yeah, sure, Mom and Dad set money aside for me, but I don't want to use it. I want to live by my own means, make it on my own merit. Besides it wasn't their money I wanted, then or now, it was their attention, their love. I moved out years ago and only ever hear from them on my birthday or at Christmas.

I pull my phone from my purse. "I'll text him. If he doesn't answer, we don't talk about this again." I go through my contacts and find his number, having stored it years ago when he called to check on me after my injury. The call had taken me by surprise; so did his concern. Maybe my brother put him up to it. I don't know. Nor do I know why I kept his number.

My fingers fly across the screen, but in no way do I expect him to respond. At least I hope he doesn't. I read over the text. *Sorry to hear about your concussion. I was wondering if you could help me with something.* Then hit send.

I set my phone down and look at Jess. "Happy?"

"Hey, I'm not the one who's going to be homeless."

Point taken. Maybe I should be hoping he *does* text back.

My phone pings, and we both reach for it. Jess gets it first, and from her smirk, I guess my wish just came true—Colin responded.

Careful what you wish for.

"What does it say?" I ask, afraid of the answer.

"It says, sure what's up?" Jess's fingers dance over the screen as she responds for me.

"What are you saying?" I ask, panic welling up inside me. "So help me, if you're telling him I need to get laid..."

The phone pings again and she holds it out for me to read.

"I asked—I mean *you* asked if you could stop by his place, and he said sure."

"I don't know whether to kiss you or choke you," I say.

Jess laughs. "I think you'll be thanking me." She stands. "Come on."

We make our way outside, and the rain has slowed to a light mist as I follow her down the street to her parked car. I hop in and question my sanity. Am I really going to ask Cocky Cannon to teach me the game?

Jess starts the car and the locks click as she pulls into traffic. Guess so.

"You remember where he lives?" I ask. I think back to when he bought the house. He had a big party to celebrate. I was invited but didn't go. Why would I? Watching the hockey players with their bunnies was not my idea of a good time.

"Of course." She jacks the tunes and sings along off-key as she drives. Twenty minutes later, she pulls up in front of his mansion. It's a ridiculously big house for one person. I stare at it, and once again question my sanity.

"Go," Jess says.

"I'm going," I shoot back. I open the door, and smooth my hand over my mess of curls. Why the hell did I do that? It's not like I'm trying to make myself presentable or impress him. We don't even like each other.

I force my legs to carry me to his door, and I'm about to knock when it opens. My breath catches as I take in Cole, standing before me shirtless and barefoot, dressed only in a pair of faded jeans that hug him so nicely.

God, he is so freaking hot—and I never, ever should have come here.

As we stare at each other, like we're in some goddamn Mexican standoff, I can't stop thinking about his 'cannon'. My gaze drops to the lovely bulge between his legs, and a moan I have no control over catches in my throat as Jess's words come back to haunt me.

You two should hate fuck.

Thank you, Jess, for planting that idea in my brain. Christ, I should have choked her when I had the chance.

His Best Friend's Girl

His Reason to Stay

Confessions

Confessions of a Bad Boy Professor

Confessions of a Bad Boy Officer

Confessions of a Bad Boy Fighter

Confessions of a Bad Boy Gamer

Confessions of a Bad Boy Millionaire

Confessions of a Bad Boy Santa

Confessions of a Bad Boy CEO

Hands On

Hands On

Body Contact

Full Exposure

Dossier

Private Reserve

House Rules

Under Pressure

Big Catch

Brazilian Fantasy

Improper Proposal

Boys of Beachville

Good at Being Bad

Igniting the Bad Boy

Bad Girl Therapy

Stone Cliff Series:

Crashing Down

Wasted Summer

Love Lessons

Wrapped Up

Eternal Pleasure Series

Instinctive

Impulsive

Indulgent

Sun Stroked Series

Seaside Seduction

Deep Desire

Private Pleasure

Captured and Claimed Series:

Yours to Take

Yours to Teach

Yours to Keep

Firefighter Heat Series

Fever

Siren

Flash Fire

Playing For Keeps Series

Slow Ride

Wild Ride

Sweet Ride

Breaking the Rules:

Hold Me Down Hard

Pin Me Up Proper

Tie Me Down Tight

Stand Alone Title:

Hands on with the CEO

Torn Between Two Brothers

Holiday Spirit

Unleashed

Knocking on Demon's Door

Web of Desire

ABOUT CATHRYN

New York Times and *USA today* Bestselling author, Cathryn is a wife, mom, sister, daughter, and friend. She loves dogs, sunny weather, anything chocolate (she never says no to a brownie) pizza and red wine. She has two teenagers who keep her busy with their never ending activities, and a husband who is convinced he can turn her into a mixed martial arts fan. Cathryn can never find balance in her life, is always trying to find time to go to the gym, can never keep up with emails, Facebook or Twitter and tries to write page-turning books that her readers will love.

Connect with Cathryn:
Newsletter https://app.mailerlite.com/webforms/
landing/c1f8n1
Twitter: https://twitter.com/writercatfox
Facebook: https://www.facebook.com/
AuthorCathrynFox?ref=hl
Blog: http://cathrynfox.com/blog/
Goodreads: https://www.goodreads.com/author/show/
91799.Cathryn_Fox

Pinterest http://www.pinterest.com/catkalen/